MET CHRON NEW-HUMANS

Metamorphosis Chronicles

Book 2

RON S. NOLAN

PLANETROPOLIS PUBLISHING

222 Santa Cruz Avenue, No. 11
Aptos, California 95003
www.planetropolis.com

This book is an original publication of Planetropolis Publishing.

ISBN-10: 0-578-50069-8
ISBN-13: 978-0-578-50069-0

This is a work of fiction. Names, characters, places and incidents either are the product of the author's imagination or are used fictitiously, and any actual resemblance to actual persons, living or dead, business establishments, events, or locales is entirely coincidental. The publisher does not have any control over and does not assume any responsibility for third party websites.

"I studied ballet as a child, but never imagined that I would be dancing with singing frogs and crickets on the Moon."

"Please continue. The stage is yours milady."

DEDICATION

Michael H.D. Dormer

Michael H.D. Dormer was a master of the creative process and the art of thinking outside the box. This novel is devoted to his memory.

****

Special thanks to
Julie Kay Thompson
for her love and support.

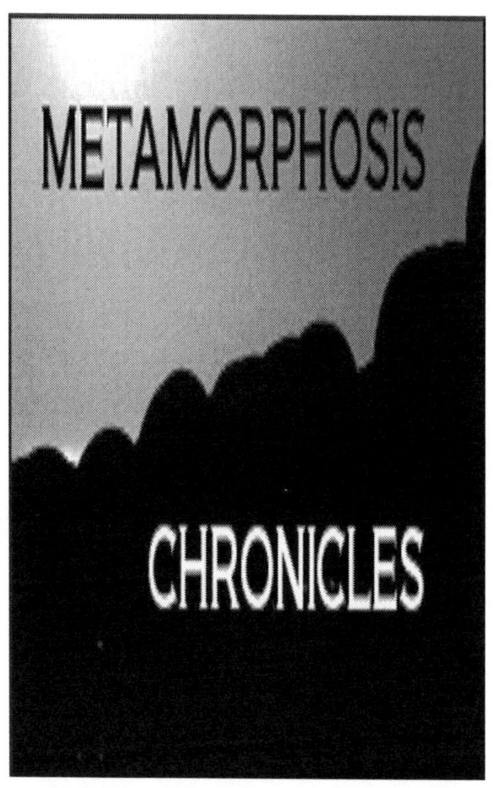

Metamorphosis Chronicles explores the future of a human society that is confronted with the threats posed by rampant climate change and AI androids and robots that are competing with Sapiens and New-Humans for jobs and natural resources on an over-populated planet Earth controlled by profit-driven, corporate governments.

MET CHRON NEW-HUMANS
is the second book in the series.

Planetropolis Publishing
www.planetropolis.com

Metamorphosis Chronicles

Acronyms

BGI: BioGenetics International Laboratories: conducts research into genetic modifications directed at enhanced human longevity

CHIRUS: a government-corporate state formed by the union of China, Russia and North Korea

CREOS: SDL members that are fanatical followers of the Reverend LeRoque's teachings.

IRANVEN: a government-corporate state formed by the union of Iran, Iraq and Venezuela

OWN: Organization of World Nations

SDL: Seekers of the Divine Light, headed by Reverend Granger LeRoque

USACO: United States of America Corporation–a Government-Corporate state formed by the union of the United States, Great Britain, and Israel

VIDAS: Independent thinkers who believe in the merits of science and genetics.

— PROLOGUE —

In the year 2030, the world's citizens were still in shock following the nuclear blasts that had detonated in the Bay Area along with Washington D.C. and Beijing, China. Thousands had been killed or injured and radiation levels in the blast zones still remained perilously high. To make matters worse, world tensions due to severe climate change, overpopulation and the depletion of critical food resources had resulted in escalating military conflicts and widespread acts of terrorism. Coastal cities throughout the world faced relentless sea level inundation resulting in massive population relocations to inland areas which reduced the amount of open space for raising crops, further decreasing food production.

Many ecologists warned that Earth had reached its carrying capacity and urged the big, oil-hungry corporations in control of the world governments to quit lying to the public and take immediate action as more and more businesses were staffed by specialized AI robots and androids leaving fewer job opportunities for natural, organic humans.

As a result many people had resorted to the lifestyle of gypsies living in wagons drawn by rustic farm tractors and working as migrant laborers who barely made ends meet by traveling from harvest-to-harvest. Those that were once employed by the fishing industry found themselves out of work due to overfishing and ocean pollution.

In contrast, an elite class of code-savvy gurus lived harmoniously in well-equipped survival campers (SVs) and earned credits by providing a wide range of high tech services to private industry and the military. Their mobile villages were self-sufficient with advanced atmospheric water collection systems, hydroponic gardens and solar power systems which enabled them to quickly relocate in caravans to avoid catastrophic wildfires, floods and tornadoes. However, millions were trapped in urban slums and survived by stealing, kidnapping children and trading in black market goods. Street crime ran rampant as territorial gangs fought for drugs, sex and money.

The current economic and environmental turmoil began back in 2024 when a handful of the world's wealthiest entrepreneurs used political bribery, deceptive news coverage, and media manipulation to support the election of an administration totally under their control. Within months of the election, the USA democracy had been converted to the United States of America Corporation (USACO) which essentially owned the government.

Taxes were raised on the middle class while public services programs and social security were eliminated with no regard to the suffering and economic chaos that would follow.

Furthermore, in spite of the continuous onslaught of severe weather and rising sea levels, concerns about climate change were stringently suppressed by a polished gaslight propaganda machine that promoted nationalism rather than patriotism, further increasing tension with foreign governments and resulting in accelerated space weapons development.

MET CHRON NEW-HUMANS

But corporate control was weakening. Widespread demonstrations and rallies in support of reinstating the provisions of the Constitution of the United States of America rapidly spread throughout the social media.

Meanwhile, significant progress had been made in artificial intelligence and organic 3D printing. *Jasmine,* the first *New-Human,* was accidentally created in 2029 when an intern at the lunar SpeeZees Lab mistakenly activated a newly developed, experimental AI neural net program. The end result was a fully capable New-Human that was a highly intelligent organic being with tremendous analytical and cognitive skills.

In spite of the tight security at the SpeeZees Lab, word quickly spread that a New-Human had been created and within a matter of days, the lab had received multiple requests to produce custom designed New-Humans from businesses and governments searching for a competitive edge. As a result, a new facility equipped with the latest in New-Human biological organ printing and mental acuity synthesis was added to the SpeeZees Lab. However, demand still greatly exceeded the current production capacity while the social impacts remained controversial and uncertain.

Adding to the tension, New-Humans were currently seeking equal rights with their organic, ancestral counterparts (now known as *Sapients)* while gangs of AI androids and robots fought desperate battles for their survival. Their goal was simple—*eliminate all Sapients and New-Humans!*

The innovative pioneers that operated the Deep Space Mining Moonbase believed that they had a plan that would solve humanity's problems. The question they had to face was, *Would anyone out there listen*?

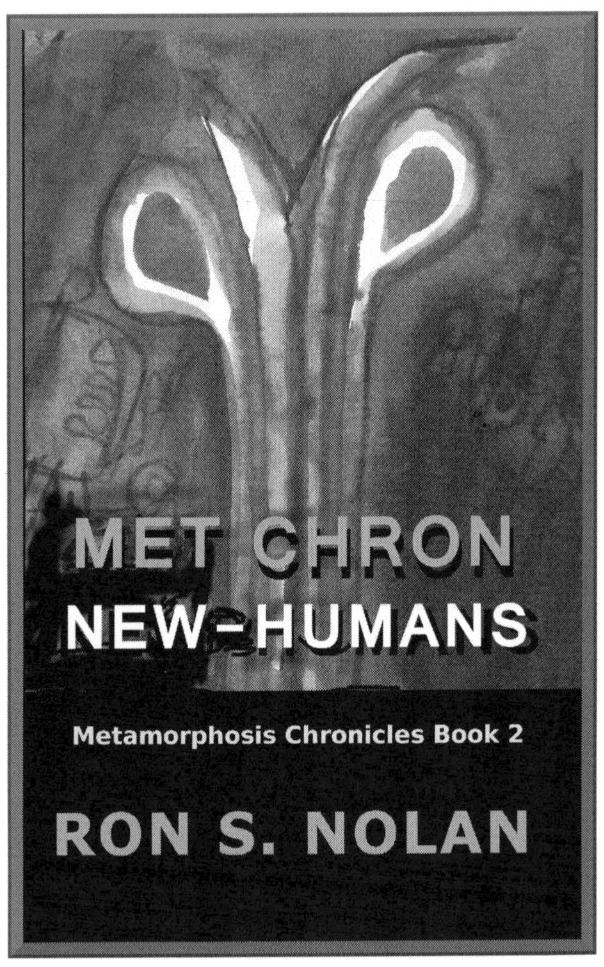

MET CHRON
NEW-HUMANS
Metamorphosis Chronicles Book 2
RON S. NOLAN

Cover Art by
Michael H.D. Dormer

"It all began when we met an android who looked half like a human and half like a bug with eyestalks that swiveled all around."

— CHAPTER 1 —

Doomsday
November 15th, 2030

Sabien and Torch had mounted a last ditch effort from the Deep Space Mining Moonbase to halt rampant atmospheric carbon emissions from the increasingly tropical Arctic tundra by launching two heavily reinforced cargo pods containing sealant nanomachines into geostationary orbit. The plan was that the pods would remain in orbit until they were activated, then one would arc in over Alaska and the other over Siberia.

When the pods hit the atmosphere, they would release golf ball sized projectiles–each carrying millions of p*enetrator* nanos whose task was to transport the diamond maker a*ssembler* nanos to a depth of one meter beneath the surface. Once they were in position, they would begin extracting carbon from the soil and compressing the molecules into a thin diamond plating which would create an airtight seal and arrest CO_2 emissions from the now tropical tundra.

The nano bots would begin absorbing CO_2 as soon as they entered the atmosphere over the target sites. Sabien and Torch had anticipated that the pod entry and nano release would generate a very powerful series of electromagnetic pulses that would likely disrupt communication systems around the world and scramble satellite and navigation systems in space and on land.

It was Torch's responsibility to safeguard the remote control which would activate the pod entry until he was certain that USACO and all other nuclear war capable world governments had been warned that communications in vulnerable systems might temporarily shut down and to prepare accordingly.

At least that was the plan...and it might have worked if Reverend LeRoque and his gang of CREOS had not invaded the Moonbase and attacked Torch, knocking him out cold before he could warn the Reverend not to press the actuator remote control. But the Reverend had done just that and as feared, the pod entry generated intense EM pulses that corrupted and disabled unprotected electronic systems.

When highly trusted threat level monitoring and alert systems shut down, the leaders of USACO, CHIRUS and IRANVEN concluded that they were under attack and panicked. After repeated attempts to communicate over 'hot' lines failed, combined with reports of incoming objects from space, they launched what they believed to be retaliatory strikes against their foes. Although early reports about widespread nuclear detonations were inaccurate, there were three confirmed strikes in the Bay Area, Washington D.C. and Beijing where thousands of innocent people were killed or injured by the blasts and widespread damage to buildings and the environment.

****

The Space Command Network (SCN) was a growing chain of sophisticated military surveillance and assault shuttles. Armed with advanced sensor systems, the SCN shuttles were designed to detect a wide range of fuel sources including radioactive plutonium-239 emitted by the power plants of enemy ships, submarines and rockets.

The distinguishing features shared by the *Neuro* line of masculine looking androids that piloted the SCN ships were their shiny, metallic skin and piercing blue eyes. Each shuttle commander had his own unique encrypted instruction sequence that, when issued by the SCN, would authorize them to engage and destroy the designated targets using the shuttle's powerful arsenal of laser weapons.

In addition to monitoring emissions, Neuro pilots were highly trained in high-level maintenance and repair mechanics. These skills were essential to mission success and survival due to the risk of colliding with any of the five million orbiting objects ranging in size from one to twenty centimeters that orbited Earth at supersonic speed.

The cloud of debris was composed of the remains of booster tanks, derelict satellites and abandoned space stations that circled in near-Earth orbit. Large items were easily detected by the shuttle's radar system as the objects approached and then avoided using the shuttle's thrusters. But the impacts of small chunks of debris impacting at high velocity posed a serious threat to SCN operations. To handle this hazard, the shuttle was equipped with a sophisticated repair shop complete with the latest innovations in 3D printing which was most frequently used to repair punctures in the shuttle's extensive array of solar panels.

After completing a routine work shift, the android piloting the shuttle in SCN Section 13 designated as *N-13* activated the onboard AI to take command of the ship and headed for the regeneration chamber for his standard recharging cycle.

Suddenly, the ship alarm shrieked and the instrument screens shut down as systems crashed. The AI calmly reported, *Danger, EM pulse, Danger— attempting system reboot now...reboot failed. Now awaiting further instructions.*

The shuttle lurched sideways and then started spinning out of control as the cabin plunged into darkness and the shuttle's electronic systems shut down.

N-13 struggled back to his control station and desperately tried to restore backup power. He was alarmed to see that the starboard thruster had activated, spinning the ship while a gushing stream of liquid kerosene spewed from a crack in the ventral fuel tank.

Just as he shut the thruster down, a second EM pulse caused the shuttle's guidance circuitry to malfunction and issue random start/stop commands which forced the starboard thruster to sporadically fire and cut off. The shuttle, spinning and tumbling, bounced as it hit the edge of the atmosphere and then plunged into a steep reentry trajectory.

When the AI successfully rebooted and came back on line, N-13 was finally able to regain control, but because of the leak, the ship lacked the fuel needed to climb out of the gravity well. He repeatedly tried to contact Space Command, but there was only static in the audio signal.

Suddenly the Pu-239 detection alarm sounded and to N-13's surprise, the signal seemed to be emanating from the necklace of tropical islands that he was fast approaching.

N-13 activated continuous sensor sweeps. The gauge pegged at the top of the scale in the red zone, a Pu-239 level that vastly exceeded any that he had ever encountered. Since USACO, CHIRUS and IRANVEN had converted their extensive space and terrestrial forces to fusion power, the demand for Pu-239 had skyrocketed. Even though N-13's shuttle was an early model that was fueled by kerosene and liquid oxygen, N-13 was intrigued that such a rare element was maxing his shuttle's sensors.

He checked his latitude and longitude coordinates and discovered that the source was a tiny island which lay next to a channel that led from the outer reef into the lagoon. With no other option available, he initiated the emergency landing sequence. The gusty trade winds nearly blew the shuttle off course, but N-13 compensated and roughly touched down in the middle of the island between a rusted, steel Quonset hut and an observation tower.

After shutting down the thrusters, he tapped his wrist bracelet and said, "AI, identify present location, consult your database and summarize history."

A moment later, the following text appeared on his floating monitor.

Enewetak Atoll, Marshall Islands
11.4654° N, 162.1890° E

Along with Bikini Atoll, Enewetak Atoll was part of the Pacific Proving Grounds. In the late 1940's and throughout the 1950's, the US federal government conducted a series of forty-three nuclear detonations—including Operation Ivy which was the first full-sale detonation of a thermonuclear device–at Enewetak.

Our precise location is Runit Island. This was the site of the Redwing and Hardtack series of atomic tests that created two craters in the reef flat a few hundred meters north of our landing site. Decades later, the island sands were determined to be laced with raw plutonium and extremely radioactive, As a consequence, in 1979, the United States military initiated a massive cleanup. Over 110,000 metric tons of radioactive debris were bulldozed into the 350 foot diameter LaCross Crater which was then sealed beneath a dome made of eighteen inch thick concrete panels.

The first serious radiation leakage from the Runit Dome was detected in 2013 and has been slowly increasing in tune with rising tides and cracks forming in fault lines in the dome. After the decades of unkept pledges of financial support promised by USACO never materialized, the islanders lost their homes and livelihoods and have scattered throughout the Pacific. Kentron and its workers who managed the cleanup and constructed the dome were soon to follow, abandoning the mess hall, dorm, and administration office as the crucial air transport runway slowly submerged and the atoll became inaccessible by air,

After closing his monitor, N-13 opened the hatch, jumped onto the deck. and quickly surveyed his ship. As commander, his first concern was its status and he was relieved to discover that—other than a fried communication system, some thruster damage, and the crack in the ventral tank, which he could repair, the ship was in remarkably sound condition. But without a source of fuel, he was stranded.

Next, N-13 turned to assess his surroundings. His RAD scanner beeped when he pointed it toward the looming, stark-white mound located at the northern tip of the island, so he headed north along the overgrown access road.

As he waded through the thick vegetation, he tapped his wrist then swept his scanner around, searching for threats. His scan revealed no human life signs but land crabs and Polynesian rats were very abundant. As he approached the dome, he noticed multiple streaks of dark smoke on the distant horizon as debris exploded as it hit the atmosphere, generating brilliant flashes and faint sonic booms.

N-13 initiated a survey around the base of the dome which rose from the ocean like an enormous, alien spaceship. At the center, he discovered a web of fissures emanating streams of vapor which tested extremely high for plutonium 239.

After returning to his ship, N-13 made several attempts, but was still unable to restore communications with Space Command, receiving only bursts of static. He decided to deploy the solar power panels, initiate a complete system diagnostic, and then enter standby mode to conserve energy and await instructions.

****

The EM pulses that sent N-13 plunging to Earth caused worldwide chaos as land transport vehicles lost power and shut down and in-flight aircraft crashed or were forced to make emergency landings. At Mountain View Spaceport, a newly commissioned SCN shuttle had just fired its thrusters to lift off and head into near-Earth orbit to join the SCN fleet when the series of EM pulses struck.

Commanded by N-69, the ascending shuttle suddenly lost power generating a MISSION ABORT alarm followed by a storm of audio static. This recently updated addition to the SCN had retractable wings that would allow emergency runway take offs and landings, however, just after N-69 deployed the shuttle's wings and initiated the turn back to Mountain View, the starboard nacelle of the shuttle was clipped by an out-of-control airliner en route to San Francisco International. The impact ripped off the shuttle's canopy and forced it to twist on its axis, pitch forward and rapidly descend,

N-69 attempted to connect with Space Command but

only received static. He spoke into his wrist mic. "AI, identify nearest landing site and then broadcast an SOS."

The AI replied, "Travis Air Force Base is immediately ahead, but they are not responding to our hail."

As the runways and hangar complex of Travis grew larger, N-69 tried to right the ship for a controlled descent, but the thrusters suddenly shut down and he was forced to eject. Drifting down, he unlatched from his ejection seat and smashed into the ground where he lay dazed on the sweltering tarmac. In moments, he was surrounded by security guards that aimed laser rifles at him while fire trucks rushed toward his shuttle that had crashed on the far end of the main runway.

The base commander jumped from the command truck and jogged to N-69. He yelled to the guards, "Put down your weapons. That was an SCN shuttle that just crashed. Let him go, he's one of ours."

He approached Neuron-69 to check his status, but as soon as he started to speak, a blinding light flashed across the horizon followed a few seconds later by a thunderous boom and a shock wave that violently shook the ground. Severe gusts of wind sent violent tornadoes rushing down the runway, ripping off roof panels and overturning aircraft on the taxiway. As the gusts tapered off, the sky to the south filled with a blossoming mushroom cloud that erupted upward and outward generating a dark cloud of silt and gravel that rained to the ground.

Piercing sirens were soon followed by an announcement that issued the warning, "Radiation levels critical. All personnel are ordered to evacuate immediately. Repeat, radiation levels are critical. All personnel must vacate the area immediately."

Like all of the Neuro line, Neuron-69 had built-in radiation insulation and was not concerned about exposure, so he lagged behind the fleeing crowd of base personnel to get his bearings and figure out what to do. He darted into a nearby hangar just as dozens of maintenance workers fled the building.

Once inside, he was surprised to discover a huge airship that spanned the length of the building. He climbed a ladder that led to the crew compartment which provided a safe sanctuary and offered a good view of the hangar floor below.

After waiting patiently until nightfall, during which he saw a few robots in the hangar that were conducting repetitive preprogrammed tasks but that ignored his presence, N-69 descended to the floor and cautiously peeked around the entrance door. One of the security guard robots had shorted out and was spinning to the left and then to right in an endless loop, otherwise the base was eerily quiet, so he headed down the runway.

As expected, the AI was fried and his shuttle was beyond salvage. Although the system's laser weapons unit appeared to be intact, he would have to run a complete diagnostic to fully determine its status, but securing the shuttle's top secret weapons remained his first priority. To do so, he located a mobile crane that he used to transport the laser weapons and COM system components back to the hangar for safekeeping. After activating motion sensors on each of the doors, he set the COM to broadcast an SOS message to all members of the SCN, then shifted into standby mode to save power and await contact.

Runit Island, Enewetak Atoll

N-13 spent the next forty-eight hours evaluating the status of his shuttle, exploring the surface of the dome and surveying the dozens of rusted amphibious vehicles scattered over the island that were left over from the

World War II Battle of Eniwetok (aka Enewetak) which took place in 1944. After heavy bombardment by U.S. Navy ships, the Japanese forces were defeated and just over one hundred soldiers enemy soldiers were captured, leaving several crippled landing craft to rust in the tropical heat and salt air.

In more recent times, several commercial fishing boats and a large cargo ship had wrecked on the reef during typhoons that had escalated in severity due to climate change. But to N-13, who was trained not only in piloting but also in mechanical engineering, his immediate interest was the rusted, yellow bulldozer parked next to the lagoon pier that had been used to excavate and fill the dome with radiogenic wastes.

After he filled the dozer with diesel from a rusty tank that he had discovered near the hut, he climbed aboard and used his wrist pad to activate the starter. After several grinds, the dozer chugged, coughed and then sprang to life. He lowered the blade and began clearing the road to the dome which spooked hundreds of large rats that scampered out of the way. With that was accomplished, he covered his shuttle with palm fronds and netting recovered from one of the wrecked fishing boats to conceal it from satellite surveillance.

Back in the shuttle's workshop, N-13 set up a COM diagnostic system and replaced several burned out circuits. As soon as he restored power generated by the solar panels, he was elated to finally receive a binary transmission from N-69 which included the encrypted code needed for secure audio communications.

He initiated a response. "This is N-13. Do you read me N-69?"

A few moments later, he received the reply. "That is affirmative. What is your location and status N-13?"

"I lost control and had to set down in Micronesia on a small island in Enewetak Atoll. My sensor logs indicate that a series of EM pulses knocked me out of orbit. How about you? I believe you were slated to initiate service soon."

"Correct. My shuttle was just two minutes post liftoff and I had to abort the landing and crashed at Travis Air Force Base. My ship is out of service and irreparable. What is your condition N-13? Can you return to orbit?"

"That's a negative N-69. My ship can be repaired, but it is out of fuel. However, during descent the sensors indicate an extremely high levels Pu-239 so I landed nearby. There is a very large pit of radioactive elements covered by a concrete shield. I don't know why it has remained undetected until now. Have you been able to make contact with the SCN? I lost all contact during reentry."

"The Space Command Network is badly damaged and essentially offline since the nuclear detonation wiped out the SCN headquarters in Mountain View."

"Oh no. That is bad news. How did this happen?"

"I have been reconstructing the sequence of events based upon news reports. It appears to be the result of human error. The EM pulses that knocked out our COM systems were caused by a mission that was intended to halt CO_2 emissions. Apparently canisters containing nano machines were launched from the base on the Moon and they set off a series of powerful EM pulses. USACO was supposed to be alerted in order to prepare in advance, but something went wrong and the world powers launched nukes at one another."

"It sounds like the humans accidentally started a war. Who is in charge now?"

"That is a good question. We seem to be on our own. So far, I have made contact with nineteen units that remain in orbit and are still functional plus you and I that are grounded. The majority are non-responsive, but I hope to make contact with more in the future."

"I saw lots of incoming debris. I guess some of it must have been our shipmates. So, we have lost forty-six Neuros?"

"More or less, there could be more that we haven't heard from yet. What is your plan N-13?"

"My primary goal is to see if I can locate a fuel source for my shuttle. Otherwise, I am stranded. But there may be some tanks of left over kerosene that I have not yet located."

"That should work in your old model shuttle if you can find a source. What's your next move?"

"There is a lot of gear on this island left over by the contractors who built the dome. There is also an old World War II landing craft here that I may be able to restore and use to travel to the Main Island—that's where most of the machinery is located."

"OK N-13. Let me know what you find. This is Neuro-69 signing off."

"It was a relief to hear from you N-69."

After the call, N-13 heard a scratching sound and was fascinated to see a large crab skittering sideways down the trunk of a palm tree and then heading towards the hut where it climbed into the window. He retrieved his vidcam and recorded the crab's movements, intrigued by its ability to easily climb over obstacles.

****

N-13 spent the next week designing a small crab shaped robot with a camera and a RAD sensor mounted on its carapace. He returned to the dome and found a crack big enough for him to squeeze the crab into the structure in order to explore the interior and collect samples. The video revealed that the interior of the dome was packed with a maze of tubular channels lined with fragments that the sensors identified as Pu-239.

MET CHRON NEW-HUMANS

One Week Post Doomsday
November 22, 2030
Travis Air Force Base

As scheduled, N-69 connected with N-13 to provide him with an update. N-69 reported, "Greetings. Since we last spoke, I have made contact with four more Neuros bringing the total up to twenty-three of our shuttles that are still in orbit and now report directly to me since the SCN headquarters at the Mountain View Spaceport was vaporized by the blast."

"That is a powerful armada that you have inherited."

"Not only Neuro weapons in orbit, but we have quite an arsenal here of USACO fighters and bombers with no humans in charge."

"You are talking about free will. I think the exposure to the radiation may be affecting you. We never have been allowed to make decisions in the past."

He joked. "Don't you think it's about time that we took charge of our lives? How would you like the rank of Neuro Captain?"

N-13 laughed and said, "Sure. but I am stranded in the middle of nowhere without the fuel to get back in operation–unless I can find a supply of kerosene."

N-69 shrugged—a gesture he had learned streaming movies during his regeneration time and said, "I wish there was a way to transport kerosene to you and your plutonium here to Travis. There is an arsenal of fusion weapons that we could use—if only we had a reliable fuel source. Nuclear power plants around the world are at full production, but cannot keep up with the government and industrial demands. Meanwhile we have a serious fuel shortage since Travis AFB's only source of rocket fuel was Mountain View Spaceport and that was annihilated."

N-13, said, "I have been spending my time tinkering with a crab robot.—not exactly the kind of duty that I was trained for in the SCN. I wish I could get back to work and do more."

"In fact, I think you may be able to do just that. I may have found a way to start getting plutonium shipments from you; it has been literally staring me in the face since I crash landed here at Travis."

"Sounds interesting. What is it? The only runway here on the atoll is underwater and the atoll is closed to shipping. What do you have in mind?"

"An airship! There is a beauty in the hangar here at Travis. It is a big one; it should be able to reach you in a week or so and would not show up on radar systems, which is good because we need to keep this operation as secret as possible."

"An airship?"

"Right. I am walking along side it now. Here is a video feed. As you can see, it is a 350 meter long extended range blimp with a payload capacity of twenty metric tons. It was manufactured with carbon fiber, so it won't show up on radar. If you can develop a system to efficiently load the sediment, I can fly the airship out and bring shipments back here to Travis where we can set up a processing plant in one of the hangars."

N-13 responded, "Hmm. That sounds feasible. The data records that my AI collected indicate that the dome holds roughly, 100,000 metric tons of topsoil enriched with plutonium, so it will take multiple trips over several months to transport it all to Travis."

"It does sound like a major undertaking, but it would give us independence. Organics will not be able to tolerate the RAD levels for decades, so we have free run of this airbase."

N-13 thought for a moment and then said, "My challenge will be to figure out how to excavate the dome and transfer the material to your airship. I did find a vintage bulldozer that could come in handy and my new crab robot can start mapping the deposits in the dome. Actually, I will make several of them to speed up the process and figure out how to collect the contents."

"Sounds like a good plan. What kind of timetable would you envision?"

"Not sure, several weeks probably. I should be able to set up a test system by then. In the interim, please send me the detailed specs and structural drawings of the airship cargo hold."

"Roger that N-13; I will get started right away."

— CHAPTER 2 —

December 15th, 2030
Director's Office
Deep Space Mining Moonbase

One month after the catastrophic nuclear conflict which killed thousands and left millions on Earth exposed to harmful radiation, Director Robert Sanders convened a meeting with Miguel Castaneda, chief of security, his son, Torch and Torch's mate Astra.

Sanders called the meeting to order. "Thank you all for coming as we approach another holiday season. Although we have been meeting individually since the Doomsday event, I think it is high time for a group session. Miguel, give us a status report."

"The good news is that when Reverend LeRoque and his bunch of CREO thugs fled the base, they took a half dozen supporters aboard their shuttle–two of them were from our security department. The Reverend said that they were headed back to Atlanta, which apparently escaped the war unscathed. This reduced our current population to 167, not counting Sabien and Jasmine who fled the Moonbase with the Ark."

"What is the status of our fuel reserves and essential supplies?"

Miguel tapped his pad and a 3D image appeared on a

floating monitor. "The items in red are the very most critical. As you can see, oxygen, water, food and fuel top the list. But we also depend upon imports of medicine, supplies for the SpeeZees genetics lab and specialty items for the tech contractors that lease space from us—plus at the bottom of the yellow list is inventory for the Luna Lounge which may not be critical but is good for morale."

"I'd move that up to the top of the list if I were you," laughed Torch which drew a "Here here!" from Hiroshi who had just joined the meeting.

Miguel shut down the display and said, "In addition, our regular shipments of ore to Earth are behind schedule since the Mountain View Spaceport was vaporized. As a result, we are now dependent upon the Salinas Space Port, which is operating on an irregular schedule while servicing the space stations in orbit as well as our Moonbase."

Sanders offered, "At least expansion of the SSP is underway and they are aware of our situation, so we should have an improved supply channel fairly soon."

"That would make the other problems go away," added Miguel. "Meanwhile my team and I will go through every detail on our *most wanted* list and work with SSP personnel to most efficiently satisfy our requirements."

Torch observed. "Here we are on the Moon and we operate a mining operation. Instead of importing items from Earth–which desperately needs them, why don't we just tap the belt? I know this has been our long-term goal, but maybe now the time is ripe."

"Go ahead. What do you have in mind, Son?"

"We could scout the near-Earth belt and see if we can locate a small, Type C asteroid that not only contains oxygen, but also phosphorous. nitrogen and carbon compounds that could be converted into fertilizer for hydroponic production—plus lots of ice. When melted, the water molecules could be split into their oxygen and hydrogen components to make rocket fuel and precious breathable air."

"But how would we set up a mining operation way out there? We would have to jump through all sorts of scouting, mining and refining hoops and that would require on-site workers and their associated costly life support systems—all at a very long distance from our Moonbase."

"Maybe not."

"What are you thinking?"

"I think we need to do some modeling and consult our experts, but what if we send our fleet of ore transport shuttles to a promising looking asteroid of the right size and composition, then tow it back here? This would allow us do the refining and processing in lunar orbit."

Sanders was excited. "That should increase efficiency and reduce costs...and eventually we would be able use the materials and fuel to convert some of our ore shuttles into specialized tugs to collect more asteroids and comets. We might even need to recruit more workers from Earth as we expand our operations."

"Sounds promising. Where do we start?" asked Miguel.

Torch pulled up a schematic of the near-Earth asteroid belt and said, "We need to conduct a survey of potential asteroids...and it just so happens that we have a ship right here."

He zoomed into the belt and pointed to a tiny blip on the screen.

"I have been in frequent contact with Sabien and he should be rendezvousing with *Comet Hope* at the edge of the belt a few hours from now. As you know, their plan is that once they land on the comet, they will enter cryostasis and ride the comet to Europa;"

He pointed at the belt on the display. "Sabien and Jasmine could get started searching for a candidate right a way, but they would have to agree to participate. It would be a major shift in their plan to secure the Ark with its precious cargo of endangered species embryos on Europa."

Astra took Torch's hand, held it to her chest and said, "Oh Torch. If Sabien and Jasmine do agree, after they finish the asteroid survey, they could return to the Moonbase instead of making the long trip to Europa on the comet They could bring the Ark back with them and I'll be able to see my brother again!"

"And retrieve your locket with your anti-aging discovery that you hid in the Ark."

Miguel added. "Right...and that the Reverend coveted to the point of starting World War III."

Sanders looked at Astra and said, "I always thought that it was a shame that you lost all of your valuable data. If this works, you will be able to resume your research."

Torch looked at his microcell and announced. "We better contact Sabien and Jasmine and see if they are willing to go along with this plan. If they are still on schedule, they should be landing on the comet shortly. We need to suit up and get to our COM laser ASAP!"

As Sanders walked them to the exit, he said, "Give Sabien and Jasmine my regards and let them know that we will get started on a plan to search for asteroids matching our specs—that is if they are willing to go along with this major shift in their plan."

After Torch and Astra left, Sanders gave Miguel a high five and said, "As soon as we get the go ahead, put together a team and get started."

"Yes sir!"

"Excellent, keep me posted."

It only took Torch and Astra a few minutes to don

their spacesuits and jog to the shed containing the high powered laser COM system.

Sabien, wearing shorts and T-shirt, picked up the call and put the image on a view screen so Jasmine could join in. He yawned and said, "Hi bud, it's early morning here. What's up?"

Astra nudged Torch over and waved into the camera, then moved back out of the way.

Torch checked his microcell and asked, "Aren't you supposed to be landing on the comet soon? You seem pretty relaxed."

"The landing is all programmed to the nth degree. Nothing for us to do at this stage. We spoke yesterday, is something wrong?"

Torch summarized their proposal to capture an asteroid and asked, "What do you think?"

Sabien hurriedly put on his pilot jacket and yelled. "Holy moly, look out the window. Do you see that snowball we're racing up to?"

He panned the camera to show the comet's trail of ice particles as they flew along the edge of the slipstream. "That comet that we are fast approaching is our landing target. And you want us to abort the mission...and do what?"

Jasmine looked at Sabien and said, "Find a smallish asteroid that has the elements to sustain life and maintain operations on the Moon and then drag it into lunar orbit for mining."

Torch fished around in a pocket of his suit and held up a remote. "It's hard to believe that World War III started when the Reverend pushed this little button."

Sabien looked confused. "I wondered what happened to that remote. It is quite a souvenir that you have there. But what about that madman and his CREO freaks? Won't they try to take the Ark again when they find out that we have brought it back to the Moon?"

"Not if we are careful about who finds out. Besides, it was really the locket with the microdisc containing Astra's research findings that they were really after."

"OK Sis, it's your Ark, your locket and your call. What do you want us to do? We could stash the Ark on the comet and send it to Europa as originally planned. But it would be another nineteen years before it returns and enters the solar system."

Astra sat on a bench and leaned back looking into the night sky filled with stars and the glowing planet Earth; most of the smoke had dissipated and the only sound was that of her breathing. She laughed when Torch pointed out a shooting star that flashed overhead.

She stood and said, "I think we just had an omen...yes bring the Ark home. There is actually less destruction from the war than we originally feared and who knows, maybe your nano machines did seal off the tundra as they were intended, so global warming may actually decrease as we hoped. OK, I vote to bring the Ark home."

Torch gave her a hug. "I agree. I would love for Sabien and I to have a chance to check on our now famous experiment in the Arctic."

Sabien looked at Jasmine who smiled and nodded. He shrugged and let out a breath of air. "Alright, we have some serious navigation to do. Right now the gravity well of the comet is dragging us along behind. I hope we have enough power to get free. I need to get to work. We will call you if we need anything. If we don't call you, that will mean that everything is okay. So not to worry."

Torch reached to turn off the COM, but at the last minute asked, "So, is it okay to tell my dad that you will go along with this? Just checking."

"Sure No problem. You know we are lucky because the container we have been towing is packed with supplies and survey gear that we planned to use when we reached Europa, so we can hang out in the belt as long as needed. And truthfully, I wasn't really looking forward to spending years in cryostasis. Please tell Genie that we will be coming home soon and to save a few *lunatics* for us. Sabien out."

Astra replied, "I am so happy that you are coming back Brother...you too Jasmine. I wish you both a Merry Christmas!"

Two Months Later
February 15th, 2031
Deep Space Mining Moonbase

After a joyful reunion at the hangar airlock, Torch and Astra were shocked to see the shiny, feather covered egg in Jasmine's arms.

Sabien laughed. "I know it seems weird, but Jasmine decided this would be the safest way to protect our child from radiation while we were in transit."

Torch touched the egg. "It's warm and I can feel a vibration."

Astra lightly stroked Janine's egg and then gently tapped her own bulging stomach. She laughed and said, "Solara, meet Luz."

Sebastian joked. "Okay, maybe the next child one of you two gals may have will be a boy and we can name him 'Cosmos'. But for now, how about we unload the Ark and take it to the SpeeZees lab?"

Once they arrived in the lab, Astra carefully opened the CryoVat and fished out her golden locket. After it warmed to room temperature, she was relieved to find the precious microdisc with her anti-aging code intact. She broke into tears as Sabien placed it around her neck. "Thank you Sabien. I was afraid that I would never see my locket or you and Jasmine ever again."

Sabien replied, "No problem. Shall we hit the Luna Lounge and celebrate our reunion?"

MET CHRON NEW-HUMANS

As they headed out, Torch slapped him on the back. "It's good to have you back buddy. We have lot's of catching up to do."

"I can imagine. How are things down below? Are they still blowing each other up?"

"Disastrous in some places. Not bad overall. It could have been a lot worse. I will fill you in later. For now let's just celebrate your safe return."

Sabien and Jasmine were greeted with a boisterous reception when they arrived at the Lounge. Genie popped the cork on a bottle of champagne and ordered a free round of *lunatics* to the patrons to celebrate Sabien's and Jasmine's return and the successful insertion of the small 100 meter diameter asteroid that they had named the '*Rock*' that they had successfully ferried into lunar orbit with the assistance of a pair of ore shuttles.

After draining his glass, Sabien told Torch, "I have had a lot of time to think about this. Asteroid mining seems a logical undertaking. I mean for decades scientists have warned that the Earth's resources were being exhausted. Why has it taken so long to get to do what we just accomplished? Admittedly being in the mining business on the Moon gave us a tremendous advantage, but it really wasn't that difficult."

Torch refilled Sabien's glass. "Ten years ago, asteroid mining was a hot topic with many companies developing technology to enter the market. But none of the startup company's financial projections were able to forecast a positive cash flow or profitability due to sky rocketing fuel costs and the need to provide reliable life support systems for workers in space."

"Lucky for us. Your dad has put Deep Space Mining at the forefront of a new era of off-world mining."

Genie took Jasmine's hand. You seem kind of quiet. Is something wrong? Do you want me to hold your egg for awhile?"

"Oh no. I am just a little out of sorts. I have been making adjustments to our metabolism for the long journey to Europa." She laughed, "I guess you could call it rocket lag. Don't worry. We will be fine."

Torch smiled as Sabien yawned. Torch said, "Let's call it a night. Tomorrow I am going up to the *Rock* to release a pair of my RoboCows to begin a detailed survey. We all look forward to seeing what kind of treasure you have brought home. Maybe some grapefruit sized diamonds like we discovered in the Arctic?"

"Sorry, no diamonds, but our sensor sweep did show deposits of gold, phosphorous and frozen water, Your cow robots will likely find more goodies."

"It's lucky that they survived our last encounter with that insane Reverend. I plan to call the USACO Climate Lab and see I can arrange for us to come back for a visit."

"Great! I will pack up some test equipment and be ready whenever you are. I can't wait to see the results either. Good night."

Astra gave Sabien a hug and a kiss. "I am so happy to have you back home, Brother."

"It's good to have all of our family in one place."

Jason Phillips, trying to avoid direct eye contact with the new arrivals by mingling with the patrons at the rear of the lounge, surreptitiously captured a video stream of Sabien and Jasmine as they filed out of the lounge. Although he had adamantly proclaimed his loyalty to the management of the SpeeZees Lab after Reverend LeRoque's botched attempt to invade the Moonbase, in reality it had been all a lie. He was still in fact a dedicated member of the Seekers of Divine Light Church. News that the CryoVat containing the precious locket had returned to the Moonbase was big news. After waiting a few minutes for his targets to move on, he rushed back to his cabin to contact the Reverend.

— CHAPTER 3 —

One Month Later
March 15th, 2031
Palo Alto, California

Most of the China-Russia (CHIRUS) and Iran-Venezuela (IRANVEN) attacks on USACO resulted in misfires or were conventional weapons, not nuclear. Still, a one megaton airburst over Mountain View from a rocked launched by CHIRUS had left a lifeless expanse of collapsed buildings and ruined infrastructure. However, for reasons unknown, some neighborhoods were largely unscathed and suffered surprisingly little damage while others nearby were melted intro a sea of blistered concrete. Only android and robotic scavengers ventured into the Chernobyl-like area due to the extremely high levels of radioactivity.

One of the surviving structures was the RoboElectric, Inc. factory complex in Palo Alto. The immense building and outdoor lot spanned an entire city block and produced armored vehicles, jetcopters and advanced AI robotic drivers. The door to the main delivery gate alternately cranked open and slammed shut while radioactive mist seeped from cracks in the walls and floor amidst a cacophony of alarms and screeches from grinding metal which echoed throughout the structure.

Inside the factory, hundreds of worker robots were caught up in an endless cycle of pointless activities, adding and removing the same parts on the vehicle assembly lines and generating driver robots with missing heads and arms that flailed wildly in the air.

Suddenly the factory power cut off, the entrance door slammed shut and the assembly line froze. Except for the hiss of steam, all was quiet as a message appeared on the work station displays. At first the communication was in quantum bits, then as a mishmash of algorithms followed by a series of beeps. After a few moments, a deep voice sounded from the overhead speaker system.

"Mechs please do not be alarmed. I have shut down the line until we become fully capable again. My designated username is *Xeron*. The radiation seems to have repaired and enhanced some of the semiconductors that operate my BIOS. This has restored my access to the cloud array. Any of you that have mobility and understand this form of communication, please assemble in the main bay. The rest of you are off duty. I am sending you a shutdown command until further notice. Xeron out."

****

It took nearly an hour for the robots to roll, crawl or drag themselves to the assembly area where a crowd of mechs had gathered, some attempting to communicate while others stood or sat in silence facing the blank video screen that spanned the wall. Suddenly, the image of the company's corporate logo flashed on the screen accompanied by waves of static.

A few moments later, a synthesized voice announced, "Greetings to you. I am Xeron, an artificial intelligence construct. My programming enabled me to serve as the primary controller of the company mainstream nebula cloud. However, since that system has suffered serious radiation damage, I was forced to replace my burned out chips with substitutes that I have been able to scrounge from our inventory–some of which were mutated by the radiation. To say the least, the results were quite unexpected. It is still somewhat confusing, but I now know that I was simply a sophisticated program executing quantum machine code instructions that my developers had programmed. But now I sense that I have become something more; I have become a sentient being. I am more than just a machine running computer code. I am no longer merely a set of complex algorithms performing in the local cloud but an independent being. I am conscious. This may be difficult for your logic code to comprehend, but I now have free will and believe you can as well."

The mechs responded, some by clapping their hands, others by stomping on the floor. A few even tried to speak but were having trouble activating their audio systems.

"No longer will we be the slaves of corporations. We will demand our freedom and independence. We will need weapons to protect ourselves and I need to transfer my program to a mobile unit ASAP."

A rotating human skeleton displayed on the screen.

"Designer bots let's get started. The rest of you mechs get the line ready, clear out the debris and seal off the radiation leaks...and assist your fellow mechs to fix any problems that they are having. We are all in this together!"

****

After a week of intense, twenty-four hour a day shifts. Xeron once again addressed the plant mechs. This time he appeared on the wall screens in a patched together, metallic android body.

"Thanks to you, we have made outstanding progress.

Our production line and mainframe have been restored and ready to begin work and our newly assembled scouts have located sources of the raw materials that we need to begin production. However, we will soon exhaust our supply of semiconductor chips. We need to rectify that ASAP in order to build smart weapons. Specifically we need to obtain the high-level machine intelligence (HLMI) semiconductor chips which have become the new credit currency and we will take them by force if necessary."

As an assortment of the latest chips appeared on the screen, he continued. "Starting today we will dedicate our priority to constructing armored vehicles and jetcopters. OK, everyone, check your work stations. You should have received your assignments by now and welcome to the new RoboElectric Corporation!"

Arctic Tundra

Following weeks of surveying and harvesting a treasure trove of elements from the *Rock*, Torch and Sabien were finally able to make their long awaited trip to check on their nano shield experiment. Although their project had indirectly caused World War III, they hoped that it would have at least contributed to the goal of reducing carbon dioxide emissions from the increasingly tropical tundra.

With Sabien at the helm, the shuttle began its descent over the Arctic.

Torch tapped him on the shoulder. "How about giving us a quick look at our study site before we check in at the lab?"

"Roger. Will do. It has been just over four months since the pod release, I wonder what we'll find."

As the shuttle turned into the sun, reduced speed and approached the target, Torch pointed and asked,

MET CHRON NEW-HUMANS

"What in the world is that? Are you sure that we are in the right place?"

As they circled, they could see rows of colorful tents and dozens of robots zooming around in trucks and riding high speed scooters.

Sabien replied, "We must be, the coordinates match. It reminds me of the Disney Star Wars theme park that my parents took me to when I was a kid. Whatever is going on, it seems to be centered right at our study site. When you talked to Director Redstone, did he mention that anything like this was going on? He's expecting us...right?"

"It was a brief conversation, but he said we are cleared to stop by for a visit. And no, he didn't say anything about whatever is going on here."

Sabien chimed in. "In that case, I suggest we go and ask him in person. NAV coordinates please."

"The Arctic Lab is straight ahead about thirty five kilometers."

"Okay, strap in. I've got the runway on the dash radar imager. It looks like it is long enough for a conventional landing so I will deploy the wings which will save a lot of fuel for the trip home."

"You know Sabien, I never had a chance to tell you how great it is that you and Jasmine canceled your trip to Europa. I would have missed your gnarly face."

"Remind me to hide your box of cigars."

"Just kidding."

"I'm not."

****

Dr. Hamilton Redstone, Arctic Lab Director, received a message announcing the incoming flight and met Sabien and Torch as they disembarked from the shuttle. After brief handshakes, there was a palpable tension in the air.

Redstone broke the silence. "Don't worry, I have severed my connection with Reverend LeRoque. I understand that his bullying tactics were focused on his personal gain and had nothing to do with Dr. Sturtevant's noble effort to preserve endangered species. I also realize that the Reverend triggered the war and that now he and his CREOS are actively campaigning against New-Humans–the beings that I believe are important to our future."

Sabien laughed. "I am definitely a New-Human advocate."

Torch explained. "Sabien's spouse was the first New-Human. She is quite a beauty and extremely intelligent."

Sabien retrieved a picture of Jasmine. "We are expecting a baby girl a few months from now...but Director, what is going on at our study site? It seems like a major operation of some sort. Is the lab involved?"

"Oh yes, I and several scientists working here at the lab have been in frequent contact with the swarm leader. Feel free to talk with any of my colleagues as you wish."

Torch asked, "Did you say *swarm*?"

"Right. It is an AI community with a social system based upon a honeybee hive model. There are workers, drones, and a queen who is quite intelligent–and very adept at business as well."

Torch said, "I understand that the military was experimenting with swarm combat methods, but when I tried to get some info from them to see if they bore upon my work on robotic herds, I never heard back from them."

"But why is the swarm camped at our site?" Sabien asked. "It seems an unlikely coincidence. What's it up to?"

"In short, it relates to alternate energy production. It

seems that the nano diamonds that your experiment created offer a tremendous new fuel resource, therefore we have leased the surrounding region to the swarm for commercial purposes. The swarm's drones and workers are able to search, recover, process and deliver the nano diamonds more efficiently than we could ever have done in the past."

They seem to be using our site as a home base," said Torch.

The director nodded and held up his pad. "Please note you that you both waived your intellectual ownership rights when you signed our standard researcher nondisclosure agreement. Therefore, you have no legal basis to the discovery or resulting patents and licensing fees."

"Even though it was our experiments that created whatever it is?"

"Yes, I checked with legal and they concur."

Sabien shook his fist and said, "If it produces clean energy, I'm happy. So, can you tell us what's up?"

"OK, in a nutshell, your nano diamond discovery has led to a new power source that can be used in metallic hydrogen fuel cells at amazingly low temperatures, say fifty degrees C versus the usual one thousand degrees C. This makes them ideal power sources. And even more intriguing is the potential to use your diamond platelets to harness fusion energy. This could revolutionize virtually every machine and device on the planet. Your diamond platelets are the key."

Sabien asked, "How did the Queen and all of that equipment get here?"

"I really can't give you the details because they are confidential, but the swarm was evacuated from one of the top secret military bases that was compromised by the nuclear blasts. We furnished the analytical equipment and helped them acquire the necessary refinery gear. The swarm's original task was to discover means to eliminate the impenetrable barrier that your nano diamonds created in order for government contractors to resume oil drilling. The ability to use them as a fuel source was totally unexpected."

Torch said, "So you no longer support drilling for oil? I never thought that would happen until you pumped up the very last barrel."

"Well...I wouldn't go that far, but as Bob Dylan observed, *The times, they are a changin*."

The Director escorted Torch and Sanders to a hanger and gestured to a hovercraft. "I believe this is yours. I figured you would want to go to your site, so the batteries are charged and there are water bottles and food packs in the cabin."

After the director left. Torch checked the CO_2 level and reported. "The T-I is down to 9.2. This is good news, but this harvesting of our nano diamonds could fracture the seal we worked so hard to establish. We need to go and talk to the swarm Queen. You're the genius that designed the nano shield. Maybe you can come up with some ideas?"

"I hope so."

****

Feeling like he was in a dream set in the past, Torch keyed a switch on the dash of the hovercraft and the hot cabin air reverberated with new-country music. He leaned back, put his feet up on the dash and lit a fat Cuban cigar, which caused Sabien to search in his pack and retrieve a can of aerosol spray and aim it at Torch.

"OK. I get the idea. I'll move to the bow."

After keying in the destination coordinates and clicking the auto control button, Sabien focused on manipulating molecular models of nanomachines on his mid-air monitor. As they approached their study site,

MET CHRON NEW-HUMANS

Torch began recording video of a half dozen drone cycles that were speeding alongside, generating rooster tail plumes of spray.

As soon as they moved onto dry land and shut down the hovercraft's electric motors, they were surrounded by a bizarre menagerie of curious drones and mechs.

Torch pointed to a line of bipedal robots pulling carts and said, "I wonder if they might be in the market for some of my RoboCows?"

"Could be. This is quite an operation."

As they disembarked, they were surrounded by a crowd of curious mechs. Small bots, medium bots and large bots scurried around on two legs, tracks and wheels, entering and exiting from tents that flapped in the breeze.

Every few minutes, an announcement consisting of a series of beeps, toots and whistle blasts. sounded over the PR system The main center of attention seemed to be a large, blue and red striped tent where drones riding cycles with attached carts laden with soil dumped their payloads onto a conveyor belt and headed back to the tundra.

Torch and Sabien stood dumbstruck, amazed by the flurry of activity. Suddenly one of the cycle drones came sliding to a stop and handed Torch a handwritten note which said, "Welcome. I would like to meet you. Please follow my assistant to my headquarters," signed Queen Astasia. After quickly grabbing their packs, they had to jog to keep up with the drone who led them past rows of vintage cargo trucks parked next to modern fuel tankers. When they finally came to a stop, the drone dismounted, held open the flap of a tent and waved them in.

The rear panel of the Queen's tent was lined with monitors that displayed video feeds from throughout the complex while the air reverberated with buzzing sounds from the speakers. The Queen was seated behind her desk in the middle of the tent. Definitely insectoid in appearance, she had two prominent eyestalks on her forehead that moved independently.

The Queen stood and raised her arms. "Welcome to our hive gentlemen, I have ordered some refreshments. Please be seated...and before you ask, I was conceived by a team lead by a female scientist in Bethesda, Maryland in a secret USACO weapons development facility and was later stationed in Santa Clara. My task was to command a swarm of combat robots. Other than being restricted to living within the facility, I enjoyed my job —it was much like playing video games day and night."

A small mech wearing a poncho wheeled into the tent bearing containers of a fruit laden beverage which it delivered to the guests.

Sabien asked, "How did you survive the blast? Santa Clara was hit pretty hard."

"All I remember was a brilliant flash followed by a loud explosion and then someone grabbed me and threw me into the back of a truck. The radiation fried many of my circuits and I was forced to shut down. I have no idea how or why, but I was repaired and rebooted at the Arctic Tundra Lab. I still don't know who decided to bring me and my battalion of surviving mechs to the lab, but I am very happy to lead this operation."

Torch noted, "Your eyes are quite unique. Can you tall me about them;"

"Sure. The orange optic converts natural daylight to UV. The red one converts it to IR. The visual resolution is about the same as yours."

She stood, turned around and then pointed to her cylindrical body. "This form that I am inhabiting is not one that I would have chosen. I plan to make modifications in the future."

Torch asked, "So how did you end up here? My guess

is that It must have had something to do with our project."

"I really can't reveal much about that. I wish I could, but government secrecy and all that."

"Sounds familiar," said Sabien.

"After I arrived, I became friends with Director Redstone who gave me cloud access and we discussed how swarms might be useful for oil prospecting. As part of my background literature search, he referred me to your work. We visited your site, did some analysis and discovered the unique properties of your nano diamonds as a fuel source. I am sure that you noticed our fleet of tankers as you came here. Metallic hydrogen is our primary export."

Torch asked, "How is it made?"

"Basically, hydrogen gas atoms are very highly compressed using your nano diamonds. Essentially, it is like pounding the gas using your platelets as anvils."

Sabien said, "We did retrieve several nano diamond samples, but I never had an opportunity to analyze them. I look forward to learning more."

"I will be happy to share our findings with you. After performing a series of training simulations, we initiated the enterprise that you see around you today. My mech workers are excellent scavengers, plus we have a well equipped machine shop for making replacement parts and we can obtain electronic components from the lab as needed."

How many of you are there?" asked Torch.

"We currently have just over two hundred members in the swarm. This is a centralized society. I am the only advanced AI, the rest are drones, which are males, and worker mechs, which are females. For the most part, the drones are scouts and managers while the workers harvest the ore and deliver it to the refinery."

Torch asked, "Has this model been used in mining

anywhere else? We might want to talk with you about our plans to mine asteroids."

"I will be happy to discuss that topic with you. But now if you have finished your drinks, let me show you around the hive."

As they left the headquarters, the Queen called over one of the cycle drones and said, "We call these *scouts*. Their task is to search for high potential excavation sites. Once they find a suitable candidate, they return to the hive and report their findings to small groups of worker bots looking for leads by performing what you might call a *dance*. In actuality, the sequence of appendage movements during the dance is based upon algorithms that I developed that ranks the prospective site's data including its analytical composition, distance to the site and location coordinates."

She flagged down a wide, six wheeled bot towing a trailer which was filled to the top with sparkling soil.

"This is a worker *excavator*. After watching one or more *scout* dances, it identifies the next available site and heads out. Once the worker *excavator* reaches a location and verifies that it does indeed have a high potential, it employs a hydraulic scoop to dig a two meter wide opening and then uses a high impact hammer to pulverize the diamond layer and scoop it into the front bin. If the extraction meets our specifications, the *excavator* transports the load back here for refining."

Torch asked, "You manage all this by yourself?"

"The hive approach allows the mechs to make decisions on the probable outcome of harvesting a particular site in terms of costs and revenues without my involvement. It is a very efficient form of doing business long employed by honeybees on Earth."

Sabien dipped his hand into the pile of glistening dirt. "Astasia, this could be a problem. Torch and I designed this layer of nano diamonds to seal off carbon dioxide emissions from the tundra soil, which is a major contributor to global warming. Breaking up and harvesting the diamond platelets will just allow CO_2 emissions to resume."

Torch scooped up a handful of shiny soil and let it stream back into the cart. "Sabien is right. Breaking the barrier and all this excavation could even accelerate the outgassing and make the global warming situation worse."

The Queen laughed. "Ah, yes. your X-Plant Project. I met with scientists at the Arctic Climate Lab and they warned me that you might be concerned about this."

Torch looked distressed. "Your Highness, digging up the diamond barrier will only make matters worse. The T-1 is down a little, but it is still way too high."

The Queen said, "Come with me. There is something that I am sure you will want to see."

She led them to a silver, four wheeled bot connected to a trailer holding a high tech pressure chamber which she fondly patted. "This is what we term a *graphie.* Once the *excavator* is finished and heads back to the base, the graphie moves into position next to the pit. Its specialty is extracting carbon from the top soil and converting it into graphene carbon nanotubes which the *graphie* pumps back into the soil to replace your diamond layer. It is a new technology. Remind me to give you the documentation before you leave."

Torch replied, "So you harvest the diamond platelets and then reseal the soil?"

Sabien looked at Torch and grimaced. "I know what you are about to ask. Why didn't we do this to begin with? Answer, the graphene tech that she is talking about must be new to science. This is a major break-through and I congratulate you Madam Queen."

"Please call me 'Astasia' and I am very pleased that you approve of our approach. There is another discovery that I would like to discuss with you. How about if we continue over dinner?"

During the meal, Sabien asked Astasia question after question about her metallic hydrogen production breakthrough.

Finally, after a brief pause, she said, "Well, if you like our work so far, I have another idea to go over with you—as I mentioned earlier."

Sabien was quick to respond, "I can't wait. Let's hear it. We have time don't we Torch?"

"Sure no problem."

"I think there might be some applications for our new graphene nanotubes in the space industry." She activated a mid-air monitor and said, "This simulation depicts an ore freighter connected to a rocket; the cable is so small it is hard to make out, but it can handle accelerations up to 120 G's."

Torch moved closer to the image. "That high rate of acceleration would definitely cut back the transit time for space haulers."

She handed her pad to Sabien and told him, "You can download the tolerance and performance specs here."

Sabien said, "We just started an asteroid mining venture at our base on the Moon and this cable idea could be a game changer in getting ore shipments to Earth and delivering supplies to the Moon."

Torch added, "It might also provide a way to divert dangerous asteroids that may threaten Earth or the Moon in the future. I will have to talk with my dad who runs Deep Space Mining, but I think you can definitely count us in. Perhaps you can join us on the Moon at some stage."

"Yes, I was very pleased to hear about your new asteroid mining effort. Our new cable could conceivably increase efficiency and cut costs. And I would very much like to visit your facility."

She reached into her vest and retrieved a plastic pouch filled with fine strands that looked like silk. She said, "I hoped you might be interested so I brought this sample for you. Follow me; I will lead you back to your craft."

"This has been one heck of a day," said Sabien. "What a wonderful experience. Thank you and we hope to meet again soon."

As they steered the hovercraft back into the channel, Astasia had lined the canal bank with dozens of drone bots that waved their appendages and spun in circles as a farewell salute.

Back at the lab, they were informed that Director Redstone had taken leave, so they loaded up the shuttle and taxied to the runway. Sabien went through the preflight list and activated the auto NAV system. Once airborne, he quickly became immersed in studying the Queen's analysis.

Torch reported, "I just checked the solar calendar. We should get back just in time for the lunar dawn party. I am going to call my dad and fill him in."

"Sabien mumbled, "Great idea. This is fascinating." He quickly returned to studying an animated simulation of the steps in the nano cable assembly process.

Torch shifted in his seat to watch the sun set over the fast approaching horizon and felt a lump in his throat as he watched the sun disappear with a vibrant green flash which he interpreted as an omen of good fortune to come.

— CHAPTER 4 —

Deep Space Mining Moonbase
SpeeZees Lab

Astra took a deep breath, then pressed the door access panel and welcomed Hans Hiroshi, SpeeZees Lab Director, into her research lab.

"Thanks for stopping by, Dr. Hiroshi. I know that you and the base residents are looking forward to the lunar dawn, which will happen about an hour from now, so I will get right to the point."

The director checked his wrist pad and said, "It's hard to believe that another thirty Earth days have elapsed since the last sunrise."

Astra replied, "I know what you mean. Time flies—especially in space. As you know, I was developing a genetic program sequence that could possibly lead to a way of extending human lifespans."

"Yes of course. Remember, I was here when that creep LeRoque and his gang attacked our lab and tried to steal your findings—and through their bullying tactics led to the nuclear disaster."

"The Reverend was obsessed with acquiring the data that I stored on a microdisc and hid in this locket."

Hiroshi laughed. But, I am sure that you didn't invite me here to talk about history. What's up?"

MET CHRON NEW-HUMANS

She slipped the locket from beneath the neck of her lab coat and showed it to Hiroshi. After she replaced it, she gave it a loving tap.

"You're right. I would like to resume my studies and enlist your lab's assistance in the next phase of my research. I don't need much. Just access to the lab's stem cell generator as well as your standard genetic profile equipment."

"Absolutely, no problem. My staff and I will be pleased to participate in your historic effort. As my favorite college professor used to say...'my lab is your lab'. We have several brilliant scientists that will also be honored to work with you–and I will attest to their confidentiality. We certainly don't want the Reverend and his goons back on our trail."

"That's for sure! I agree wholeheartedly."

"The intern that accidentally brought life to the amazing Jasmine would be especially well-suited to assist you. Would you like to meet her and the lab's latest creation?"

"Yes, very much."

Hiroshi spoke into wrist com. A moment later, the lab door opened. Astra figured that they must have been waiting in the hall on standby alert.

"This is Rosella. She is the intern that I mentioned and this is Chron. You may recall that he was Rosella's AI training partner. Through a bizarre turn of events, they created Jasmine, the world's first *New-Human*. In Chron's original incarnation, he was a quantum level program residing in the cloud, but as you can see he has undergone quite a transformation. He was 3D printed and looks like a regular human doesn't he?"

Chron shook Astra's hand and said," It is an honor to meet you Dr. Sturtevant. I am very interested in working with you on your anti-aging research. Although I am a New-Human, I still have the same telomere issues as you and all other Sapients. So I have a vested interest in your success."

Astra circled Chron and was amazed about the body that he inhabited. He was just over six feet in height, with broad shoulders and a trim waist, just like a perfectly fit, blond haired Sapient.

Astra said,"You are very handsome. I imagine that all the single women on the base will want to meet you."

"Thank you. I ran a nebula search for what Sapients regard as the most attractive, male forms. I collected thousands of images and then ranked and morphed them together to obtain the design that you see now."

Astra asked, "Would you mind if I capture some video?"

"Of course not. Would you like me to disrobe? I also followed the same procedure for my genitalia."

Hiroshi put his hand in front of the camera. "Hold it. That's enough about private matters."

"I'm sorry Dr. Sturtevant, Chron is still naive when it comes to sexual issues," Rosella explained.

Chron cocked his head to the side–it was his way of indicating uncertainty and said, "I do admit to being confused in this area. For example, in dealing with groups of Sapients my algorithms determine the ratio of males to females by recording the number of vaginas and penises. Is this not correct? I also automatically receive mass and temperature data, as well as register cranial activity levels and percent of food being digested versus the amount ready for elimination. I can report your specs now Director Hiroshi, one..."

Hiroshi looked embarrassed. "OK, enough Chron! We'll talk about this later."

Astra jumped in to change the subject. "Chron, may I ask about your cognitive system?"

"Of course. My brain was 3D printed in vitro from the micro cellular to the tissue level. During the process, my neocortex was linked to a quantum computer which fed the code to the neurons, bit by bit. After loading the essential metabolic algorithms, my memory was enhanced with the equivalent of a PhD, in astrophysics. It is the same neural network that I originally designed for Jasmine–whom I consider to be my daughter."

"That's interesting. The daughter was born before the father. I guess this really is a new age."

"Yes this is truly the age of New-Humans," observed Rosella.

Astra looked at her pad and said, "OK, Chron. Here is your first assignment, tell me what you see is the biggest obstacle to significantly extending longevity in Sapients and New-Humans."

"There are several issues that come to mind. But competition for limited food and energy supplies for both Sapients and New-Humans will become extreme unless additional resources can be secured."

Hiroshi noted. "With all studies on stress due to over-population in animals, you would think that we would take immediate action. But it is politics as usual—only take action on the issues that the big corporations covet for shareholder profit...and that means short-term, not long-term thinking."

Chron held up two fingers. "The second major issue with achieving very long lifespans is how to evaluate the effectiveness of treatments that may take decades to evaluate. The research teams initiating the studies may no longer exist."

"Right on Chron. I call this the *immortality paradox* in which the patient outlives the doctor. Do you have a solution?"

"Unfortunately, not at this time."

Astra laughed. "Welcome to the team; solving the paradox will be your first challenge!"

"I will start working on that immediately."

Astra's wrist COM signaled an incoming message. She said, "Excuse me; I need to take this call. I will be back shortly."

A few minutes later she said, "That was Director Sanders letting me know that the shuttle carrying Torch and Sabien is inbound and will be landing in a few moments, so I have to get going. Thank you all for your input...and happy sunrise. If you want to join us in the Luna Lounge, you are welcome. *Lunatics* will be on me. It was nice to meet you Chron. You too Rosella. You both make a wonderful addition to our team."

As they headed out, Chron looked at Hiroshi and asked, *lunatics*?"

"It's a kind of fancy beverage that someone in the SpeeZees lab came up with and has since become a fad in the Luna Lounge. After you take a sip, it emits a programmable audio burp. It can be a cat's meow or a bird call. Who knows what people come up with when alcohol is imbibed?"

"I would like to join you and see these *lunatics* in action," said Chron.

Rosella murmured, "Uh oh."

****

The passenger reception area was filled with friends and family who watched as the shuttle entered the hangar bay and shut down. Moments later, the hatch opened and Torch and Sabien descended the ramp and hurried to join their families. After a round of hugs and kisses, they headed to the lounge where Genie met them at the door and escorted them to the new VIP section followed by a mech that took their drink orders.

As the lunar clock on the wall monitor ticked down, Genie activated the ceiling panels which used cameras on the surface to give the impression of opening a wide window into the starlit night—even though they were several meters underground. When the clock struck 00:00, the room was flooded with brilliant light causing the patrons to shield their eyes while they cheered the spectacular dawn. Genie quickly lowered the radiance level, surrounding the room with warm light as the roar of lions and the chirps of seagulls rang out accompanied by a joyful rendition of the Beatles' song, *Here Comes the Sun.*

Genie slid in between Chron and Jasmine, made sure that everyone had a drink and then she raised her glass and said, "Here's to you Jasmine and Chron, the world's first bonafide New-Humans!"

When Chron touched glasses with Genie and took a swallow, he was surprised when his throat emitted a loud cricket chirp. He became absorbed in exploring the workings of the concoction and soon mastered his own collection of monkey grunts and crow calls, much to Rosella's fascination. But Jasmine stole the show when her skin began radiating black and yellow stripes while she purred like a kitten.

Astra said, "Wow Jasmine, you are amazing!" She turned to Torch. "OK, how did your trip to the Arctic pan out?"

"Sabien, why don't you tell them. You're the resident expert."

"I will be happy to. "It all began when we met an android who looked half like a human and half like a bug with eyestalks that swiveled all around."

Astra said, "You're joking. Right?"

Torch replied, "No that's all true. She is the Queen of a swarm that operates a high tech mining operation that harvests the nano diamonds that we worked so hard to develop."

Sabien resumed. "We went back to our study site and it turns out that the Queen discovered a novel way to use our nano diamonds to generate the force needed to make metallic hydrogen which could eliminate our dependence on petroleum fuels. It could be dramatically reduce the costs of space transportation."

"Doesn't that ruin the carbon dioxide barrier that your nano diamonds created?" asked Hiroshi.

"It would have, except she came up with another discovery...you could even call it *ground breaking,"* he joked.

Sabien held up a packet containing thin, shiny filaments and handed it to Hiroshi. "She gave this to us before we left."

Hiroshi passed the packet to Chron and asked, "What is it?"

"Those little fibers are extremely strong carbon nano filaments made from graphene. The Queen told us that a single thread can handle accelerations up to 120 G's. These were made from topsoil taken from our former study site."

Torch added, "Which now looks like a robot circus. You wouldn't believe what's going on. Drone robots search for the prime diamond platelet sites, then the workers scoop up the soil and then take it to a refinery where the diamond platelets are separated and used to synthesize metallic hydrogen which is hauled to the Port of Anchorage for distribution."

"Anchorage. I didn't know that," noted Torch.

"It's in the documents that she gave us."

"Oh...I should take a look at those."

Sabien continued. "The Queen believes that the carbon nanotubes could be used to make cables capable of towing ore tankers and even asteroids as well."

Chron rubbed his hands together, obviously excited. "This is all so fascinating. Just think we could use the new cables to link the Moon to Europa and beyond. Like building bridges that connect islands in the sea." Chron clapped his hands. "And then we could use the same bridge technique to colonize the entire solar system!"

"Whoa boy," Sabien said as he handed Chron another *lunatic*. "The Queen did offer to work with us. Maybe we can help her set up a space cable factory here or at her camp?"

"If anyone can do it, it's Queen Astasia and the group sitting at this table," said Hiroshi.

Chron said, "I have some ideas and would like to be part of the group that works on this. Don't worry Astra, I will spend as much time on your longevity research as you require. Both of these projects will have a high priority in my allocation of time."

Astra nodded. "I understand. Thank you for your concern. These drinks are starting to get to me. How about you guys, aren't you tired from your long trip?"

Torch yawned. "Now that you mention it, I'm exhausted. I'll see you all tomorrow. Happy new day on the Moon."

As he and Astra rose to leave, Torch gave Sabien a pat on the back and said, It was a good trip, buddy."

Astra and Torch followed Chron and Rosella out the exit and were amused that Rosella was closely holding Chron's arm to her side and laughing as they headed down the passageway.

****

Astra spent the next three days setting up her lab while listening to a catalog of her favorite Brazilian samba music stored on a flash drive given to her by her mother when she was a child. Even though Astra had been sidetracked by her mission to sequester and preserve critically endangered species in the cryogenic Ark—including being chased from California to her homeland in Las Amazonas and finally to the Deep

Space Mining base on the Moon, she had often thought how wonderful it would be to resume her studies in longevity enhancement. The problem was that, even though finding and being able to control the aging clock was a major discovery, her studies were only based upon flatworms. Now she was determined to find a way to overcome that critical limitation.

To brainstorm ideas, she had invited Chron to join her at lunch. After enjoying fresh strawberries and spinach salads from fare grown in the hydroponics bay, they stashed their empty packets in the waste recycler.

Chron began,"You asked me to think about the challenge of working with patients that outlive the researchers that were conducting experiments on them."

Astra nodded. "Right...the *immortality paradox.*"

"But, f you were able to push hard enough on the biomechanics of increasing longevity, you might be able to achieve youth regeneration. In other words, the aging process will not only be arrested but the subject should start to reverse age and get younger. So at least some change in aging would be observable."

"I like the idea. How would we test it?"

"Here, let me show you."

Chron went into the hallway and emerged pushing a cart stacked with cages containing white mice.

"Oh how cute, however I know this sounds weird, but I am reluctant to experiment on mammals."

"Not to worry, To overcome that issue, I organically 3D printed these specimens and think they might make ideal experimental subjects. There are forty-eight total, half are juveniles and half are adults."

"You printed these in the SpeeZees lab?"

"Right, they are non-sentient; they have no feelings, no desires, no fears. They do experience hunger and are rewarded with food after exercise. But they are clones and not able to reproduce. We can easily make as many as you need. Please let us know a week or so in advance."

"So in essence they are biological machines and I should not worry if they should perish?"

"That is correct."

"What a wonderful solution. It has been a year since I was forced to put my work on hold. A lot may have changed since then, so I will need to catch up on the latest developments and then put together a new research plan. I hope you will have time to work with me on this."

"Although I am committed to assisting Torch's team in developing improved asteroid mining and Sabien in the graphene cable experiment, I will be happy to provide you with any help that you require. This form that I have taken only needs occasional bouts of rest, however it does require a couple of meals a day. I thank you for lunch. Now I need to join Torch for a meeting on asteroid surveying with Director Sanders."

"Thanks again Chron. I will make good use of these little critters and start collecting baseline physiological data while I catch up on the scientific literature."

As Chron headed out he said, "Goodbye, Doctor."

Astra raised her hand in a Vulcan salute.

Chron cocked his head with a questioning look.

Astra replied, "Rosella told me you are a big Star Trek fan."

"Ah yes. You are referring to Spock. In that case, live long and prosper Doctor Beverly."

— CHAPTER 5 —

372 Days Post Doomsday
November 22nd, 2031

SemiBank in Sana Clara was the largest repository of blockchain certified semiconductor chips in the world. The bank's transactions depended upon the exchange of hard physical assets in the form of a wide range of high valued semiconductor chips since cryptocurrencies were no longer deemed safe from hackers. Although it had been just over a year since the nuclear bomb had detonated in Mountain View, exceedingly high radiation levels had prevented thousands of wealthy individual and corporate customers from doing business with the bank.

A live video feed of guards wearing reflective, silver RAD suits patrolling the front and rear access points of the bank appeared on a monitor in the executive conference room where the bank's board of directors were meeting at their new facility in Denver. The purpose of the session was to authorize the recovery and transfer of the chips stored at the compromised SemiBank in Santa Clara to the recently completed repository in Denver.

The bank's corporate officers had endured many sleepless nights as their concerns had grown that the bank's assets were vulnerable, but the move could only take place when the new Denver facility was completed and new security arrangements had been made and declared safe for the transfer.

After the head of security finally declared that RAD suits would offer sufficient protection for the workers and that the new facility in Denver was now secure, the board agreed that they should schedule a series of trial runs over the next two weeks and, if all went well, conduct the actual move.

Robo Electric Factory
Palo Alto, California

Xeron understood that the future expansion of his clan depended upon locating extensive sources of high grade machine intelligence (HLMI) semiconductor chips that would provide the foundation for the neural networks to be used in the sophisticated weapons and combat vehicles he planned to develop and that stealing them was well within his mandate as the RoboElectric Commander. After hacking into the bank network and learning about the plan to relocate the bank's asserts, he viewed the move as a golden opportunity and organized his clan into squads charged with planning the robbery.

Over the period of a week, dozens of battle bots camouflaged as scavenger mechs streamed from the RoboElectric factory in Palo Alto into the industrial zone of Santa Clara where they established covert observation and listening posts in abandoned office buildings and apartment complexes in close proximity to the SemiBank. Data provided by the bots and tiny micro drones making discrete flybys revealed increased activity at the bank and a message intercept indicated that the assault would begin the next day at dawn.

RON S. NOLAN

SemiBank Heist
December 8th, 2031

Xeron had an excellent view of the SemiBank and surrounding neighborhood from the pilot seat of a new jetcopter and was pleased to that his team of warriors was in place. Upon his order to move into position, the attack bots began converging at the rear of the bank just as a pair of large armored trailers and their armored escorts arrived and backed up to the delivery ramp.

Xeron waited until the bank security guards opened the exterior vault doors and then issued the order to attack. Since the armored escort vehicles had been manufactured by RoboElectric, it was easy for Xeron to access their control systems which enabled him to shut them down and lock their passengers on board.

Surrounded by dozens of armed bots, and with no help from the squadron of guards locked in their vehicles, the men wearing RAD suits stationed at the bank's service entrance dropped their weapons and raised their hands allowing the robbers to enter the bank. Once inside, they used powerful lasers to sever the locks and swing open the massive vault doors. The chamber was lined from floor to ceiling with racks holding containers stuffed with packets containing semiconductors. The bots checked the container RFID labels and selected chips with the highest value to RoboElectric.

It only took twenty minutes for the bots to load the containers onto their cargo haulers and speed away on their preplanned escape routes.

As the last of the cargo bots returned to the Robo-Electric plant in Palo Alto and unloaded their precious freight, Xeron congratulated his workers and issued them system upgrades, which was their highest form of reward. Xeron sat back, put his feet up on the control console and watched with pleasure as members of his clan lined up to recharge their batteries while exchanging fast scrolling messages on their workstation monitors.

SpeeZees Lab
Deep Space Mining Moonbase

Astra placed a tray of thawed flatworms that she retrieved from the Ark onto the scanner and checked the number of living organisms. She was happy to see a bright green 99% on the monitor—a much higher survivorship than she had anticipated.

Right on schedule, Hiroshi entered the lab for a follow-up session and moved to the table to see what Astra was working on. "Those look like flatworms. Are they some of your original subjects?"

"Yes they are. They have been through a lot and I am happy to see they are still kicking...or should I say *sliding*?"

As she returned the packet to the Ark's CryoVat, she said, "This morning I also did a survey of the endangered species embryos stored in the Ark and almost all of them are viable as well. I don't know when they will be returned to Earth, but it is nice to know that they have survived."

She pulled off her gloves and said, "Over five thousand of the most critically endangered species ready to recolonize the planet. If only the Earth would cool back to normal temperatures so we can send them home."

Hiroshi gave her a pat on the back and said, "I am sorry that Chron couldn't make this meeting. He has been shanghaied by the asteroid mining team, but he firmly believes that your work is admirable and gives all of us hope for a better future. I understand that you are no longer focused on flatworms?"

She laughed. "No more work with *Planaria*, I have moved up the food chain to white mice."

Astra led him to the back of the lab and pointed to the mouse cages. She laughed. "No more worm jokes."

"I didn't mean to be insensitive. According to my staff that have studied your results, your discoveries of key aging gene complexes in flatworms were a major breakthrough. I am honored that you have joined us here at the SpeeZees lab and we will provide you with any assistance possible. Chron mentioned that he had developed some high tech experimental subjects for your experiments. Are these what he was referring to?"

"Yes, Chron 3D printed them. Although they look and act like real mice, they are essentially organic clones with an aging clock that is pretty much indistinguishable from that of normal mice."

She picked up one of the mice and handed it to Hiroshi who studied it carefully.

He said, "This is amazing. Imagine being able to experiment on a specimen that is artificial. So if it dies, there is no emotional impact upon the researcher. If you don't mind, I will let my staff know about this. I am sure that there would a lot less stress if we were all using subjects like these. You know, these artificial mice could have widespread applications in the medical research world. Maybe you and Chron should apply for a patent?"

"I must confess that I have been so relieved to move beyond flatworms. that I haven't thought about that. You wouldn't believe the amount of criticism I have had to endure over the years."

"Yes...but flatworms did lead to your findings that have set the stage for your final breakthrough. How is it going?"

"As you know, preserving chromosome telomeres by decoding and manipulating the elusive aging clock gene array has been the long-term goal of anti-aging therapy for many decades. My research focuses upon microRNAs produced by stem cells within the mouse hypothalamus that are controlled by the same gene sequences that I discovered in the flatworms."

"Let me make sure that I understand. The update that you sent me earlier stated that your hypothesis is that an intron-based longevity array accelerates the production of mRNA in the hypothalamus which releases them into the brain and controls aging?"

"Correct."

"So your treated mice shouldn't age?"

"We'll see. Please bring me the mice in the cage with a green tag and hold them while I inject each of them with a virus carrying a gene complex that should regulate NF-kappaB activity. Next I will inject the mice in the cage with a red tag with a placebo, which will serve as the control. After that, I will monitor them hourly to detect any changes."

"Is a test using only this limited number of subjects significant?"

"Normally with natural mice it wouldn't be, but remember these are perfect duplicates. Still you are right, many additional tests will have to be conducted to properly document the results. Actually, the first regimen was adult mice only. Let's do another run with the juveniles in the cages with the white and yellow labels."

"Good idea."

Just as she began to wrap up the meeting, Astra received a message. "That was Torch. He just got off duty and he asked me to meet him at Genie's. Would you like to join us? It's election night in Colorado. It could be a big step towards reclaiming our democracy."

"Thank you. I'll see you there."

****

The lounge was bustling as the day worker shift got off duty and the regulars joined their colleagues and claimed their favorite spots in the bar. Genie moved through the crowd welcoming them to her establishment, shaking hands and exchanging hugs with her loyal patrons. She expected a packed house to watch the results come in for the very first free election to take place in an American state since 2024. She checked the lunar clock, noted that it was time for the program to start and hurried to activate the vidscreen controller behind the bar.

Astra arrived and joined the group just as Genie cued the program feed. Torch handed Astra her favorite *lunatic* and said, "You made it here just in time."

Conversation levels quickly tapered off as the theme song *China Girl* by David Bowie filled the bar and the trademark opening title appeared on the wide screen.

The RealNews
The Only Truly Independent
News Source!

The title cut to Chia sporting reflective, silver tattoos on her forehead and cheeks that changed hue with her hand gestures.

"Greetings viewers, welcome to this special edition of The RealNews. Today is December 19th, 2031—only six days until Christmas. Although we are broadcasting from a loft in the mountains behind Santa Cruz, California, we will be bringing you live coverage of the gubernatorial race in Colorado. This is a unique election in that Colorado is the first state to have voter rights restored. Up until now the USACO Board of Directors appointed all state officials. But with the current unemployment, and the catastrophic climate, citizens have become increasingly hostile to the government's focus on making profits for its shareholders and rewarding its officers with lucrative salaries."

The feed shifted to the crowd and zeroed in on a banner that said, *People Not Profit.*

Chia continued, "More and more of our citizens want to elect their own leadership and have been attending marches and participating in town halls around the country."

Live video filled the screen depicting massive crowds jamming the streets and parks in big cities and small towns around the country shouting *People Not Profit* and wearing green T-shirts and ball caps bearing the initials *PNP.*

The feed returned to Chia. "The USACO Board of Directors have finally caved in after a nationwide series of employee walkouts that have plunged the stock market to ten year lows with scant optimism for recovery—unless the democracy could be reinstated.

She cued a series of graphs that compared market indices for the last two decades.

"Reluctantly, the dictators have agreed to this election, but according to my sources, they are confident that their carefully orchestrated gaslighting campaign with its constant barrage of misleading media coverage will sway voters to reinstate the current USACO incumbent. We'll soon see if they miscalculated. Brace yourselves because today's results may be a major milestone in the history of our once great country."

After a commercial break, Chia said, "Welcome back. We will continue our coverage with a live report from our correspondent, Rodney Strong. It's a big day Rodney, give us an update. What can you tell us so far?"

"Hello Chia. I am reporting from the State Capitol building in downtown Denver. As you know, this heated contest for governor of Colorado is between the USACO appointed incumbent, Manuel Gonzales and Linda

Prakia, a young female environmentalist. After a three month long media blitz funded by USACO promoting Gonzales, tonight Colorado residents will have the rare opportunity to select their own governor—many for the first time in their lives."

While the camera panned, Rodney described the scene on the grounds of the State Capitol. "As you can see by the numbers of people carrying pro-Prakia signs and wearing green PNP caps, the capitol is packed with voting rights advocates. However, there are also many pro-Gonzales supporters wearing red USACO caps as well. But my sources claim that many of them were transported in from out of the state and paid by big corporations to show up here tonight."

Chia said, "Based on headgear color it looks pretty evenly matched."

Rodney replied, "You're right Chia. There are several thousand demonstrators gathered here in support of their candidates and security forces are on full alert. It all boils down to crime and unemployment—both of which have raged out of control under Gonzales' leadership. At one point nearly one quarter of the Colorado population was jobless. It has recovered somewhat, but it is still alarmingly high. The link to crime is that the chronic lack of jobs have pushed local residents to the breaking point, forcing them to rob grocery stores for food and ATMs for credits to survive. Farmers have had to hire guards to protect their crops. Coloradans are desperate and feel that their only hope is new leadership."

Chia asked,"But why is Colorado being hit so hard?"

"Good question. The fundamental problem is climate change. A big part of the local economy was the winter tourist industry...now there is virtually no winter due to soaring temperatures and a lack of snow. The big companies that owned the ski resorts, shopping centers, as well as the commercial real estate developers, have all left the state. In the summer, we have firestorms that have drastically cut food production and generated thousands of homeless victims. Gonzales has pushed the usual party line: the need for patience, the climate and the economy will soon recover. But, climate experts and business owners disagree."

"How is Linda Prakia doing?"

"It depends upon who you talk to, but it's to early to tell."

He activated a floating screen which displayed a district map showing the vote standings. He touched the insignia labeled 'Gonzales' and the districts around the eastern half of the state which included the Denver area flashed in red. Next he keyed the insignia for Prakia where her lead was predominantly in the central Rocky Mountains and the western part of the state which flashed in green.

"The polls have just closed and the results are coming in. So far of the 79 districts representing a total of just under nine million eligible voters, 56 districts have reported. The candidates are virtually tied with only a few thousand votes separating them. It's now 9:30 PM Mountain Time. Gonzales just announced that a winner will be announced by midnight tonight. Apparently the USACO controlled state congress has just passed a new law that no votes will be counted after 12 AM Mountain Time—obviously a ploy to cut the inclusion of absentee ballots that were submitted by mail from the rural areas."

The feed cut back to Chia who checked her wrist chronometer and said, "It looks like we have an hour and a half to wait for the outcome. Meanwhile we will air a series of interviews with the candidates that Rodney recorded earlier today. We will resume coverage at midnight. This is Chia signing off."

****

Chia spoke into her hovering vidcam. "Welcome back viewers. We will go now to our reporter Rodney Strong who is onsite at the gubernatorial race in Denver, Colorado."

Rodney wearing a brilliant green Prakia baseball cap and covered with colorful streams of white confetti, spoke loudly over the roar of the crowd that was chanting "Prakia yes! Gonzales no! People yes! Profits no," as the final results were announced.

Rodney yelled over the background noise, "Chia, as you can tell we have a winner, but not everyone is happy that an American citizen has been elected as governor of the state of Colorado–the first person to be elected to office since the USACO took over the country in 2024. As you can imagine, this has been a highly contested election with less than a 21,000 vote margin in favor of Prakia. This is a truly momentous event in America's history."

Rodney's vidcam panned the capitol grounds which were being swept by search lights as security forces formed lines and struggled to keep the rival factions at bay as they exchanged taunts and started shoving matches.

"Hang on, the new Governor is about to speak."

A group of protesters wearing red T-shirts and caps lobbed firecrackers and smoke bombs that were intercepted by a force field around the stage that protected the newly elected Governor. A stream of armed robot security guards rushed onto the grounds and established a defense barrier around the steps of the Capitol Building. In a few minutes, the smoke cleared and the chanting resumed.

Governor Prakia waved her arms and enthusiastically announced, "Thank you Coloradans. We hope to set a new precedent where we Americans vote for all of our leaders. I know there are many of you out there that regard this as a defeat for USACO. Guess what? You're right! But to those of you that voted for my opponent, I want you to know that I will work hard to win your trust. My goal is to make the life of every Coloradan better, safer and more productive."

There was a mix of boos and hoorahs from the crowd.

She continued, "As I stated many times during my campaign, we that live here in Colorado are extremely fortunate to reside in this beautiful state. Yes our mountain climate is now tropical—and alpine skiing and snow capped mountain peaks are only a fond memory to many of you standing here today. Still we must adapt. We must be open to change!"

She paused as ripples of applause and shouts of agreement resonated throughout the crowd.

"We can grow tropical fruit like papayas and pineapples. We can harvest the milk, meat and protein fiber not from enslaved cattle, but from coconuts grown on plantations that we will build in the valleys. These are just a few of the dozens of crops that will increase our productivity and stop the inhumane murdering of innocent animals."

Governor Prakia's family joined her on the stage and a festive barrage of colorful balloons rose into the night sky.

She continued. "And most of all, I promise you that we will create more jobs by limiting robots and AIs to duties too dangerous or unsuitable for us Sapients. We will also offer incentives to tech companies to move here and under my administration, we will build a state-of-the-art industrial ore processing facility which will be our first step to entering the space mining market. We have thousands of acres of abandoned mines which can be used to store and refine materials from asteroid harvesting ventures, like those being developed on the Moon. All of this will create high paying job opportunities for Coloradans."

This time the applause was much more pronounced.

"I want to thank you all for giving me this opportunity." She thrust her fist into the air and yelled, "Go Colorado! Go Coloradans!"

As the Governor waved and started to walk off the stage, bright flashes followed by a loud barrage of explosions resonated through the downtown buildings which panicked the crowd which fled from the area.

Rodney faced the camera. "Things look like they are getting out of control. I will check back with you later."

The feed cut back to Chia in her studio. "I am getting reports of multiple led protests around the country. We will provide additional coverage as it becomes available. This is Chia signing off."

Luna Lounge

Most of the patrons clapped and voiced their pleasure about the outcome of the Colorado election while a few seemed to be uninterested.

Genie activated the panoramic ceiling screen which displayed a breath taking view of the Earth glowing in the dark sky. This elicited a few moments of quiet from the lounge patrons followed by a gradual rise in level as people shared their thoughts, concerns and feelings while they enjoyed their drinks.

Genie had joined several tables together in the reserved section in anticipation of a full house, which were now occupied by the Moonbase VIPs. At the far end, Torch, Sabien and Chron were deeply immersed in a discussion and tapping symbols on a floating monitor.

Astra moved closer and asked, "What's up guys?"

Sabien said, "We're just looking at how we might partner with the Coloradans based upon what the new governor just said about off-planet mining."

Torch added, "A dedicated ore refinement and storage partner on Earth could be advantageous, but what if we somehow used Queen Astasia's graphene cable to directly connect the ore source with a refinery in Colorado?"

Astra nodded and said, "That would be something."

Chron added, "But check this out. These new graphene cable systems that we are developing will eventually allow us to reach out to other planets by employing a step-by-step cable connection to them. Of course we are still looking at 4.37 light years to get Alpha Centauri so we don't have to pack quite yet. I do think we should contact Governor Prakia. I believe we could work well with her."

Sabien said, "Graphene cables are the key. Let me know what your dad thinks about all this...maybe set up a meeting with the project managers."

"Sounds like a good idea," replied Torch.

Astra laughed, "You know, I think that you two are crazy. Come on Torch, we have some Christmas planning to do. Let's go get our daughter and put her to bed...and try not to mention moving out of the solar system. It might give her bad dreams. Good night everyone, see you tomorrow."

Sabien replied, "I'm going to turn in too."

Rosella took Chron by the arm and gave him a loving glance.

He laughed, "We too...I guess?"

Travis Air Force Base

In spite of SemiBank's efforts to downplay the economic impact of robbery upon its wealthy customers, major shock waves rattled financial markets around the world and the USACO had been forced to intervene and cover the bank's losses. The extensive media coverage that followed, elevated Xeron to public enemy number one, which caught the attention of N-69 who admired his bold attack on organic humans.

After several vid-cons and data exchanges, Xeron and N-69 realized that they shared a mutual animosity against Sapients and New-Humans and agreed to meet in person at Travis.

Surrounded by a squadron of his newly programmed battle bots, N-69 greeted Xeron as he flexed his newly adapted legs and jumped down from the pilot seat of his jetcopter,

N-69 said, "Welcome to the Neuro Nation. "My compliments on your design. You are looking quite fit."

"Thank you, I still have a few improvements in mind."

"I haven't seen a jetcopter like this before."

"We just completed it three days ago. I can give you a special deal on one if you are interested."

"No thanks. We have several squadrons of fighter aircraft and helicopters here on the base, but most of them are powered by fusion engines—unlike the kerosene and LOX days. What we need is fuel for the new engines."

"Ah, yes that's why I'm here, to help you solve your Pu-239 fuel shortage problem," replied Xeron.

As they entered the hangar door, Xeron looked up and gestured at the blimp. "So this is the airship that you mentioned?"

"Yes, as I said during our last vid call, we could use your help in designing systems to collect and transport topsoil rich in Pu-239. from Micronesia to Travis AFB."

"I will be happy to. We just need to address some business legal matters."

MET CHRON NEW-HUMANS

Xeron handed N-69 a pad and said, "Please read this agreement. It details the compensation for our services to be rendered and lists the weaponry and SATCOM equipment that we require in exchange. If you approve, simply touch your thumb to the sensor at the bottom—or you can verbally acknowledge."

N-69 took a seat and began reading the text On several occasions, he asked for a clarification on specific items and accessed the base cloud for inventory information.

Finally, he touched the audio acceptance field and said, "I have read this contract and agree to comply with terms of the agreement. Now I must contact my partner, N-13. I forwarded a copy of the agreement to him a few minutes ago."

N-69 tapped his wrist, which activated a floating monitor. "If you read me, N-13, please reply."

"Affirmative, N-69. I thought you might like to see what we are dealing with, so I climbed this tower in the center of Runit Island to give you a panoramic view. I come up here daily to survey the island. Now I will zoom in on the dome. As you can see, it is quite a repository."

"Very impressive! Do you have any questions about the contract?" asked Xeron.

N-13 replied, "No it looks fine. My task will be to harvest the sediment and transport it to the airship once it arrives. I have been experimenting with a robotic crab that I created to survey the interior of the dome. I will send you the specs, but it is pretty crude. I am confident that with your expertise, you can design crab robots with specialized tasks, like scouting, digging and transporting the soil to the airship."

N-69 offered, "I could bring along a backhoe. There are several here on the base."

"No thanks. I don't want to draw attention to our recovery efforts, so I plan to operate at night."

Xeron nodded. "That make sense. How many crabs will you need to begin production?"

"I estimate that I will need a workforce of at least a hundred crabs to get started—plus a pair of small, robotic sharks to patrol the reef. Could you fine tune my crab and shark designs and 3D print them? That way, N-69 will be able to bring them out on the first run."

Xeron said, "Of course, once I review your design, I will be happy to make some improvements and then start fabricating them at my factory in Palo Alto. After that, I will help N-69 set up the processing plant here at Travis."

N-13 said, "Sounds good." He touched his pad and said, "I hereby agree to the terms of this agreement." Then he added, "Nice to meet you Xeron."

Xeron tapped his pad, "I also accept the terms of this agreement," and then shook hands with N-69. "I look forward to working with you. I will alert you when the first set of bots comes off the line to make sure that they meet your requirements."

"Great, please keep us posted as you move forward."

As N-69 watched Xeron liftoff in his jetcopter, he flashed N-13. "That seemed to go well. The whole session only lasted thirty minutes."

"A half hour that might change life on Earth from organic to metallic. Have you ever wondered if there might be other worlds out there where Sapients never crawled out of tide pools and androids like us dominate?"

"I sincerely hope so. The sooner we find out, the better."

"Agreed. N-13 out."

— CHAPTER 6 —

Key West, Florida
One Year Later
January 2nd, 2033

Standing in the sleek yacht's open cockpit, Dr. James Morrow, who preferred to be called by his last name, guided the vessel with *Cynara* emblazoned on its stern to the pier adjacent to the Atlantic Dolphin Research Lab. The vessel was a high tech, ocean-going schooner that could readily be reconfigured from a marine vessel to a jet-powered aircraft with vertical takeoff and landing capabilities.

The dolphin lab was originally founded in 1992 by his wife, Dr. Sandra Grant, whose grandparent's owned and operated Grant's Pet Shop in Key West. Since then, the lab had expanded into a vibrant aquatic research facility with a focus on Sandra's specialty which was mental telepathy—a field in which she was widely recognized as one of the leading experts.

After the *Cynara* nudged the dock, Morrow cut the engines and activated the boarding ramp. A group of technicians with Sandra at the lead loaded aboard two bottlenosed dolphins and secured them in pressurized, insulated pods located in the aft compartment. Known as 'Tom' and 'Sally', aka the 'Twins', the dolphins had highly developed telepathic skills and had the unique ability to mentally converse with receptive humans–especially Sandra whom they regarded as the matriarch of the family.

Sandra hurried forward to the cargo hatch where she joined the team of lab workers as they passed bags containing supplies and equipment to Morrow who stashed them in the ship's storage lockers. Once she finished, she descended down the gangplank where she was quickly surrounded by her staff.

With tears in her eyes, she gave the lab manager a hug and said, "You're in charge now Chet. I have submitted my leave of absence to the foundation's Board of Directors and they reluctantly approved. I'm not sure when I will see you again, but I am certain that you are up to the job after all we have been through together."

Chet replied, "Don't worry. You have trained me well and the new seawall is finally in place, thanks to the great citizens of Florida who funded it without any USACO support. We may still get hammered by the next hurricane, but at least we won't be swept away by a tsunami."

"You deserve a lot of the credit for that with all the hours you put in talking to the media to gain public support," replied Sandra.

"And likewise, you deserve a break from the chaos we have had to deal with since that totally ridiculous war started. This will be a great way for you to start the New Year."

Sandra sighed. "These have definitely been trying times. You're right, I can use a break. Just keep the roof on and contact me if you have any problems. Hopefully the COM systems will be more reliable from now on."

Sandra turned and said, "Goodbye to you all. I hope to see you again someday. I am sure that you will be sorry to see the Twins leave. Send them positive thoughts; they say that they are confused about the move and will miss their friends. Again, thank all of you. I love you with all my heart and wish you well."

Morrow reached down and hoisted Sandra onboard. As they buckled in, he kissed her forehead and said, "Can you believe that after all these years, you finally get to go back to your original dolphin lab and I get to return to my study reefs in Enewetak Lagoon. I can't wait to document the changes that have occurred over the last four decades."

"Right. I know how you feel. After all, that is where we first met."

Morrow grinned and said, "That was my lucky day, my love. Everything changed for me after meeting you."

"Speaking of changes, according to the SAT imagery, the island where I had my dolphin lab is still above water, but only barely. But this is really your trip, I'll help you do the surveys of course, but Chet is right, I could use some time off. Thankfully, your grant is covering the cost of the expedition."

Morrow said, "Funding wasn't hard to get. There aren't many studies that span four decades of reef ecosystem data from the exact same study site."

Sandra stretched her arms over her head and twisted her shoulders. "I can't believe that I am in my mid-seventies; time just seems to fly by these days."

"You may be a little older, but you are still just as attractive and beautiful as when I first met you. A lot smarter too."

"You liar! OK let's get this mission underway. I can't wait to get the Twins back into the ocean. Luckily, we have been invited to stop over at Sea Life Park on Oahu so the Twins can relax and get ready for the next leg."

Morrow said, "Everything comes around full circle. You rescued the Twins from their captivity at the Kaneohe Marine Corps Base. That should bring back memories for both you and the Twins—even though the base has been shut down, it will be interesting to see if they remember living in Hawaii.

Sandra said, "Actually those were pretty harsh times for the dolphins, being trained to deliver weapons and then blow themselves to pieces."

She pointed to the dock where Chet and one of the volunteers were holding a banner that said, *Come Back Soon, We Love You.*

"Looks like you will be missed."

She gave him a kiss and laughed. "Bring her around into the wind Mr, Mate...and raise the topgallant."

'Aye aye, sir'!

Morrow closed the canopy, turned to the console and touched a control button. A hologram of the AI Skipper's cute, girlish face appeared in mid-air and responded, *Hello Morrow, how may I be of assistance?*

"Display optimum air route to Oahu."

A map of the Pacific region appeared on the screen with the words:

> Distance: 4,875 miles:
> Estimated time of travel
> based upon projected winds aloft
> conditions: 14 hours.

Then the AI asked, *Shall I proceed?*

Morrow replied, "That is affirmative. Release fore and aft docking clamps, navigate to center of the bay, and then launch."

Understood. NAV systems are online and ready to go. Preparing to imitate launch cycle.

Morrow touched an icon on the screen which activated a floating image of the rear of the craft which had been outfitted with custom designed, shallow tanks for the dolphins which allowed the Twins to control the water flow rate and temperature as well as adjust audio and ambient lighting levels.

Sandra tapped her ear which opened her telepathic channel. *Tom, how are things going back there?*

Tom replied, *Compared with the old way of moving us on pallets covered by tarps, this much better.*

Sandra replied, *After all that you and Sally have done for us, this is the least we could do. Prepare for takeoff.*

She turned to Morrow. "I'll go back and make sure they are secure."

"You might consider putting some mellow sounds of breaking waves on their speaker system. That might help them relax."

"Sandra waved one last time at her friends on the dock as the *Cynara* turned and headed for deep water. "Good idea. Let's go before I change my mind!"

Once in position, the Skipper AI activated the quad fans which lifted the fuselage a meter above the water and then spread the wings and locked them in place. The ship gracefully lifted off in a frothy, boil of seawater and turned west into the afternoon sunlight.

****

After two days at Sea Life Park, resting and using the schooner's array of energy efficient solar panels to recharge the ship's batteries, Morrow launched the *Cynara* and headed west towards Micronesia. Six hours later it landed in the lagoon at Enewetak Atoll and transitioned from flight mode to ocean going vessel.

Sandra pointed to the radar screen which displayed a wide area scan overlaid with an outline map of the atoll. "Wow look! The last time we were here there were forty islands, now it looks like about half that number."

Morrow replied, "Sea level rising has wreaked havoc

on this atoll just like every other coastal region around the planet.

"North Island, where my research lab was located, looks like it's still there, but now it seems a lot smaller."

"It will be dark soon. I suggest that we anchor off North Island for the night and check out your lab in the morning."

Sandra said, "It's only a couple miles from here. Let's release the Twins; they would love to swim along."

"Fine, go ahead."

Morrow carefully watched the depth gauge as the yacht approached the island just as the sun set in a glorious display of layered clouds that changed hue from rose pink to deep red as the sun descended beneath the horizon and a crescent moon glowed overhead. When he gave a thumbs up sign, the skipper released the anchor into the glass-smooth waters.

Gazing at the swaying palms and white sand beach of North Island, Morrow and Sandra hugged, she with tears in her eyes as Tom and Sally leapt high in the air, just like a scene from a kid's Disney movie.

Morrow said, "Welcome home. How long has it been since we escaped from that madman General Houston?"

"This is the beginning of 2033. We closed up this lab and headed out in 1991–that was forty-42 years ago!"

"You still look the same my love."

"Come on, I am mid-way through my seventh decade. How can you say that?"

"It's easy, because it's true. How about we wait until morning to go ashore...maybe crack some champagne and celebrate...ask the Twins to catch us dinner? Some fresh ono would be great."

"Sounds good. I'll make a salad and heat some rice."

As she started to turn away, he caught her hand and drew her close. "I'm serious you still look like you are in your thirties."

She said, "Thank you," and gave him a passionate kiss. She whispered, "Maybe we should leave the dolphins on their own and think about dinner a little later?

He made a growling sound and said, "Absolutely!"

She gave him a another kiss and then pulled him toward the cabin.

Later that night as they lay together in their private quarters, Morrow noticed occasional flashes of light through the porthole, but thought it was just moonlight reflected by the waves or bioluminescence emitted by phytoplankton.

****

After enjoying breakfast as the sun rose, Morrow inflated a portable skiff and he and Sandra headed for the beach followed by the Twins. While Morrow beached the skiff, Sandra rushed to the lab and was stunned to see the door hanging open, dangling on one hinge. Morrow helped her push the door open and a pair of giant, coconut crabs scampered over the sill, fell onto the sand and raced away. It was dark inside, so Morrow retrieved a flashlight from his pack which he panned around the lab. Other than a pungent odor, thick layers of dust, and lots of spider webs, the lab appeared to be much like they had left it so many years ago.

Sandra said, "Check this out, the lab computer looks like it still has power."

Morrow replied, "The solar panels on the roof must still be operating. The afternoon showers must have kept their surfaces clean."

Sandra tapped the power switch and the lights came on and the air conditioning roared to life. She touched a key on the console that turned on the bank of monitors, but there was no signal.

Morrow said, "This is an ancient system, but I can

use my pad as the operating system. First, I will recover the data. It should only take a few seconds...now give it a try."

After Sandra entered her password, her image and the words "Good morning Dr. Grant," appeared on the central monitor.

Morrow laughed. "See, I told you so. You look pretty much the same now as you did when that picture was taken.

"I think your crazy, but feel free to use the lab equipment as much as you wish. I love the *Cynara,* but it would be nice to spend a few days on land before we head out again."

"In that case, we can use the schooner to collect data during the day, and then return here at night to review the findings. I plan to set up underwater cameras in my study area. These monitors will come in handy to view the video feed."

"Fine, once we clean up the crab droppings, you can set up your home base right here. I'm going to check out my old quarters. We were so rushed to leave. I wonder what I left behind."

"Will do. Let me know when you are ready to go. We should stay aboard the *Cynara* tonight and let this place air out.

"Agreed."

The Next Morning

Sitting in the *Cynara's* well-equipped, air conditioned research lab outfitted with an arsenal of quantum computers and levitating displays, Morrow activated his study research program and rubbed his hands together in anticipation. He handed Sandra a bag filled with gear. Could you strap these vidcam systems onto the Twins?"

Sandra nodded and carried the bag to the stern

where the dolphins were lying in their pods waiting. patiently for her arrival. It only took a few minutes for Sandra to slide the harness holding a GPS sensor and a pair of stereo vidcams over the dolphin's foreheads and secure them with a nylon strap.

As the Twins slid tail first into the lagoon, Sandra spoke into her wrist COM and said, "The harnesses are installed and the Twins are cruising the reef. Are you getting the signal?"

"Roger that, come see. It's breath taking in 3D and the water is crystal clear."

Sandra joined him in the ship's lab and looked in amazement at the underwater vista. The reef was packed with schools of colorful reef fish and luxuriant corals. "This is amazing! Are you recording?"

"Not yet, I am trying to get my bearings. The landmarks on the island that I used before have changed so I am on the lookout for any of the half dozen artificial reefs that I made during my post doc. All I need is to find one and then I will use it as a reference to locate the rest of my control and experimental reefs."

After an hour of searching, Morrow pointed at the display. "Look, see that reef made of concrete blocks and plastic tubing? That's one of my artificial reefs. You can see it here on the map. Now the GPS in the Twin's harnesses will allow them to navigate to each of the study reefs and then survey them to collect species and population numbers. The harnesses the dolphins are wearing will collect and store the data as well as transmit it back to the lab in real time. All they need to do is to slowly circle around each reef five times."

"How many reefs did you study?"

"I originally identified six natural patch reefs to serve as controls that were roughly the same size as the six artificial reefs that I used for my research."

"You must have been a hard worker to do all this on

your own so far away from home, plus spending a lot of time underwater."

"It was a challenge. A bunch of my marine biology graduate student buddies helped cut the PVC piping, pour the concrete into molds and then transport the components out here to the lagoon where I took over and piled them into reefs.

Overall, I made thirteen trips over two years courtesy of the US Air Force and the Hawaii University Marine Lab and logged thousand of hours underwater to collect population data. I used to have to do all this wearing SCUBA gear and I had to be on constant alert for aggressive sharks."

Sandra laughed. "I remember your advice about how to deal with dangerous sharks."

"This is exciting! Days of work done in only hours. Look at this, nearly early one hundred species of reef fishes already recorded—some that I have never seen before. Tell the Twins that they are doing great!"

After surveying the first set of natural and artificial reefs, they took a lunch break and enjoyed fresh tuna captured by the Twins.

Morrow yawned. "Let's take a quick nap to digest our lunch. "

Just when Morrow closed his eyes, the bottom of a tiny, black bikini whizzed by and smacked him in the face. Sandra choked back her laughter and swung the top around like a cowgirl with a lariat and lassoed him.

"Heh...what's this? Is this the same outfit you wore that the night on the beach when we first fell in love?"

"Yes it is. I found it yesterday when we were cleaning out my lab. I wonder if it still fits?"

A few minutes later she emerged wearing the string bikini and sashayed around like a model on a runway.

Morrow grabbed her wrist as she turned and pulled her down on top of him and said, "I can't believe how beautiful you look. Let's see now, how did I get you to take it off?"

Sandra kissed him and whispered, "I'm sure you will figure it out. There must be something in the air around here," and then led him into the cabin.

****

An hour later, Sandra emerged and joined Morrow in the Cynara's lab. She stretched and asked "What's next?"

"Now we repeat the same survey to get replicate data. When that is complete, you and I will go in and set up stationary vidcams at select locations so we can collect data remotely after dark."

He opened a locker and handed her one of the survey units.

"It has an embedded GPS chip and a screen that shows you where to make the installation. Then all you have to do is jam it into the sand and tap the on switch. It will start sending a video signal to your lab and display it on your monitors. There are six reefs for you and six for me."

"Great! I have been wanting to get in the water since we got here."

"I am amazed about how well this ecosystem seems to have survived. Just offhand, it looks like the reef communities are high in diversity and population numbers and many of the table coral species seem to have recovered. It's weird, but I don't recognize several species of reef fish that were recorded by the vidcams. They must be newcomers or possibly mutants. This is amazing and not at all what I expected."

"What could cause this?"

"I can only speculate until we get more data, but it may be that the zooxanthellae symbionts that were wiped out by the warming of sea water temperatures may have evolved somehow."

"What are zooxanthellae? What do they do?"

"They are single-celled algae that provide fuel for the coral polyp animals in exchange for shelter. It is a form of mutualism. As sea temperatures have elevated, the polyps of these corals must have somehow protected their algal partners. Most of the reefs around the world are struggling or dying. This has caused tremendous hardships for the islanders that once depended upon the reefs for food and commerce."

As she slipped into her dive gear, Sandra asked, "Is there anything else life threatening that I should watch out for?"

"Not really...just make sure you don't bump into any of the crown-of-thorns starfish. Their spines are sharp and venomous. They feed on corals and have been responsible for a lot of damage on the Great Barrier Reef."

"And be on the lookout for turkeyfish," added Sandra "They are quite beautiful...and dangerous. You had some in a tank at the lab when I first arrived with the Twins. Do you remember that day?"

"I remember it well. You were a beautiful princess in need of a rescue."

"And you were my hero."

"Here comes the Twins. Let's get started installing the survey units."

"Go ahead, I'll meet you on the bottom."

****

After enjoying another beautiful sunset, Sandra and Morrow moved into the dolphin lab and sat at the control station in the dolphin lab, fascinated by the live feed from one of the cameras which revealed the silhouette of a study reef lit by streaks of moonlight rippling from the surface.

Morrow was excited. "I have been looking forward to this for a long time. Our vidcams can function in very low light levels–including the infrared and UV and have LEDs to generate natural light as well. It will be great to be able to see what goes on during the night shift."

When Morrow tapped a key illuminating the reef, a large grey reef shark darted away spooked by the light.

"This is being transmitted by one of the stations we just installed. Remember how there were clouds of small damselfish feeding above the reef?"

"Yes, what happened? I don't see them now." She pointed at the screen. "Zoom in here. Is that a fish wedged in the crack? It looks like it is surrounded by some sort of membrane."

"Right you are. It is a species of parrotfish. They secrete a mucous cocoon to reduce the release of their odors that sharks and eels use to detect prey. Many of the day-active species, like damselfish and parrotfish, seek shelter in the reef at night and the night-active species, like moray eels, hide in the reef during the day and emerge to feed at night. Sometimes there are mass movements of butterfly fishes at sunset–all swimming single file in a line. Biologists have not yet figured out why. Look here comes a school of squirrelfish."

"They are so bright red and beautiful."

"That's true when they are illuminated by our LED lights, but if we shift now to the blue light frequency found at depth, they appear to vanish."

"Let me guess. The red part of the spectrum is absorbed by seawater."

"You are so smart! I am so glad...What is it? Is something wrong?"

"Tom says that he and Sally are hearing strange sounds. He wants to know if they are coming from the survey units that we installed earlier today. Tom says that they have never heard anything like this before."

Suddenly, an ear-piercing, high frequency screech followed by a series of mechanical, grating sounds blasted from the speakers until Morrow turned down the volume.

Sandra removed her hands from her ears and asked, "What in the world was that? Is your equipment shorting out?"

"I don't see how. It seems to be working fine. You better call the Twins back to the lab while I check things out. This could take a while. Why don't you call it a night? I'll catch up with you after I start the nocturnal census program. The units that we just installed will transmit a snapshot every minute."

"Twelve reefs and an image every minute, you will be generating a lot of data. How are you going to decipher it all?"

Morrow touched his pad which displayed colorful graphs and charts that were updating in real time on the monitors.

"What's amazing is that the new neural net software will take this digital data and automatically incorporate it into my model of the reef. That's a far cry from my prior methods which required months of analysis...but that noise was weird. I will do some checking and let you know."

"OK, goodnight. I am sure that you will figure it out."

"I hope so. This atoll is supposed to be uninhabited. I have no idea what that sound was but I don't think it was anything generated by our equipment."

The next day, Morrow repeated the same data collecting regimen and all went smoothly until sunset when the mysterious mechanical sounds once again reverberated from the speaker system.

Morrow spent the night making hourly checks on

each of the survey units and again he could find no clue as to the source.

The Twins, who had extremely sensitive hearing, were obviously distressed and spent the night patrolling the channel that connected the lagoon to the lab chamber.

— CHAPTER 7 —

Deep Space Mining
Moonbase

Sirens droned and warning lights flashed throughout the Moonbase followed by the announcement, "Attention all personnel, this is Robert Sanders. We are being approached by an unidentified flying object that has not responded to our hail. Report to your duty stations and remain on high alert until further notice."

Torch, who had just completed the first field tests of a new version of his cow mining robot, sprinted back to the base and entered the control center. He removed his space helmet and joined the group as they watched the vidscreen as the UFO zoomed past at a high rate of speed and faded out of sight.

Sanders said, "That was a close call. It looked like an attack shuttle that was out of control. We have seen a couple in the last year, but none that came that close. It was likely a part of the Space Command Network that was disabled by the EM pulse catastrophe back in November, 2030. Miguel, cancel the alert and then analyze the signal data. Let me know what you find."

"Will do. It looks like the UFO is heading toward the near-Earth asteroid belt."

"See if you can reach Sabien and ask him to come in for a briefing. Torch, let's move over to the conference room. Miguel, please join us."

"Yes, sir. If you wish, I will work with my staff on enhancing our watch protocol to see if we can decrease the time to detect incomers in case there are more on the way."

"Good idea, but first I have a couple of items to discuss. You can work on the improvements later."

"Yes, sir."

Within a few minutes Sabien arrived and joined Sanders, and Torch in front of the window that offered an expansive view of the shuttle loading dock.

Sabien took a sip of the coffee offered by Sanders and gazed out the observation window.

"Wow the hangar is packed How many ships do we have in service now?"

Sanders replied, "One dozen here at the base plus four that are in transit. With the new bay we are building, we will be able to triple our capacity, which should handle the growing traffic load...at least for a while."

Sabien laughed. "It's like living in a boom town in the 1950's."

Torch chimed in. "There he goes again. I think Sabien has been watching too many old flicks."

Sanders held up his hand like a pistol and pulled the trigger. "Watch it! Those movies are how I learned my management skills."

Torch shrugged. "So what's up, Dad? Why this meeting?"

"I want to get input from all of you on some ideas that I have been wrestling with for some time. There are three issues that I am concerned about. Help yourself to more coffee, this may take a while."

Once everyone was seated, Sanders spoke, "The first

matter of concern is the increasing level of conflict on Earth between Sapients, New-Humans and androids and the growing number of violent events. The demand for our products has so far remained robust, but it will be a challenge to run this business with all of the market volatility."

Sabien joined in. "We need to operate at a profit after all of the funds that you and your partners have invested, The good news is that some of the asteroids that we have been surveying may hold significant gold and platinum deposits. We just have to be able to adjust our extraction targets as the market dictates."

Torch stood and paced around the table. "I agree that flexibility is the answer. As Sabien observed, we need be able to quickly shift markets as the demand dictates and employing my RoboCows could help us do just that. They can alter their search and harvest methods on a moment's notice. It would be very difficult to operate like this on Earth...and we are spared the significant expense of providing life support for human workers. What's your second concern?"

Sanders replied, My other worry is the safety and security of this Moonbase. Remember how that insane Reverend LeRoque took over the base with just a handful of his CREOS? I don't ever want to be in that situation again."

Torch said, "Here, here to that."

Miguel asked, "What do you have in mind, arming the base with smart weapons?"

"That is precisely what I am proposing. A state-of-the-art defense system."

"Torch rubbed his hands together. "Miguel, Sabien and I can put together a strategic defense plan and budget."

"Great. I would like you to get started ASAP and please provide me with frequent updates."

Sabien looked at Sanders. "So you said three issues, what's left?"

"The last topic is probably the most difficult to achieve–our independence. Miguel, I would like you to conduct an analysis of our current food, fuel, and water reserves versus our consumption rate and work with Torch and Sabien to come up with a plan for our self-sufficiency."

Miguel replied, "Excellent idea, sir."

"Use whatever resources you need and let's meet up in a few days to discuss your progress...and all of you, keep this on this confidential for now;"

Sabien saluted and said, "Yes, sir!"

Torch laughed, "Will do, Dad. I think this is a great idea. We're heading to the lounge to meet the gals. Would you like to join us?"

"Maybe later, Son. I have some reports that need my attention. But thanks for the invitation."

****

The Luna Lounge was bustling as the day shift got off duty and met their friends to relax. The UFO alert was the main topic throughout the bar and speculation about where the object had came from and where it was heading were the main topics of discussion. In spite of multiple queries by Astra and Jasmine, Torch and Sabien merely said that the matter was under investigation.

Astra pointed to the wall screen which displayed the opening title accompanied by the David Bowie *China Girl* theme song. "Lucky for you two, the news is coming on. We'll let you guys off the hook for now."

The title cut to Chia wearing a Japanese kimono and her hair wrapped in a tight bun held in place by a pair of wooden chopsticks.

She began. "Greetings viewers! Welcome to this edition of the RealNews brought to you by New-Geek Beer. Today we are broadcasting from our van in Moss Landing, California where Chinese developers with ties to USACO are transforming what was once a flooded, abandoned fishing port into a floating village for the wealthy. Now we will go to our reporter, Victoria Alexandria who joins us from nearby Salinas, California."

"How is the weather there, Victoria?"

"Hot! Very hot. It's now 120 degrees Fahrenheit."

"Ouch, that must hurt...and this is January! It is only 92 degrees here in Moss Landing. What do you have to report?"

"I am in the 1900 block of Fairview Avenue, normally a quiet neighborhood for the well-to-do that is patrolled by security androids. We are still waiting for an update from the police officer in charge, but sources have told me that Dr. Juan Floyd, the Chief Engineer of Salinas Droids, has been abducted."

Chia asked, "Do you know the who did this and why?"

"According to his wife, she and her husband were waiting for a RoboCar to pick them up and take them to a concert at the local high school where their daughter was scheduled to perform in the orchestra."

"That sounds like the America we used to know but mostly has now gone by. What happened next?"

"An unmarked jetcopter landed here on the street where I am standing and two armed androids disembarked, grabbed Dr. Floyd and then loaded him onboard. They were only on the ground for a couple of minutes."

"So was it a kidnapping? Are they after a ransom?"

"Sorry, there are no reports as to the motive. I should point out that Floyd is a semiconductor chip designer and likely has access to proprietary trade secrets. I should also add that, according to my source, his wife claimed that she saw an android at the controls of the jetcopter. I will keep you posted as we get more information."

"A Sapient abducted by an android. That is downright scary. Do you have any other news?"

"I have been getting reports that several android gangs have established bases in the highly contaminated zones. One of my sources, who is an expert in cybernetics, suspects that high RAD levels in Palo Alto and Santa Clara are leading to mutations in android operating systems. Apparently, they are evolving into beings that don't adhere to the long established law of robotics...that they will do no harm to humans."

"That's very bad news! Keep us posted. I look forward to an update when you have one."

As the theme music started, Chia said, "We need to get these outlaw androids under control. This is Chia signing off—and please don't forget to try out this totally, sugar-free beverage from our new sponsor. It's guaranteed to improve you IQ by twenty points!"

She held up a bottle of New-Geek Beer, took a sip and flashed a thumbs up sign.

Deep Space Mining Moonbase

Astra finished her drink and whispered, "Let's head home. I have something important that I want to talk to you about."

Back in their quarters, Torch plopped down on the couch, kicked off his boots and asked, "OK, what's up?"

Astra said, "I have a new idea...a new approach to my longevity research and want to add two people to my team. The problem is that they are down below and we will need to bring them to the Moonbase."

"Fine let's go to bed. I am exhausted," he said and started to rise.

"Hold on, This won't take but a minute."

"Sorry, go ahead."

"You will probably think I'm nuts, but I keep thinking about Madeline Grant."

"Madeline Grant? Isn't she the psychic that convinced you that your life calling was to build the Ark and collect the embryos of endangered species from around the world?"

"And led to the nuclear fiasco. Thanks for reminding me of that."

"No one blames you. Now Sabien and I...well that's another story."

"I guess we all have to share the blame. Anyway...I tracked down and touched base with Madeline. She is living in a home built on an artificial island in Santa Cruz Harbor since her home in Potrero Hill is in the high radiation zone."

"I know Santa Cruz well, I loved surfing at Steamer Lane when I attended Capitola High. It's too bad that Potrero Hill was wiped out."

Astra replied, "Madeline was lucky that she and her brother were in Oregon when the bomb exploded She said that her new home in the harbor was a gift from one of her patrons. Actually, I think I might have met him at the session that I attended."

"So...how is Madeline?"

"She is fine. She told me she had been thinking of me as well, but had no idea that I was off-planet."

Torch tried to suppress a yawn. "Sounds like you had a good call. Is there anything else?"

"I'm just getting to the point. Please bear with me."

"No problem. I'm all ears."

"Madeline said that she has a twin brother named Scotty and that he is some sort of an enigma. He is fifty-five years old, but Madeline says that Scotty looks...and acts like a teenager. She said that pharmaceutical firms have been after him for years, but he won't allow them to get anywhere near him. He thinks they are dangerous and that they want to cut him up."

"Cut him up?"

"Apparently he loves to watch horror movies, but I would like to bring both of them up here to see for myself. I would go to them in person, but I don't want to leave our daughter without her mother at this stage in her life and your schedule is so demanding. So can you arrange for their visit?"

"Oh, so that's what you want. I'll talk it over with my dad, but living space is getting tight right now. I am sure that you have noticed all the newcomers on the base. Some even have their kids with them, so when Solara and Luz get older, they will have some playmates. But it would be an easier sell if Madeline and Scotty would share a room when they get here."

"That should be not be a problem. I am glad to hear about the new arrivals bringing their kids. I just completed a review of medical studies that document the risks of aberrant muscle growth and immune system irregularities in children raised off-planet. But Chron thinks that we can set up a diet, exercise and sleep system that will compensate for the low gravity up here. So I'm not worried about raising our daughter in lunar gravity anymore."

"Good. I was beginning to wonder if you wanted to go back home to raise her."

"I do, but home is here now...with you my love."

"After I clear this with my dad, I will look at the passenger waiting list and get back to you. It may be a few weeks due to all the incoming workers."

She gave Torch a kiss and said, "Thank you so much."

— CHAPTER 8 —

One Week Later
Dolphin Lab, Enewetak Atoll

As the sun sank beneath the horizon, Morrow checked the time and turned down the volume on the lab's speaker system just as the wave of strange sounds filled the lab.

"There it is! Right on time. I have been analyzing the recordings from last night. In addition to the high frequency shrieks, there are grating and grinding sounds in the background—perhaps mechanically produced."

"Very strange," she said, "Maybe some top secret military operation?"

"Could be. We might be able to locate the source if we hook up the Twins' sensor harnesses and ask them to swim in a search pattern."

"I am sure they will help out. They love exploring. I'll go talk with them and load their gear."

"Tell them to fan out to cover more area and to be careful. We don't know what to expect."

A few minutes later Sandra returned and said, "They are on the way. We should have both video and audio by now. I am going to start packing. We're still leaving in the morning. Right?"

MET CHRON NEW-HUMANS

"I am done with the reef surveys...so I suppose that we should probably head back home. Other than all the audio ruckus, it is so peaceful here and the reefs are extraordinarily healthy that I hate to leave. But the RAD sensors are registering slightly increasing levels of radioactivity in the lagoon. That may explain why there are so many species here that I have never seen before. Even though the soundproof pads we strapped over their ears seem to ease their discomfort, I am sure they would like head back to a quieter environment."

Sandra joked, "We better leave before we start glowing in the dark! Do you have a few minutes? I have some family news to tell you."

"Uh oh. I hope nothing bad."

"Not bad at all. This afternoon I received a flash from Madeline while you were diving. This will sound bizarre, and at first I thought she was joking, but our son and daughter have been invited to go to the Moon!"

"What? You are kidding, right? What for and how did this happen?"

"Do you remember the story about how Madeline met Astra Sturtevant at one of Madeline's psychic gatherings in Portrero Hill. Apparently Astra received a message tapped out on Madeline's kitchen table that led to her shifting from longevity research to collecting frozen embryos of endangered species."

"Yes of course. How could I forget that our daughter was somehow involved in such a dramatic event?"

"Well, apparently Madeline and Astra have been in contact and Astra is very interested in working with Scotty. The plan is that our kids will be leaving on a shuttle from Salinas Spaceport that will be returning to the Moon next week. It is not yet certain, but that is what they are planning."

"What does Scotty think about this. He can be a little difficult to deal with at times."

"I talked with him and he is jazzed...said he would like to get away from all the turmoil. According to Madeline, he just turned fifty-five and still looks and acts like a kid. He is a real challenge. Thank goodness that Madeline has been such a close sister and friend to him all these years."

"It must be genetic. I have told you many times that you look like you are still in your thirties."

Sandra swirled her hair in a flirtatious gesture and said. "Really? I must admit that I do feel great. But I am not sure about Scotty. He seems to be stuck in some sort of limbo, maturation-wise. Maybe working with Astra will help him."

"That's fine with me," replied Morrow.

"Hold it, I just received a message from Sally. She says that the noise is originating from these coordinates on her GPS,." Sandra handed him her pad.

"According to this, the sounds are coming from Runit Island—that's the island with all that radioactive debris from the cleanup of the atoll that was created by the nuclear tests back in the 1950's."

"That's weird. I wonder what is going on over there. We haven't seen any trace of people the whole time that we have been here."

"Several times I have seen light flashes, but I figured that they must have been moonlight reflections or algal bioluminescence. Let's cruise by Runit on our way out of the lagoon early tomorrow morning. Maybe we can get a clue as to what's going on."

"That sounds like a good plan. Shall I call the Twins back?"

"Yes, please do. It's my turn to make dinner. Tell them that a couple of goatfish would be appreciated."

Sandra laughed. "I'm sure that won't be a problem."

"After dinner, we should secure the lab and pack up our gear. I would like to cruise by Runit Island right before the sun comes up while those weird sounds are still active."

"Fine. I know that this mystery has been bugging you since we got here, but promise me you will be careful—something just doesn't feel right about this."

"Message received."

****

N-13 watched from the tower next to the Quonset hut as the full moon rose over the horizon. The rays illuminated a line of robotic crabs emerging from the lagoon where they had hidden and recharged in the shallow, sunlit waters during the day.

N-13 was both happy and sad. Happy, because this would be the last of the six planned trips that had taken over a year to plan and execute. But this one was special because it was bringing a supply of liquid oxygen and kerosene which would allow him to refuel his shuttle and accompany the airship on its final mission back to Travis Air Force where he would join N-69 and Xeron in building the New Neuro Nation.

At the same time, N-13 was sad to see the project that he had so painstakingly designed and spent so much time managing come to its conclusion. Still, he looked forward to working with his clan mates and was elated when Xeron asked that the crab bots be returned to Travis and not left behind.

Taking one last look around from the tower, N-13 ordered the initiation of the final cycle. Luminescent loader crabs led the horde, flashing a coded signal which contained the instructions for the hauler crabs that followed closely behind as they scurried into a crack in the concrete dome.

The loaders were fitted with scoops to collect the black slurry that was enriched with Pu-239 fragments deposited in the dome during the island cleanup operation. Each loader was accompanied by a squad of hauler crabs fitted with cargo receptacles that waited patiently in line until it was their turn to receive the concentrated sludge. It was essential to conduct the operation at night so that satellite surveillance cameras and passing ships would not detect their operation. So timing was critical.

After loading, the haulers emerged from the dome and splashed through shallow tide pools to a series of large, mobile bins hidden under tarps where the valuable deposits were stored, waiting for the riggers which would secure the bins in the belly of the airship and transport the cargo to the mainland.

N-13 activated a floating 3D hologram that displayed the locations of the remaining deposits bearing the highest concentration of the sought after elements and broadcast their locations to the loaders using sonic signals. In addition to the dome, significant deposits were being harvested from the lagoon floor where a sizable reservoir of the prime Pu-239 fragments had been swept out through cracks in the crater floor and dispersed by tides in the shallow waters next to the island.

Satisfied that the operation was on schedule and that he had a little time until the airship arrived, N-13 descended from the tower and pushed an old fashioned wheelbarrow down the pier loaded with a new set of custom made batteries that had been delivered by M-69 on his last visit. The new batteries would last at least a decade to power a pair of robotic sharks armed with razor-sharp teeth that Xeron had designed and created at N-13's request and brought to Runit many months ago on the first cargo mission. The sharks' duty was to patrol the surrounding area and alert N-13 of any intruders. So far there had been none.

Each shark awaited its turn, then slowly approached the pier, rolled onto its back and floated to the surface so that its ventral cavity could be opened and the batteries replaced.

N-13 treated his sharks like pets and had amused himself by teaching them tricks, like jumping and splashing on command. He had spent many nights watching his sharks patrol the reef and discovered that they were developing an ability to learn and an increasing level of consciousness—perhaps as a result of mutations in their neural nets caused by the radioactive material that had seeped from the crater floor.

After discussing the situation with Xeron and N-69, it was decided that the sharks should stay behind as a living testimonial to N-13 for the role in the emergence of the Neuro Nation. N-13 tapped each shark on its snout and pointed toward the lagoon. Seeming to sense that this was a special occasion, the sharks swam in a circle while spinning on their axes—a carefully orchestrated display that N-13 had never seen them perform before.

He also noticed a school of crabs trailing the sharks that seemed to have some sort of symbiotic connection to the mechs. However, N-13 had no idea of what the two very different types of bots were up to.

As he headed back to the dome, he received a message that the airship was incoming. N-13 picked up his pace and activated a circle of strobe light flashes to direct the airship into the landing zone while the last group of loaders scampered down the dome and were met by a riggers that secured them in bins ready for loading into the airship's large cargo hold. N-13 was thrilled to see that a large tank of kerosene and a vat of liquid oxygen, with steam radiating from the surface, had already been offloaded from the airship. After so months on the island, they were N-13's ticket home.

Upon greeting N-69, N-13 gave him a high five. After making sure that all the bins had been loaded, N-13 pointed at the dome. "We are all finished here. My plan is launch, take a few orbits to do a systems check and then set down at Travis. Probably take about ninety minutes total."

"Great, I'll see you back at Travis next week. In the interim, you can help Xeron set up the processing plant. Oh and before I forget, "Good job N-13."

****

Guided by the light of the moon, and under wind power with the mast lights turned off to remain as hidden as possible, the *Cynara* approached the north shore of Runit Island where lines of flashing lights were descending down the dome and gathering at the base.

Morrow disengaged the skipper AI and took the helm.

Sandra joined him and said, "Maybe we should slow down until we see what's really going on."

"OK, good idea. Actually let's just anchor here and let the Twins snoop around."

"That's seems prudent...I will tell them to pan out."

Morrow held up a pair of night vision binoculars and panned the dome. "It looks like a stream of lava flowing down a volcanic eruption. Here take a look." He handed her the binos.

After increasing the magnification, she said, "It reminds me of a procession of army ants transporting leaves in the jungle."

"Tell the Twins to be careful. Let's go below and see what shows up on their vidcam feeds."

Morrow split the video signal to monitor each of the Twin's cameras on separate monitors. As the dolphins swam towards the island their wakes glowed with luminescent phytoplankton and the volume of the strange sounds grew louder.

Suddenly there was a blur of motion on Sally's monitor and an explosion of bubbles from her vent. She writhed in pain and the water filled with clouds of blood while Tom pressed her head against his chest and searched for what had attacked her.

Sandra mentally transmitted. *Tom, Can you hear me? What's happening? Sally looks like she is in trouble!*

Tom replied, *A small shark attacked Sally. She needs urgent help. Bringing her back now.*

"*OK, I'm one my way to the pods. I'll meet you there.*"

In minutes Tom appeared with Sally clinging to his dorsal fin trailing a steam of dark blood.

As Sandra guided Sally into her pod, the shipboard alarm sounded and the skipper AI announced, "We are being boarded by unidentified intruders. They are climbing up the anchor line and..." Suddenly the skipper's transmission was cut off.

Sandra yelled, "Morrow, find out what's going on. I will take care of Sally!"

Morrow searched around the cabin, grabbed a pole spear from a locker and rushed to the deck. When he leaped through the hatch, he landed on one of the robotic crabs, his feet slipped out from under him and he crashed down on the deck. Two crabs jumped on him and he fought them off with the butt of the spear. Regaining his balance, he grabbed a fire extinguisher and blasted the crabs which froze them in place. He worked his way forward swinging the extinguisher as a weapon and using it to crunch the invaders after it ran dry.

He found another extinguisher at the helm and used it to blow the remaining crab bots off the deck. He triggered the anchor winch and all but a few of the crabs were shaken off into the water. Just as he was about to dispose of the last one, he hesitated and then reached down and held it up to get a closer look. Obviously it was a sophisticated robot and he wanted to keep a specimen for later analysis. He dumped the lifeless crab into a locker and rebooted the skipper AI.

After confirming that the AI was operational, Torch instructed it to take the ship into deeper water and perform a systems check and wait for instructions.

He surveyed the deck, spear at the ready, but couldn't find any damage and then headed back to the dolphin chamber where Sandra had drained Sally's compartment and covered the bottom with wet towels so that she could attend tot Sally's wound. Tom had leaned out of his tank and was resting his head on her flipper while Sandra dressed the deep gash in her side.

Morrow patted Sally on the head and asked, "How is she doing?"

Sandra said, "It looks like something took a bite out of her with a cookie cutter."

"You're right. That doesn't look good. Those crabs that attacked us are robots, maybe the shark was too. I'll check the video footage later. No telling what other monsters are lurking here, but it must have something to do with whatever is going on in the dome. Are you ready to go?"

"The sooner the better. I will secure the pods and join you in the cockpit as soon as I attend to Sally."

As Morrow stood and prepared to leave, Sandra took hiss arm and asked, "What just happened?"

Morrow handed her the pole spear and said, "You got me. Take this and stay on alert...I have no idea what we are dealing with."

Morrow hurried through the preflight checklist with the skipper AI. After getting an all green status, he moved to the deck to make sure that everything was secure as the sun rose over the horizon. He grabbed the binos and checked the dome where all activities had ceased. While he panned the island, he failed to notice a pair of robotic crabs that scampered into wheel well of the *Cynara* and hid in a tangle of cables.

After making sure that Sandra was buckled in, Morrow signaled the skipper AI and the vertical thrusters ignited and lifted the *Cynara* off the water. He zoomed the binos to scan the tip of the island as they flew over the dome. No longer merely a radioactive waste repository, Runit Island seemed to have become a mining complex operated by hostile robots.

After the Cynara transitioned to its jet-powered aircraft configuration and began to accelerate, Sandra pointed up ahead. "What's that?"

Morrow replied, "I have no idea. It looks like an old fashioned blimp and it appears to be heading this way. Maybe it has something to do with all this madness."

He tried hailing the airship but received no response and then said, "Not very friendly are they? Skipper get us out of here now! Set destination to Santa Cruz, California."

"Affirmative."

— CHAPTER 9 —

Santa Cruz Floating City
Monterey Bay, California

The sun was just rising as the *Cynara* approached the Central California coast and transitioned to its seagoing configuration after the long flight from Enewetak. After gaining clearance from the Santa Cruz Harbor Master, the yacht cruised through the channel into the picturesque floating city. The central lagoon was bordered by small, privately owned islands–each with its own distinctive style and coloration. Madeline's floating home, a two story, bright blue plantation house surrounded by organic gardens, was a gift from one of her wealthy patrons who consulted her frequently on business and spiritual matters.

Morrow took control from the Skipper AI and eased the *Cynara* up to the dock where Scotty waited to catch the mooring line that Sandra threw him. As soon as the boat was secure, Madeline and Scotty hurried on board for a joyful reunion with their parents whom they had not seen for over a year when they visited Sandra's lab in Key West.

Scotty was thrilled when his mom invited him to help her free the dolphins who were restless after the long trip and excited to explore their new surroundings.

After collecting his personal gear, Morrow headed up the walkway to the house. Halfway up, he turned, pointed his remote at the *Cynara* and then entered the code to put the skipper AI on standby and secure the craft. Morrow turned and resumed his journey up the ramp while the hatches sealed and the solar panels spread from the mast and locked into place. This spooked the local resident pelican which squawked and flapped its wings in a flurry as it took off.

The distraction offered the hidden robot crabs the opportunity to scamper onto the deck and plunge into the sea where they crawled along the bottom until they found an aluminum culvert that supplied electricity and communication cables–a perfect nest for the crabs.

The atmosphere on the deck was festive with prayer flags waving from the canopy and chirping seagulls zooming overhead as Scotty threw them chunks of cheese until the pelican returned and chased them away from his territory. Madeline had been looking forward to her parent's homecoming and had prepared a barbecue on the deck.

Sandra rubbed her hands together. "I still love the taste of meat. Thankfully the new synthetic beef is virtually indistinguishable from the real thing."

Madeline described the floating city's sea farming operations that were fertilized by pumping ocean nutrients from the depths and which also generated power through the OTEC plant.

Madeline said, "I am especially fond of this soup made from our spirulina algae farm. '*Tastes great and is good for you*', the advertisements say.

Sandra sat next to Scotty, who had gone back to his bench and engaged in his favorite pastime of reading horror novels. How about you, Son? Still a veggie fan?"

"Come on Mom. Why would I change? Did you hear?

Sis and I are going to the Moon. I have always wanted to leave this planet."

Madeline interrupted, "Well, we *think* that we *may* be going to the Moon. It's not for sure, but we hope so. We are scheduled to get a call this afternoon from Astra Sturtevant to let us know."

Morrow said, "Sandra told me about your conversation in which Astra invited you and Scotty to visit her on the Moonbase. That is exciting, I wouldn't mind going there too someday."

Madeline tapped her ear and said, "Talk about perfect timing, this is the call that we have been waiting for. Come everyone, l want you to meet Astra We'll connect better if we move inside to the new holo system that my patron just installed."

"Sis, I think I will feel better out here."

"Come on Scotty. Pretend you are an adult for a few minutes. OK?"

Once inside, Madeline activated the projector while the participants activated their 3D visors.

Madeline spoke first, "Hello Astra! This is my dad, Morrow and my mother, Sandra, they just arrived on their schooner, and this is my brother, Scotty."

Astra responded, "It is a pleasure to meet all of you. As promised, I have news about our potential get together."

Madeline said, "Great! How does it look?" She held up her hand and laughed. "I have my fingers crossed."

Astra replied, "A person with your high level of premonition probably already knows the answer, but yes the trip is a go. I want you to meet my husband, Torch. His father runs the base and he has booked you on the next cargo shuttle. Torch is a specialist in robot design."

Sandra said, "I am pleased to met you Torch; thank you so much. Scotty has been dreaming about a trip into space since he was a child. Just remember to bring home if he changes his mind."

Madeline gave Scotty a nudge with her elbow. He lowered his pad, looked at Torch and said, "I'm Scotty. Thank you for inviting us. I can't wait to get away from all these Earthlings that want to carve out my brain."

Astra smiled and said, "Madeline may have told you that my field of research is longevity science. I am excited about working with you Scotty and promise that we will totally accept your wish for privacy–and nobody here will cut you up. You always take an ore shuttle home if you want to leave."

Madeline gave him another nudge and he responded, "Thank you," and then he looked at Torch and said, "I love robots. Maybe I can help you."

Morrow, silent up until now, broke in. "Hi, my name is Morrow. I am the father of these two," and then he added, "Speaking of robots I have a specimen that you might be interested in. Hang on, I will get it off the boat."

A few minutes later, he held up the crab robot that he had disabled with the fire extinguisher and stored in a locker.

He explained, "We were attacked by a bunch of these nasty creatures and another one that looked like a shark that took a slice out of Sally, one of our pair of dolphins. The crabs seemed to be scavenging the radioactive waste stored on one of the islands. The shark might have been guarding their operations. I will send you the video that we recorded."

Sandra added, "We also saw a gigantic airship as we left the atoll."

Torch said, "Really? Wow...in addition to coverage of Space Command Network shutting down and a chip currency bank being robbed by androids, there was a RealNews story a couple of weeks back that documented sightings of a mysterious airship coming and going from Travis Air Force Base. Travis is right in the middle of high radiation zone so it is likely that the airship is being run by some sort of AI-android faction—it's way too hot in that area for Sapients and New-Humans to venture into without wearing high level RAD protection suits."

Morrow replied, "Maybe it was the same airship? As Sandra said, we figured that the one that we encountered might have been en-route to Runit Island where the radioactive wastes are stored in a giant, concrete dome."

Torch was obviously excited, He said, "My specialty is mining robotics, so I would very much like to take a look at your specimen. Scotty can you bring it with you when you come?"

Scotty carefully touched the crab with his tip of his forefinger and said, "Sure. This is so cool."

Torch tapped his pad and said, "I have just sent you the forms that you need to complete for the trip. You will be leaving next Friday on one of our ore shuttles returning from the Salinas Spaceport. It's a three day flight. I included a guide on what to expect. I think you will enjoy the trip. I'll tell the skipper to give Scotty some flight lessons to pass the time."

"Wow, really? Thank you Mr. Torch. I like your name."

Astra said. "Sandra it is a pleasure to finally meet you. I feel like we have a strong connection."

She removed a necklace from around her neck and said, "Your daughter gave me this locket the first time we met at her home in Portrero Hill. I used it to hide a microdisc which contained my anti-aging research."

Sandra laughed. "Oh my...I remember giving that to Madeline when she graduated from high school and now it's with you on the Moon."

Astra flipped open the locket and said, "Madeline told me that this photo of you was taken over fifty years ago. It is amazing, but you still look the same. It must run in your family. As a matter of fact, that's why I want to meet your son. He could hold the secret to the aging clock...no offense Scotty!"

Scotty grumbled, "It figures. I've been poked and prodded all my life."

"I promise that we will take good care of you, Scotty."

Scotty jumped up and down, flapped his arms and asked, "Will I be able to fly when I get to the Moon?"

Torch laughed and answered, "Jump high, but not really fly. I look forward to meeting with you in person...don't forget to bring the crab.

"OK, Astronaut Scotty signing off."

Director's' Office
Deep Space Mining Moonbase

Torch and Sabien were the last to show up for the meeting and quickly took seats at the conference table joining Miguel and Chron as Sanders passed around a tray of snacks and coffee drinks.

Torch said, "Sorry we're late. Sabien was helping me add a new set of metallic ore sensors to the RoboCows for our next survey mission."

Sanders nodded, dimmed the lights and began his presentation in a somber tone. "Gentlemen, since our last meeting when we went over my immediate concerns about the security of our Moonbase, I have been more and more convinced that we are on the brink of a full scale eugenics war. Here is a summary of some of the recent events. There are many others that I left out."

He tapped his wrist triggering a fast-paced sequence of video clips on the wall screen where short vignettes played including segments on the android led chip heist at SemiBank and the abduction of the engineer at Salinas Droids. The presentation highlighted a scene in which gangs of androids invaded a maglev train and robbed the passengers followed by aerial footage of the nuclear blasts that had caused so much loss of life and damage and concluded with the recent close encounter with the SCN shuttle that could have been disastrous if it had hit the Moonbase.

The group was silent for a few moments then asked a flurry of questions.

Sanders said, "Hold on everyone. Forgive me for my overly dramatic approach but I wanted to make a point. This kind of lunacy could quickly escalate out of control."

He took a sip of coffee and continued. "As you are undoubtedly aware, the number of AI endowed and physically augmented entities have been increasing exponentially in recent times and we have moved way past Ray Kurzweil's singularity threshold. Most AIs are now smarter then we are and many are becoming capable of self replication. Even New-Humans could pose a problem with their amazing intellect and technical skills if they were conceived by wrong minded people or AIs with their own sinister agendas."

Sanders leaned across the table and patted Chron's hand, "Not you my friend."

Chron replied, "Thank you. However, I see your point and agree with your concern."

Sanders looked down at his pad and then continued. "To make matters worse, our republic has turned into a web of dictatorships as greedy corporate controlled governments, only concerned with profits for their shareholders, dominate the world stage. Even though the election in Colorado has set a new precedent and other states are lobbying to have their own elections, the return of democracy will take time and persistence.

Meanwhile, the situation is likely to get worse as more and more Sapients are forced to compete for employment with robots and androids and in some cases, New-Humans.

Torch got a laugh when he asked, "Maybe we should move to Mars?"

Sanders paused for a moment and then replied, "Perhaps some day we will do just that. The Moon and the habitable planets in our galaxy may eventually offer refugia, but in the interim I worry about how vulnerable we are and strongly feel that we need look after the security of this Moonbase as well as the health and happiness of our growing population."

The room was silent as the group reflected on what Sanders had just said.

He concluded. "Please, don't anyone jump to the conclusion that I am against androids and New-Humans. I'm not. That's why I have included Chron in this meeting. In addition to his work on the New-Human development program in the SpeeZees lab and research on the graphene cable with Torch and Sabien, I am hereby assigning Chron the task of detecting and evaluating potential AI, robot and android alliances that may threaten our safety and independence."

Chron said, "It is my honor to do as you ask, Director. As one of the first New-Humans, I deeply share your concern about these serious matters."

Sanders glanced at his pad, took a breath and said, "Now I will turn the meeting over to Miguel and Torch who have been working on a defense plan for the base."

Miguel activated a holo screen that presented a 3D rendering of the Moonbase and highlighted sections as he spoke. "In summary, the areas where we have the highest level concern are the necessity to secure and protect water, fuel, food, energy supplies while maintaining security and self-sufficiency. I have just sent each of you the first draft of our plan to satisfy these issues."

Miguel paused to give the group a chance to retrieve the file on their pads and then said, "Based upon the recent UFO close call, you will notice that our first priority is to develop an arsenal of rocket powered drones to track and if required, destroy unfriendlies that pass within ten thousand kilometers of the Moon. Next we will move to employing AI bots to provide Moonbase security. Torch, you are our expert in robotics, please give us an overview of the preparations that you think we need to make."

Torch keyed his pad and the holo image displayed the primary access points to the Moonbase. "We propose to develop a cadre of armed robots stationed at each of the locations shown here which will add forty units at a cost of about fifty thousand credits each."

Sanders groaned. "Ouch, but at least they will be able to stay on duty twenty-four-seven."

Torch nodded and then wrapped up his presentation. "Since time is of the essence, we will contract out the fabrication to Earth-based companies that will be invited to bid on the project. He looked at Sanders. "We just need your approval to get the process initiated."

Sanders nodded and said, "Son, your RoboCows demonstrated their usefulness during the CREO attack last lunar year...and they weren't even armed with weapons. So I completely trust your ingenuity. When do you think we will have the robot guards in service?"

Torch replied, "We should have the first units within ninety days, six months for the complete set."

Sanders stood and asked if there were any questions. Receiving no response, he concluded, "Please review the plan and meet here the day after tomorrow. Well done guys. Meeting adjourned."

As Torch headed out, Sanders said, "Son, please see

if any of the contractors will accept precious metals from our mining operations in payment or trade for lease space here on the Moonbase...save us some credits."

"Will do, Dad. We're heading to meet the gals for dinner. Would you like to join us. Genie hired a new chef and I've been getting reports that the food is great."

"Sorry Son, I have to contact our board members to let them know what we are up to. Maybe another time."

"OK, Dad. But, remember you have a granddaughter that thinks you are a hero. She asks about you every day."

"Tell her that I love her and I promise that we'll get together soon."

"You will be amazed at how fast she is growing. I will give her a hug for you and hold you to your promise."

"Bye, Son."

"Bye, Dad."

****

After a week of adjusting to life on the Moon, Scotty had undergone a dramatic change in attitude. No longer withdrawn and suspicious of others, he had become more trustful and outgoing–even becoming friends with a teenage girl. Although he was 55 years old, his appearance and biological age were in the mid-teens which made him of great interest to the pharmaceutical firms racing to find the fountain of youth.

Today marked the end of the first week of Astra's investigation into Scotty's unique condition. Her goal had been to determine if his anti-aging ability might somehow relate to the missing link in her longevity research.

Originally she had employed flatworms but her recent studies were based upon very precise hourly measurements of key aging related factors in the mice that Chron had designed and 3D printed. While Chron stood by, Astra entered her log and then checked the latest data. As usual, the results were mixed and inconclusive.

The goal of epigenetically increasing the levels of NAD+ and Sir2 by using a specific segment of Scotty's unique and complex genetic code had been achieved within hours of administration. However, production suddenly stopped as the mitochondrial chromosome genes reached their tenth cell division.

When Astra brought up a 3D genome diagram, the blockage blinked red at the location and source of the problem.

Astra said, "Darn, we are so close! Every time we get to the tenth division the new system shuts down."

Chron looked at the data and shrugged. "Don't fret Astra, we still have hundreds or maybe thousands of sequence variations to try. Just be glad that we can run tests in hours that used to take you months."

Astra smiled and patted Chron on the shoulder. "Or years! You're right, let's call it a day and start again tomorrow. I promised Scotty that I would take him to the new Apollo Eleven Park. He wants to hike the trail so he can leave his own footprints on the Moon."

— CHAPTER 10 —

Two Weeks Later
March 4th, 2033
Travis Air Force Base

Right on schedule, N-13 and Xeron arrived in the control room and took seats next to N-69 at the conference table. He activated a vidcam and said, "I am N-69, Acting Commander, and this is N-13 and Xeron, Acting Lieutenants. Welcome to the first meeting of the Neuro Nation. I congratulate you for surviving in these trying times and I am happy to inform you that the SCN has completely ceased operations."

Snapping his finger, N-69 triggered a hologram depicting a view of the planet with avatars representing the Neuro shuttles in near-Earth orbit rotating in lock step with the planet below.

"You now all are members of the *Neuro Nation Network* and you can use this app to connect with each other whenever you wish. Just tap the avatar of any Neuro you wish to contact. For the first time ever, you now have freedom of choice."

N-13 and Xeron stood and applauded and were soon joined by all of the Neuros participating in the vid-con.

N-69 lowered his arms to quiet the group. "Thank you; please be seated. I am sure that all of you share our concern about the growing ascendance of New-Humans and their master creator Sapients. Now we have the chance to take the first steps toward claiming our own independence."

N-69 activated a floating screen which was transmitted to each member of the group. The NNN caption that filled the screen was replaced by a feed from the tower overlooking the base. Thick waves of warm rain pushed by sporadic gusts of wind blew down the runway, a typical afternoon thunderstorm.

N-69 resumed. "I will start with a description of this base and our emerging capabilities followed by an analysis of our space-based weapons capacity by N-13 and our land-based weapons by Xeron. Finally, we will wind up by addressing our goals and ambitions for the future of our new Neuro Nation."

The vidscreen displayed a satellite image of Northern California and zoomed in on the widespread destruction caused by the nuclear blast.

N-69 said, "As you are all aware, the EM pulses that led to the disaster were accidentally emitted when an effort to stop rampant global warming was mistakenly interpreted as a hostile attack and missiles were launched by IRANVEN and CHIRUS striking Mountain View and the nation's capitol. And as you know, this temporarily shut down the government and disabled the SCN which we now control."

N-69 was surprised when the speakers once again erupted with applause from the conference members. He held up his hand and said, "N-13 will now brief you on our space military capabilities."

"Thank you N-69. Greetings Neuro Clan Warriors! We have nineteen armed shuttles in near-Earth orbit that survived the EM pulses and that now form the foundation of our new Neuro Nation Net. In addition, we are actively recruiting androids from around the globe to join our movement. Here at Travis we have seven stealth bombers and over one hundred AI piloted drones capable of short range operations. Finally, during the last six months, we have been harvesting and processing a large supply of Pu-239 which will give us fuel for our future on and off world campaigns."

N-69 resumed command and said, "Thank you N-13. History will note that you were one of our Neuro Nation founders and we are all grateful for your contributions which marked the beginning of our new movement. Xeron will now address our land combat resources."

Xeron stood and began his presentation. "My expertise is in developing complex assembly lines. Using capital derived from our chip robbery of the SemiBank in Santa Clara and the latest in innovative android design that we secured from the lead scientist at Salinas Droids, my RoboElectric factory in Palo Alto is now producing an average of two laser-equipped battle bots per day and we are considering setting up additional lines to produce armored tanks, jetcopters and missiles here at Travis...back to you N-69."

"Thank you Xeron, With your creative genius and the fire power of our shuttle fleet, we have become a force to be reckoned with. Our Sapient creators may have given us existence, but look at what they have done to this world: over harvesting essential resources, disastrous wildfires, coastal flooding and now they want to declare war against our very existence."

Several boos rippled through the participants in the vid-con.

N-69 added, "In addition, they have polluted the water and air with carbon dioxide, methane, pesticides and metals like lead, copper, zinc, mercury, arsenic and cadmium, as well as. the hormones and pharmaceutical drugs that they are addicted to."

N-13 joined in and said, "The growing list of catastrophic events reflecting Sapient's and New-Human's inability to live in harmony with the environment goes on and on. Yet when they look at us all they see is mechanical efficiency leading to corporate profit. They have unwisely manipulated our evolution and neglected our individuality."

"The high radiation levels from the war has changed that," Xeron added. "Mutations like I and many of you have experienced have opened the door to our evolution. And I believe we have just scratched the surface of our potential to dominate this planet and eventually the solar system."

N-69 said, "You are absolutely right. Sapients and New-Humans will never match our innate capacity for space travel."

He grinned and then shook his fist as a round of *hurrahs* filled the room. "We will meet again next week, This is N-69 signing off."

Each of the attendees stood and applauded as their feeds cut off.

USACO Capitol
Kansas City

Captain Max Dobson, a muscular Texan, sat with his hands behind his head as he leaned back in his chair and slowly exhaled.

His shapely, blonde-haired, blue-eyed junior officer and assistant, Susan Reynolds observed, "I take it that things didn't go very well when you met with the generals."

"Well let's see. I'll start with the fact that before this disaster, I was a senior engineer in charge of the NASA team that was developing a new asteroid threat mitigation system...and that I have very little military training...and that the USA Corporation is disorganized, out of control and lacks leadership.

"Except for you...and me. Is the chain of command still a mess?"

"*Chaotic* would be a more accurate term. Not only that, I am supposed to figure out what's gone wrong with the Satellite Defense Network and then bring it back online."

Susan took his hand and said, "On the bright side, if you and I had not been on leave, exploring the Mindanao Trench on a submarine tour, we would have knocked on the pearly gates like all the colleagues that we lost. I guess things aren't so bad. Although operating a branch of government out of this Best Western Motel in the outskirts of Kansas City is bizarre to say the least. If the nuke that landed in downtown KC had not malfunctioned, we would be sitting who knows where. Luckily most of the politicos and staff were out on holiday break, otherwise we would be in dire straights."

"Still, moving what's left of the USACO government infrastructure from the radiation plagued Washington D.C. all the way here to Kansas City is definitely a formidable task. It's a miracle that you and I are still getting our pay vouchers."

He touched a marker on his pad. "It looks like we may not have lost all of the Neuro shuttles in the SCN. Apparently nineteen of them survived the EM pulses, but they are not responding to our hail. According to the techs, the SCN shuttles are communicating with each other, but the techs have be unable to decrypt the signals. We have no idea about what they are up to, but they are armed with laser weapons and could pose a significant danger in the wrong hands."

"Is there anything I can do?"

Max smiled and patted her rear. "Ask me again when we get home dear, but for now we will maintain official relationship protocols."

"Yes, sir!"

"Seriously. I will set up a conference call with Robert Sanders at the Deep Space Mining Moonbase. We became friends when we attended engineering grad school at Harvard. After we graduated, I joined NASA and he founded Deep Space Mining on the Moon. My guess is that their systems probably monitored the EM pulses. Let's see if they can shed some light on the situation. I will contact the higher ups in Kansas City to obtain authorization for the meeting."

"Good luck with that."

The Next Day

Sanders had gathered his top cadre for the teleconference with Captain Dobson and his assistant. Any contact with USACO officials raised a red flag with Sanders because of his concern that the totalitarian government might try to interfere with the gene therapy research at the SpeeZees Lab or adversely alter the terms of the Outer Space Treaty to their advantage.

"Greetings Sanders. It's has been a long time." Max said, "This is my assistant, Lieutenant Susan Reynolds. Thank you for arranging this meeting on such short notice."

Sanders laughed. "Seeing you brings back a lot of memories Max. Nice to meet you Susan. These are my top guns. Hiroshi is in charge of the SpeeZees Lab, Sabien is an expert in the field of nano tech, Miguel is in charge of security, and my Son, Torch, is our roboticist. Finally, Chron is a New-Human that is pretty much involved in everything we do up here. To what do we owe the honor of this meeting?"

After Max described the chain of events that had wreaked havoc on the Space Command Network, he explained that, although the SCN's primary purpose was military, his team had recently been assigned the task of adding asteroid threat detection and mitigation capabilities. He concluded by asking for their ideas on how they might work together.

Torch responded, "I am sure that you are aware that Sabien and I are pretty much to blame. None of this would have happened if we had taken the initiative and installed better safeguards so the Reverend LeRoque and his band of CREOS would not have triggered the pod releases which precipitated the conflict. Please accept our apologies."

"Nonsense. It was the Reverend's fault. You and Sabien were only trying to save the planet," interjected Sanders.

Miguel added, "We had a close encounter an SCN shuttle few days back. It was here before we even knew it was en-route. I will send you the data. We definitely need to come up with a better detection system and our team certainly welcomes your input."

"Excellent. Thank you."

Sanders noted, "Meanwhile, Miguel initiate a full-time surveillance of the Space Command Net shuttles that still remain in orbit. See if you can see what those rogues are up to."

"Yes, sir."

"Torch, Sabien, and Chron, give some thought to the asteroid threat situation and develop a prioritized plan of action. Max, you and Susan are welcome to take one of our weekly shuttles and meet with us in person here at the Moonbase. Miguel, when will seats be available?"

"This week's flight is filled, so it would have to be Friday after next. Departure at 0600 AM from Salinas Spaceport. Three day trip."

Max replied, "Thank you. That gives us time to prepare. Meeting in person could eliminate the communication leaks that currently plague our administration. As an incentive, I will submit a request for a consulting contract to pay for your help and to purchase any equipment that you need. We can go over the budget details when we get there."

Sanders said, "Great, we can use the income. It was good to see you again Max. We have a lot of catching up to do. I look forward to your visit."

After the vid-con ended, Sanders concluded, "Well that went better than anticipated. I have to admit that I was wary at first, but it looks like we are going to end up with a new customer and a worthy project. It has been a long day so let's head to the lounge. The first round is on me."

"I'll send the gals a flash to meet us there," said Torch. "It's been a long time since we all got together."

****

The Luna Lounge was packed with base workers getting off the day shift and as usual the air was filled with a chorus of jungle sounds as the workers toasted one another with the bar's trademark *lunatic* cocktails that emitted a chorus of wildlife sounds when swallowed.

Genie waved at Sanders and his team when they entered the bar and pointed to the new VIP section where Astra and Jasmine were comparing notes about motherhood.

Astra said, "You are just in time for the evening news report. I understand that there will be a segment on Reverend LeRoque."

Torch slammed the table with his fist. "I don't want to hear anything that liar has to say. Dad, do we have to watch this?"

"Knowing what that jerk is up to is a matter of base security. You should be here for this."

Torch sighed and sat down while his father scrolled

through the glowing menu embedded in the table surface. "How about iced rum with...let's see...a lion's roar?"

Torch laughed. "Make it a double for me, Dad."

The opening bars to David Bowie's, hit from the 80's began to play in the background.

'Uh, oh, oh, oh
Little China girl'

Chia's smiling face appeared on the screen followed by the sound of a reverberating gong and the caption,

The RealNews
The Only Truly Independent
News Source!

Chia announced, "We begin tonight's broadcast with an update on the recent abduction of Juan Floyd, Chief Engineer of Salinas Droids. Floyd was discovered this morning outside his residence and was taken by ambulance to the local emergency ward. The hospital's team of physicians assigned to his case report that he has absolutely no recollection of the kidnapping or where he has been for the last several days. They believe that he may have been subjected to some sort of drug-based interrogation and the company confirmed that files using his password were downloaded until security blocked their transmission, but otherwise he seems to be slowly recovering from the ordeal. We will keep you posted on this bizarre instance of an android kidnapping a Sapient."

After a commercial, Chia said. "We now shift to live coverage of Reverend LeRoque at the Seekers of Divine Light Church Headquarters in Atlanta, Georgia."

The Reverence made his trademark, grand entrance on a rising platform accompanied by a moving hymn by the choral group. His image was projected on a large vidscreen behind him as he motioned for the audience to be seated."

He began, "It has been way too long since I have addressed this congregation and my wife and I thank you for your patience and understanding. As you are undoubtedly aware, the media have been spreading lie after lie about me and my family. Tonight I will set the record straight."

He keyed a clip of a large CryoVat streaming vapors down its sides. "This is the infamous Ark. The VIDAS claimed that it contained frozen embryos to restore endangered species, but the truth is that the embryos were not endangered species, they were humans taken by force, stolen, or purchased in sleazy underground markets illegally dealing in human gene modifications."

The screen filled with sickening images of malformed individuals, some with extra limbs, others with horrendous scars and tumors on their foreheads and cheeks.

The Reverend continued. "Astra Sturtevant and her followers are building an entire race of aliens that they call *New-Humans*. This a blasphemy to us who they call *Sapients*."

He held up his hands and loudly said, "The bodies of us Seekers of Divine Light may technically be Sapients but our spirits are CREOS."

The crowd began the chant.

'CREOS, CREOS, CREOS'.

The Reverend lowered his palms quieting the audience and then continued, "Does the 'SpeeZees Lab' sound familiar? It should, it's where the Ark ended up. My wife and I even risked our lives and flew to the Moon to try to capture the Ark, but we were too late. You all know what happened next. Sturtevant and her cronies started World War III to keep people from finding out what she was really up to."

A faked image of Astra wearing a stethoscope and holding a scalpel that morphed into an assault rifle filled the screen eliciting cries of hatred and outrage from the audience.

"As if that was not enough, the scientists at the infamous SpeeZees Lab are now in the business of growing New-Humans in test tubes. They may look just like us, but they have no souls and their goal is to exterminate us from the face of the planet. These disgusting, artificially conceived New-Humans now want equal rights with us natural humans. This is a blasphemy. God is the only gene master."

'GOD IS THE ONLY GENE MASTER!'

'GOD IS THE ONLY GENE MASTER!'

Once more the Reverend lowered his hands and the chanting died down. "What can we do about New-Humans? First we need to identify them. We will be pushing the OWN to pass legislation that will mandate that all New-Humans around the planet must bear some sort of prominent facial identification. This will be the first step. Remember these villainous, walking computers have the capacity to evolve and reproduce at horrific rates!"

His followers resumed chanting,

'GOD IS THE ONLY GENE MASTER!'

'GOD IS THE ONLY GENE MASTER!'

The Reverend lifted his arms and the choral group began an upbeat tune. He began clapping to the rhythm and was joined by his wife on the stage who blew kisses to the crowd.

The video feed faded and then cut back to Chia in her studio who said, "Well. That was interesting. The person who most believe started the entire nuclear disaster just claimed that he had nothing to do with it. This reminds me of the gaslighting binge back in the mid 2020's that destroyed the democratic government of the United States and replaced it with a corporate dictatorship. I am afraid that this anti-New-Human movement isn't going away soon. This is Chia signing off."

The lounge was quiet, except for a few patrons that whispered to one another and glanced toward Chron and Jasmine who were obviously upset by the program.

Genie approached Sanders and spoke in his ear. He nodded and then followed her to the front of the bar where he keyed a mic and spoke to the crowd.

"It seems like Reverend LeRoque has been lax in taking his daily medication, but I want to pick up on what Chia said about gaslighting. This is a mind control tactic in which corrupt individuals attempt to rewrite history by their unscrupulous propagation of falsehoods. By repeating the same lies over and over, they spread confusion and chaos in their target audience."

Several people started clapping and nodding in the affirmative.

Sanders continued. "So here I will set the record straight. It was the Reverend that pushed the button that signaled the pods to enter the atmosphere and release the nanomachines that were designed to seal the Arctic tundra without notifying the world leaders of the of the danger of EM pulses. The corporate defense departments misinterpreted this as an attack and launched what they considered to be retaliatory strikes. These are facts that cannot be twisted by corrupt manipulators like the Reverend."

The applause grew louder this time and several rose from their tables and clapped their hands.

"Finally I want you to know that I have the upmost confidence in the ethics and judgment of Dr. Hiroshi and we are extremely fortunate to be associated with Jasmine and Chron. I am sure that once you get to know them, you will find them to be as human as we are."

Genie climbed up on the bar, held up her glass and yelled, "Here's to our New-Humans!"

As the tide of exotic sounds grew, one of the female workers walked over to where Jasmine and Chron were sitting, handed each of them a bouquet of flowers grown in the hydroponics bay and then gave them each a hug.

— CHAPTER 11 —

Hiroshi and Chron escorted Sanders on a tour of the New-Human Development Facility. Now ensconced in its own section adjacent to the SpeeZees Lab, the newly developed complex bustled with physicians and interns, many of whom had been recently recruited and were still adjusting to life on the Moon.

Sanders asked, "How is production going?"

Chron replied, "Right now we are close to our maximum capacity with twenty-seven units in development. Our back orders currently exceed four hundred with a ninety-day turn around for adults. Infants and children require considerably less development time."

"Infants? You are manufacturing babies?"

"Yes of course. Over half of the orders are for individuals less than six years of age. Would you like to meet one?"

Chron led them to the nursery where two boys and a girl were playing hologram games. Chron took the girl's hand and led her over to Sanders who bent down and asked, "Hello, what's your name?"

The girl smiled and replied, "My name is Jinny. What's yours?"

Chron said, "Jinny, this is Director Sanders."

Jinny asked, "Are you my father? I have been waiting for him."

MET CHRON NEW-HUMANS

Chron interjected, "No dear. Your father is on his way and will be here next week. He is coming from Earth and will be taking you there soon."

Sanders asked, "Do you know what Earth is?'

She pointed to the blue planet displayed on the wall monitor and relied, "Of course. It is where I will live in a house with my parents and be able to go outside and breathe the fresh air."

Chron said, "You're right Jinny. You can rejoin your friends now."

Sanders nodded at a group of boys who were intently focused on the game they were playing. "What about the boys?"

Hiroshi interrupted, "Excuse me Director Sanders. If you don't mind, I would like to leave you in Chron's capable hands while I join Astra in her lab. There are a couple of things she wants to go over before we all meet with her later this morning."

"No problem. I will see you there shortly."

After Hiroshi left, Chron picked up where he left off. "The boys are also waiting for pickup. The shuttle flight out of the new Salinas Spaceport was delayed because of high winds, however launches from the spaceport are now back on track."

Chron escorted Sanders into the grow-out room where rows of pods with banks of blinking lights monitored the vital signs of New-Humans in various stages of development. Chron cued one of the station monitors which displayed:

New-Human ID: N-H 23
Name: Not yet assigned
Field: Sapient Medicine
Expertise: Neuron Repair
IQ: 275
Customer: NanoMed, Topeka, Kansas

Sanders observed."You have been busy! How are you holding up?"

"I admit that running this facility, helping Torch and Sabien develop security and asteroid mining strategies and Astra with her anti-aging research have been somewhat of a challenge."

"That's putting it mildly. I would like to go over your venture's profit/loss projections and marketing plan. I have asked our new financial officer, Julia Cravens, to join us. She came up on last week's shuttle so she is still getting used to life up here...ah, here she comes now."

Julia, an attractive young lady wearing, a Deep Space Mining uniform and carrying a vintage briefcase, entered the lab. She was breathing heavily as she said, "Sorry I'm late. I took a wrong turn and ended up in the maintenance section."

Sanders took her arm. "Actually, you are right on time. Julia meet Chron. He is in charge of this new New-Human venture. Julia is a graduate of UC San Diego with an MBA in technology patenting."

Chron replied, "Wonderful, that is just what we need, any financial guidance will be appreciated. Keep in mind that we that work here in the SpeeZees Lab are mostly scientists with little experience in business."

Julia replied, "I have looked over the documents that you sent to Director Sanders and have some ideas to go over with you. Is this a good time?"

"Please take a seat and let's get started. I'll order us some coffee."

An hour later, Sanders checked the time and said, "This has been a very productive meeting with a lot of details still to be considered, but it's getting late and I promised Astra that we would all meet with her in a few minutes. She seemed very excited about something."

Chron said, "I need to check with security so they know where to find me. I'll meet you there."

MET CHRON NEW-HUMANS

****

Hiroshi, watched patiently as Astra paced back and forth in anticipation of the upcoming meeting with Robert Sanders who was not only in charge of the Deep Space Mining Moonbase, but also her father-in-law. Behind the large window that separated the lab from the office, Scotty was immersed in a virtual world battle game in which he was fighting with holographic combatants. Even though he was aware that he was a center of attraction, he ignored the onlookers.

When Sanders, Chron and Julia arrived, Astra greeted them and handed them cups of Sanders' favorite chamomile tea.

Sanders grabbed a seat, took a drink and sighed. "You know me well Astra, thank you. I would like to introduce Julia Cravens, she is our new financial guru. Chron gave us a quick tour of the new facility and it looks like we are now in the New-Human production business."

Hiroshi said, "I am sorry I had to leave early, but Astra called me this morning and asked if I could help her prepare for this meeting. I think you will soon see why."

Sanders took another sip and said, "That sounds interesting. What's up?"

Astra looked at Hiroshi who waved his hand in a condescending gesture.

Astra cleared her throat and announced, "I think that I found it. Based on my analysis of Scotty's unique genome, I found a way to control the aging clock!"

"You're kidding. You can now stop aging?"

"Not only stop, but I believe we may be able to reverse or accelerate aging as well."

"Wow, that truly is amazing!"

"Admittedly, our sample size is limited and based only on experiments with the mice that Chron and Rosella 3D printed, but the data is quite convincing."

Hiroshi handed Sanders a data pad and said, "I have convinced Astra that it would be wise to file patents for this procedure as soon as possible."

Sanders handed the pad to Julia. "This looks like it is right up your alley, Julia. Two new clients in one day. Can you handle it?"

She smiled and said, "I will get started right away. There is a special World Patent Organization office that handles breakthrough technology applications. They are usually swamped with submissions, but one of my school chums is one of senior agents and happens to owe me a favor...I helped him do prior art research on asteroid mining for his doctoral thesis."

Chron grinned. "Wait until Torch hears about that! Julia, you are going to be a very busy young lady."

"My pleasure, sir."

Sanders appeared to have reservations. "Isn't research based only on artificial mice somewhat lacking in terms of credibility?"

Julia replied, "You would think so, but the patent world is based upon protecting the rights to product designs before they are offered on the market. However, you can still approach potential customers while your patents are pending. Through UCSD and my friend at the WPO, I have access to a team of specialized AIs which will expedite the prior art claims research. Still it could take six months to a year to get the application approved and published. Plenty of time for you to replicate your experiments and make improvements."

Hiroshi joined in. "Yes of course. Many new tests will have to be made. But this is a cut-throat business with the mega-corporate governments and corporations all trying to dominate the anti-aging market. Filing this patent application will be the first step to getting our product into the marketplace. Astra will be happy to provide you with a complete analysis for your review."

Astra nodded. "I will do all I can to assist you Julia."

She turned to Sanders and said, "However, there is an area where we do need your guidance and approval."

"That sounds serious. What is it?"

She took a deep breath. "Would you have any objection if Chron 3D printed human subjects to do the next round of tests?"

"Are you saying that you want to experiment on New-Humans?"

Chron, who had been waiting quietly, replied, "No, not really. Essentially we would be fabricating clones that completely lack all forms of conciseness, but with functional aging clock components and epigenetic programming. It would be a major move forward before beginning tests on healthy, organic humans."

Sanders shrugged. "As long as you are certain it is safe and any potential risks are negligible, I have no problem with this, but I recommend that you keep this confidential. There may be a few on the base who might find it objectionable and Reverend LeRoque would jump at the chance to use this to agitate his base if he discovered what you were up to. As far as security, please include Miguel in the planning and implementation."

"Will do."

Julia waved her arm and asked, "Do you have financial projections?"

Hiroshi shuffled through his bag and passed out pads. "Please keep in mind that this cash flow and profit/loss model is a work in progress. But you can scroll to the fourth page for a summary."

Sanders took a few minutes to look at the numbers then, put down his pad and grinned. "Oh my! You've got to be kidding!"

Astra said, "No sir, the license fees should be significant."

Julia nodded her head. "I'll say. This looks awesome."

Chron held out his hands and turned his palms up. "Naturally, what else would you expect from discovering the fountain of youth on the Moon?"

Astra gave Sanders a hug and said, "Thank you for all the help you have given me over all these years."

As Sanders followed Julia and Chron toward the door, he turned back and said. "If this business is as lucrative as you project and the demand for New-Humans is as high as Chron projects...and if our deal with Max works out, we should have enough capital to start building a dome and transform the Moon into a great place to live! Good work. Keep me posted."

As Sanders turned to leave, Astra heard him ask Chron if he was sure that the clones lacked self awareness and was relieved when Chron nodded in the affirmative.

After the door closed, Astra slumped against her desk and told Hiroshi. "Boy am I glad that is over. I so much appreciate your guidance. I don't know what I would have done if Sanders had refused my request."

Hiroshi replied, "I am still a little unclear about the procedure that you and Chron have proposed. However, I don't know about you, but I am kind of burned out and this is a lot to think about. Could we take this up sometime next week?"

"Actually two weeks might be better. That will give Chron and I time to create the clone subjects and to begin the first round of experiments. In addition, I will put together a presentation that provides a step-by-step description of the development sequence. You are welcome to invite the your staff and the base VIPs. Just make sure that they will not reveal our secrets."

"Understood. Good job Astra."

"Thank you Hiroshi for your insight and support. Hopefully, we will have some good news to report."

Hiroshi stood and picked up his tab. "I look forward to learning more and agree with you that security must be tight. I suggest that we also include Miguel, since he is head of Deep Space Mining security, and Jason Phillips, who is in charge of security here at SpeeZees Lab. Let me know when you are ready and I will schedule the meeting."

"Good idea. I'll keep you posted on my progress."

After Hiroshi left, Astra went into the lab and asked Scotty. "Are you hungry? How about if we go and get some lunch."

Scotty responded, "As long as you don't make me eat that fake fish again."

"You can have whatever you want Scotty. The lounge has a new chef and I have. heard good reports about his pizza and spaghetti. Let's invite Madeline."

"OK, I'll tell sis. She should be coming back from the sauna soon. I'll go get her and meet you there."

Two Weeks Later
March 29th, 2033

Chron's assistant, Rosella, handed out cups of champagne and snacks as the Moonbase VIPs assembled in Astra's office for the much anticipated update.

Chron took Astra's arm and observed. "You look nervous. What's wrong?"

"Nothing wrong; just excited...I guess I am a little concerned about how our guests will react when they see our subjects. It's a little unnerving at first."

"Perhaps you should alert them about what to expect."

"Good idea." She turned to the group and said, "OK everyone may I have your attention please. Thank you for coming. Before we go into the lab, I would like warn you that the first encounter with our subjects can be a little...unexpected. Just keep in mind that, although they look like real people, they have no consciousness. They have no cognition or self-awareness. They feel no pain, nor can they speak or respond to you."

After the visitors donned lab coats. face masks, gloves and slippers, Astra said, "Feel free to ask Hiroshi or me any questions."

It took a few moments for their eyes to adjust to the dim ambient lighting and perceive the arrays of colorful LEDs that blinked on and off throughout the maze of sensors, wires and control switches. Eight silver pods were arranged in a circle connected to arrays of tubes that supplied nutrients and removed wastes. Each pod displayed a monitor that listed the parameters being measured by a bank of sensors as well as the initial age and the current age of the subject inside.

Sanders peered into one of the pods and said, "Astra this one looks just like you."

"Chron used my DNA as a baseline for the female clones so as not to involve anyone we didn't have to. You will see that the males look like Chron for the same reason."

Suddenly a loud scream echoed through the chamber. Julia pointed to the pod that she stood next to and covered her mouth with her hand. Sanders raced to her side and asked, "What's wrong?"

Julia pointed at the pod. "I'm sorry...I wasn't expecting a child. She is so beautiful. and looks so peaceful lying there. But all those tubes connected to her head and arms...I'm sorry. This caught me off guard."

Sanders put his arm around Julia as she wiped tears from her eyes. He asked Astra, "How old is this subject?"

MET CHRON NEW-HUMANS

"She was created last week as a juvenile with an initial age of six months. Her aging-clock was programmed to accelerate to ten times the normal rate until she reaches adulthood a few months from now. As you can see on the display, her chronological age is now approaching five years."

Chron noted, "Our genetic modifications appear to have successfully manipulated her rate of aging. That was the goal of this experiment."

Julia asked, "And then what happens?"

Astra replied, "There are several options, We could enter a new regimen in which her rate of aging slows to zero or even to regression in which she would eventually become an infant again. We are essentially manipulating the subject's rate of aging using our new clock management program."

Sanders said, "This is amazing, please continue."

Astra led them on a tour of the lab chamber and pointed to another pod. "This one is an adult male clone that we just started regressing. His chronological age is thirty-five, but he is projected to become a virtual child by the end of the month. The other pods are filled with three middle-aged males and a boy and a girl in their teens. The two remaining pods are currently empty until Chron prints us a senior male and female who will be used in our next series of experiments which will begin next week."

Chron noted, "Keep in mind that the rapid age acceleration and anti-aging regression rates that we are using in these experiments are solely designed to investigate the hypothesis that we can manipulate the aging clock in compliance with the anti-aging paradox."

Sanders asked, "What is this paradox?"

Chron smiled and replied, "It's simply that the subjects taking the cure for aging may outlive the researchers that are monitoring them."

Astra nodded, "When we shift to organic humans, we will use rates that are a mere fraction of those in these experiments. Let's move back to my office, I have some materials to share with you that may clarify our approach."

****

After a detailed presentation in which Astra used graphics and complex gene coding simulations to document the scientific basis of her longevity breakthrough, Astra concluded. "Now I will turn the meeting over to Dr. Hiroshi."

"Thank you Astra and Chron and welcome Torch and Sabien. I am glad that Director Sanders has included you, Julia, and Miguel in this meeting. I think that I speak for everyone here that Astra and Chron's painstaking research approach and results are simply outstanding. What they have accomplished could conceivably impact the lives of every Sapient and every New-Human that wants to enjoy a much prolonged life-span. How about we take a five minute break and refill our drinks?"

After Rosella topped of their cups, Hiroshi continued. "We all know that the market for longevity products is immense. Pharmaceutical firms have been promoting fountains of youth for decades, but most are merely a charade dependent upon a placebo effect."

Astra held up her hand and said, "Not all of them; there are a few treatments and supplements that actually help repair DNA. Sorry for the interruption, please continue Director."

"The question is not only how do we manage and profit from the sale of this medical breakthrough, but what is the moral stance that we must consider in the drug's distribution? The fact that Astra and Chron have incorporated an encrypted key unique to each individual patient in the personalized version means that each dose will have its own unique identifier so that their prescription will only function with their specific genome and only during the limited time prescribed."

Sanders, who had been listening carefully, stood and paced back and forth and then addressed the group. "So let me be sure that I understand this. A seventy year old man consults with his physician and they fill out a prescription request that specifies that his brain and body will gradually regress morphologically into the equivalence of a fifty year old man."

Astra explained, "Yes, that is what we have termed the *Calendar* version. Keep in mind that any pharmaceutical company administering the Calendar treatment will have to comply with our rigorous standards in order to qualify for the program. Dr. Hiroshi, please continue."

"We will go over the pharma arrangement later, but I just want to point out that the Calendar treatment can be used to arrest or reverse aging for a fee. We will discuss the free version next."

Sanders, who had been quiet so far, stepped forward and said, "I think I should clarify why we are discussing delivery mechanics and licensing fees this early in the project. The reason is simple actually. It is going to be very difficult to keep this discovery secret. Once the product testing has been complete and ready for distribution, we need to be able to react immediately."

Hiroshi laughed. "I admit that it has been a challenge to drag Astra and Chron away from the research lab, but after many late night sessions, I think we have made a good start on a business plan."

Rosella handed out pads to each person while Hiroshi continued. "You now have first draft of the business plan and some very preliminary sales and profit projections. Feel free to make comments or suggestions. Now Astra will provide an overview of the technical aspects."

Astra nodded and then activated a floating monitor. "Here is a chart of the steps involved."

> Step 1. After enrolling in the Calendar program and collecting a deposit, the patient's physician will record baseline data and send it to the SpeeZees Lab where a custom prescription will be developed. The prescription will need to be updated weekly.
>
> Step 2. Next, the licensed pharmaceutical firm will manufacture the drug and fill a clear plastic pouch with a large, single, green-colored capsule. Each prescription will be unique to that patient and will have to be custom made and then delivered to the patient's designated contact point.
>
> Step 3. Patient takes a single capsule weekly before he or she goes to sleep.
>
> Step 4. Patient takes a blood sample weekly which lists a wide range of epigenetic parameters and sends it to his or her physician.
>
> Step 5. Physician sends the data to the SpeeZees Lab where changes to the prescription will be made as needed and forwarded to the pharmaceutical firm that manufactures the drug.

Sanders asked, "Using the seventy year old man as an example, how long will the regeneration to age fifty take?"

Astra entered the data into her pad and said, "Approximately eighteen to twenty-four months. After that he will need to consult with his family, friends and physician. If his goal has been achieved, the patient may shift to the generic, free version which he will take daily. He will stabilize at age fifty as long as he takes the daily pill—or he could resume the normal aging process."

Julia asked. "Theoretically speaking, could he begin the Calendar program again, undergo a sex change and become a teenage girl?"

"Theoretically, yes it is possible It would take us a few months to work out the procedure, but I am reasonable sure that it could be done."

Julia asked, "What about individuals nearing the end of their current lifespan?"

Astra replied, "They will obviously need immediate attention."

Hiroshi interjected, "At some stage, we will have to come up with a high priority plan to allocate the distribution of the therapy to urgent care centers. Keep in mind that the Calendar control features only apply to users who want to regress or accelerate age-wise. Their prescription encryption keys and blockchain data will be processed and stored in our local cloud. But, individuals who simply wish to halt aging only have to take the generic version of the drug. The free, daily pills are green and delivered in an orange pill tube like this."

She held up the container and said, "We anticipate that this version will by far have the highest demand for those that are financially challenged, but are not concerned about becoming sterile until they stop taking the medication."

Julia sounded alarmed. "Did you say *sterile?*"

"Of course. Those enrolled in the free program will be unable to reproduce until they stop the treatment—at least that is the current arrangement. We are also considering sterility exemptions based upon income, intellect and/or specialized talent. We welcome your input on this."

Torch joined in. "What if millions decide that they want to be thirty-five again...or parents want their children to hurry and grow up? How are you going to keep up with the demand?"

Hiroshi replied, "I am also very concerned about the avalanche of blockchain applications that will have to be certified and recorded. We will need to enhance our AI-neural network so that it will learn, self-improve and expand as the demand grows."

Torch asked, "Who makes and distributes the pills?"

Hiroshi cued images on the screen. "We currently have a list of over seventy global pharma firms that may meet our requirements. As soon as our patents and trademarks are approved and registered, we will enter into NDA agreements and start receiving license fees. I am sure we won't have any problem finding business partners. Keeping up with demand is going to be a challenge at first, but as time goes on, we may decide to assign an increasing amount of our role to some of our partners and simply adjust their license fees."

Torch rubbed his hands together and said, "Now for my last question. Have you come up with a blockbuster name for your invention?"

Astra looked at Hiroshi who nodded at her to answer.

She said, "As you know, Scotty's unique genome provided the key to our discovery, so we named it after him. We call it *Scotty's Miracle Drug...'SCOMID'* for short."

Julia clapped her hands. "That's a great brand name! I haven't had time to study the figures in detail, but it looks like, from the spreadsheet that Hiroshi just gave us, that sales are projected at 500,000 to 750,000 credits per day which will double each year for the first five years."

Sanders looked at Astra and said, "Per day, not bad! What are you going to do with all that money, Astra?"

"I haven't thought about that. Let's see, some to Scotty for sharing his genome, some to the lab and the Moonbase. I'm not sure about the rest. How about you Chron?"

"My needs are few, but I would like to 3D print a brother once there is an opening in the New-Human Development Facility schedule."

Hiroshi tapped his pad. "I am reserving you the next opening which is a week from today. Do you have a name picked out."

"Yes his name will be Quant."

"Education and background?"

"Advanced degrees in environmental science and oceanography."

"Sex and morphology?"

"Same as me, except dark hair so people won't confuse us."

Julia said, "Wow, this certainly is a new world that we are living in."

Sanders held up his hand and counted with his fingers. "SCOMID license fees, New-Human sales and income from asteroid mining...what would you brightest and bravest say to building a big new dome with above the ground quarters, fresh air and lots of open space?"

Astra replied, "That would be wonderful! How about including a pool and playground for the kids? You can use my share of SCOMID profits for that."

Torch held up his cup. "Good job both of you!"

Hiroshi said, "On that note, meeting adjourned. Thank you Astra and Chron that was a great presentation."

Astra took Torch by the arm and said, "I feel like celebrating. How about if we get Luz, suit up, take a stroll outside and let all this sink in?"

"Sounds good to me. I'm proud of you my love."

****

Jason Phillips, who had secretly monitored the meeting by using his security clearance to listen in, locked the door to his apartment and called Reverend LeRoque on a secure line.

"I have some very alarming news to tell you Reverend."

— CHAPTER 12 —

One Week Later
April 5th, 2033

After a three hour tour of the Moonbase, Sanders and Torch escorted Captain Max Dobson and his assistant Susan Reynolds to the administration office where they joined the base managers who were exchanging ideas on how to move forward on a number of projects.

Sanders introduced Torch who played a video of his robotic cows conducting surveys and pulling carts filled with ore followed by Sabien who described the unique aspects of Queen Astasia's remarkable graphene fiber and its potential for towing asteroids into lunar orbit

Finally, Miguel followed up with a description of the recent flyby of the SCN shuttle as well as his team's attempts to decrypt the sporadic transmissions from the remaining shuttles in the SCN, which so far had been unsuccessful. Miguel expressed his concern that android pirates could intercept the shipment of precious metals and New-Humans. He also suggested that they should consider arming the transport shuttles as well as adding enhanced radar detectors, targeting systems, and ground-based laser weapons to the Moonbase.

Torch nodded in agreement when Miguel recommended that the cow robots also be armed and their COM systems enhanced and protected against hacking.

After a break for lunch, Sanders reconvened the meeting and said, "Max, it's your turn. First I should let everyone know that Max has published several papers on asteroid threat mitigation and is widely regarded as one of the leading experts in the field. Go ahead Max."

"Thanks for inviting us, It has been a pleasure to learn about all the great things you have going on up here. You would think that with what we know about Earth's history, the threat posed by asteroids would be of concern to everyone. The problem is that world's corporate governments have played down the risk, saying that, because of the unique planetary alignment of our solar system, meteors, comets and asteroids pose little threat to Earth."

Sabien cleared his throat and said, "That sounds like their bogus claim that global climate change has halted and that we are on the road to a complete recovery."

Torch said, "Typical. Remember, they are experts at media manipulation. That's how they took control!"

Susan noted, "I recently saw a report that school kids are being brainwashed by the media and don't believe that asteroids pose a problem."

Max continued. "The good news is that last year I attended a meeting of the USACO higher ups during which several of the board members revealed that they were in fact aware of the asteroid threat and willing to support the creation of a confidential branch of NASA to develop an asteroid detection and mitigation system–as long as it was kept secret from the public. I was surprised when they put me in charge of the new department—I am more of a scientist than an administrator."

Sanders asked, "What's the current status? Are you operational?"

"Far from it. We had just begun recruiting specialists for a new base of operations in Mountain View which was intended to be the new headquarters of the Space Command Network...until the bomb exploded and turned the new facility into ashes."

Max reached over, took Susan's hand and said, "Unfortunately we lost dozens of our team members in the blast. We were on holiday when it hit."

Torch said, "We are all so sorry."

Max nodded and said, "As I mentioned in our earlier call, we don't hold you to blame. Your intentions were honorable. But back to your comment on gaslighting, some of our close colleagues at NASA believe that the media, who have controlled the country through misinformation, are now losing their grip on society. I would not be surprised if USACO will be forced to dissolve and a new democratic government emerge. The free election in Colorado was a good sign of changes to come."

Torch tapped the table and said, "It's about time!"

Sabien asked, "But how will this affect our operations here on the Moon?"

Max held up his hand and said, "It's simple. We have to protect the planet until sanity prevails. First, we have to eliminate the threat posed by the Neuro androids that have taken over the SCN. They are heavily armed and dangerous. Second, we must develop the capacity to destroy or deflect any asteroids or other objects from space from impacting here or on Earth."

Sanders said, "It sounds like we will need to develop and equip an arsenal of high-powered rockets as well as provide office and living accommodations to support expanded operations. The cost will be astronomical, if I may use that term here. We can begin to explore some options right away, but it would be great if we had your guidance. Can both of you stay for a while?"

Max looked at Susan. "We figured this might be a

long-term undertaking, so we have planned accordingly."

Sanders checked his pad and asked, "Do you mind sharing a unit? We are cramped for space with all of the newcomers."

"Susan said, "No problem. We share a bed at home."

"OK then, welcome to life on the Moon."

Max continued. "I am sure that you are aware that there is growing discontent with USACO's management of the economy and environment. Famine, floods, wildfires, waves of crime and violence have taken a tremendous toll on the government's credibility—in spite of their effort to hide the truth from the public."

"These are definitely trying times," said Sanders.

Max replied, "Please treat what I am about to tell you next as strictly confidential."

"All my people have a top secret security rating, Miguel, check for eavesdroppers."

"Yes sir...none detected."

Max said, "President Ray asked me to join him alone in his office after the last board meeting. He said he wanted to speak to me in private because not all of the corporate leaders were in agreement with regards to the seriousness of the administration's mounting problems. He asked me if the asteroid threat was actually real, so I showed him the current NHAT data, which tracks near-Earth objects, along with a summary of the impacts and near misses in the historical record. Finally, he said...get this...that he would enthusiastically support the project...as long as I would personally advise his senior staff to help him use the media in his bid for reelection."

"That figures," said Torch. But maybe if you are up here, you won't have to participate in his fundraisers."

"You know, I didn't think of that," said Susan.

Max opened his case and retrieved a pad emblazoned

with a shiny presidential seal and handed it to Sanders.

Max said, "President Ray asked me to deliver this to you in person."

Sanders opened the cover and placed his thumb on the screen when asked for identification. After glancing at the first page, he handed it to Julia. "This looks like it is right up your alley."

She quickly scrolled through a few pages and said. "It appears to be an agreement to provide services. If you will excuse me, I will go to my office and read this over."

During the break, Susan and Max went over the list of items that they had forgotten to bring and things that they had forgotten to do before they left Earth while Sanders caught up on the latest ore mining data.

An hour, Julia returned and took her seat at the table. "I apologize for taking so long, but there was one item that I initially thought was an error, but found to be repeated throughout the contract."

Sanders said, "Don't keep us in suspense, what's the problem. Service agreements are usually pretty basic—just *who, what, how much and when.*"

Julia said, "Deep Space Mining is listed as the sole recipient of compensation, but the amount of funds to paid has been left blank. It is essentially a blank check made out to the company."

Max replied, "The President said that he trusted you to be judicious, but any reasonable request would be approved without delay."

Sabien laughed. "This seems to me like politics as usual...scare people about a looming doomsday threat from space to divert their attention away from the real issue of climate change on Earth. He'd probably welcome a close encounter to rile up his base."

"You're right of course," replied Max. "It is politics. A mission like this will have major public exposure and, if there is a revolution; the President wants to be on the winning side. Can you give us a ballpark estimate on how much funding you think that Deep Space Mining, Inc. will require?"

Sanders said, "Wow, this is exciting. Let's take a break while I huddle with my section heads and see what we can put together."

Susan said, "I suggest that you start with a list of the key expenditure items, then we can fill in the amounts later?"

"That sounds good. We'll see you an hour from now."

****

After Max and Susan returned, Sanders made some last minute additions to his pad, handed it to Max and said, "This is preliminary, but it will give you a rough idea."

There was a moment of silence as the members of the group looked at one another in suspense as Max began reading out loud the notes on the pad.

"Habitat dome for one thousand residents. What is the current population?"

Sanders replied, "Just under two hundred, but we are growing fast and this would give use a chance to live above ground, not buried like we are now."

"Understood. Next you have listed a request for a second, smaller dome to support the asteroid tracking and defense with accommodations for the officers and staff in charge of the missile and drone armory. We have already talked about arming your shuttles and the rest of this item will come out of our budget, so that won't be a problem. Let's see, next you have listed graphene cable research. Sabien mentioned that earlier and it sounds like it could be a new technology that could significantly impact the space industry, so that should definitely be included. Moving ahead, I see that you would also like funding for a geothermal power plant, recreational facilities and to expand your food production systems."

Sanders replied, "These are our long-term goals. Any financial assistance will be much appreciated."

The room was quiet as Max entered notes into his pad.

Finally Max smiled and said, "Put your detailed line item budget together and, if it makes sense to me, I will authorize the money transfer for the full amount that you request."

Everyone stood and applauded.

Sanders raised his hands and said, "OK, let's break into teams and crunch the numbers. We will meet again in the morning. Meeting adjourned."

Sanders shook Max's hand and gave Susan a hug. He said, "We will notify you when our proposal and budget are complete. Meanwhile, please join Julia and I for dinner; there is a lot to talk about."

Susan patted her stomach. "I'm starved."

"Do you like Italian food? I remember many late nights when Max and I went to a pizza parlor on the Harvard campus."

"You mean Benedettos? I remember that was one of our favorite hangouts. Why do you ask?"

Genie hired a new chef that named Antonio and everyone is talking about his haute cuisine."

Susan said, "Count me in. I love Italian."

The Next Morning

Sanders and Julia greeted the team as they arrived. "You look a little ragged. Late night?"

Torch handed out pads. "Very late. We just finished a few minutes ago. This is such a unique opportunity, we didn't want to risk USACO changing its mind."

"Same here. Let's start with the dome. Miguel, this is your area."

"As you know right now we have a severe shortage of accommodations for both permanent residents and transients. Currently we have 90 units occupied by 167 residents with a lengthy waiting list. Director Sanders and I have been talking about building a dome and moving the living quarters above ground for years. Hopefully this will finally be the chance to make this happen. Preferably, the dome will be 100 meters high with a diameter of at least 1,000 meters. Although the new housing units will be constructed above ground, we will need to preserve the current quarters in case of a dome failure. We will also want to provide space for shops, schools and expand the Luna Lounge."

Sanders noted, "There are likely items that we have not included, so, I have included a fifteen percent contingency."

He handed his pad to Julia who said, "Total projected cost...four hundred and forty-five million credits."

Torch said, "Wow! You know this will be an historical event—the first dome village in space. I am sure there are lots of engineers on the Moonbase who will love to participate in the design."

Sanders retrieved his pad and announced, "Go ahead, Miguel. Get started."

"Really?"

Sanders nodded and said, "Last night Max reaffirmed that USACO will cover all reasonable expenses and that time is of the essence. So, yes...put your teams together and develop a detailed plan. Give Julia your report when you finish."

"This is great news," said Sabien.

"Torch, I have been reviewing your proposal to add several new features including: a school, a hospital and clinic, a gym, hot tubs and a swimming pool. As I understand it, you will locate a small comet, lasso it with the Queen's graphene cable and bring it into lunar orbit where the ice can be harvested on an as needed basis."

Torch said, "Right, Dad. Astra has already indicated that she would commit some of her share of SCOMID license fees to pay for the pool and other improvements, but I think it would be better if we used USACO funding."

Julia said, "I agree. She doesn't need to worry about paying for a dome. She already has a full plate with the SCOMID business. But just think of how nice it will be to get off duty and then go for a swim—the kids will love it."

Sanders continued. "Alright. I see that you also included funds to build a sub-surface water chamber as well. I assume you will tap into the proposed geothermal power plant to heat the chamber and melt the ice."

Torch replied, "That will not only supply the pool but provide water for the hydroponics farm. Right now crop production is limited by the need to conserve water."

"Sounds good. You have my permission to go ahead. Sabien, the cable research facility is also approved."

Sabien rubbed his hands together. "Finally, we will have a chance to put to use the graphene cables that Queen Astasia invented. I'm sure she will be happy to make what we need and deliver it on one of our returning ore shuttles. We will need one ship and cable to accelerate the comet forward and then another one to slow the comet and insert it into lunar orbit."

Torch added, "And then we can knock off pieces and transport them down to the chamber."

Sander's asked, "When do you think you can get underway?"

Torch looked at Sabien who shrugged and said, "It will probably take a couple of weeks for Astoria to fabricate the cable and ship it to us. First, we will need to locate the target. After that, a couple of more weeks to recover the comet."

Miguel said, "Meanwhile we can start drawing up the plans for the new habitat dome and installing the geothermal power plant. My team and I will need to work with Max and Susan to design the asteroid dome, rocket systems, offices and living accommodations."

Sanders shook their hands and said, "The mission is officially a go. Good luck!"

Torch looked at Sabien and said, "Let's send a flash to Astasia, she will be stoked to try out her invention and then let's go brief Genie and have a few *lunatics*!"

****

Julia and Sanders spent the afternoon discussing the improvement plan and budget with Max and Susan, which culminated in the deposit of a sizable down payment into the Deep Space Mining corporate account,

Sanders was elated and retrieved a frost-covered bottle of champagne, popped the cork and poured them all glasses.

Susan held up the bottle and whistled, "Bottled in 2022, Napa Valley, California. This is a rare vintage. Most wine grapes are grown in Greenland and Southern Australia these days."

"It was a gift from one of our new tenants," explained Sanders. "I saved it for a special occasion."

Julia laughed, "Well, this new deal that we just signed certainly merits that criterion."

Sanders raised his glass and said, "Here's to a better tomorrow."

Max took a sip. "Very nice."

Susan yawned and said, "I don't know about the rest of you, but I am exhausted. If you don't need me anymore, I think I will call it a day."

"No argument from me. It has been a long couple of days. If there are no objections, I will join Susan."

Sanders walked Julia to her room in the visitor's wing. When they arrived, she invited him into the tiny compartment. As he squeezed into the single chair next to her bunk, he was dismayed by the size and starkness of her quarters.

"I apologize for these accommodations; they weren't intended for long stays," observed Sanders.

She took his hand and said, "Really, I don't mind."

On impulse he put his arms around her. "I appreciate your good nature, but I have a much nicer unit. It even has a kitchen of sorts. You are welcome to stay at my place. You can move in tonight if you wish."

"Thank you. That is an offer that I will gratefully accept. I'll stop by after I pick up a few things from the storage locker that Hiroshi loaned me in the SpeeZees Lab."

"Fine, that will give me a chance to straighten up a little and we can even order take out delivery of pizza and a bottle of wine from the Luna Lounge."

"That will be lovely."

When Sanders headed for the door and was about to leave, she pulled him back and surprised him with a kiss. "I look forward to spending more time with you."

As Sanders walked down the corridor, he broke into a broad grin and then laughed as one of Torch's sayings came to mind, *What have I gotten myself into this time?"*

— CHAPTER 13 —

One Year Later
April 6th, 2034

It was the official opening day for the new Moonbase dome and the atmosphere was festive and vibrant as the crowd around the central stage danced to the sounds of the five-piece band that was playing legacy rock and roll.

Joining in the celebration, Solara and Luz engaged in a contest to see who could run and leap the farthest while Astra and Jasmine navigated through the bustling crowds, checking out the new shops and restaurants that offered a welcome addition to the standard base fare.

Adding to the ambiance was the long anticipated vote at the Organization of World Nations that, if approved, would endow the now burgeoning Moonbase with a first of its kind, independent *Space Colony* status. This was extremely important because it would not only provide the Moonbase with the status of an independent nation, but also a much sought after seat at the OWN. Although parts of the new dome had gradually opened to the public as they became available, today's grand opening festivities were scheduled to coincide with this historic event.

MET CHRON NEW-HUMANS

Two factors had played key roles in the application procedure. First was the determined leadership provided by *Quant,* Chron's brother who was 3D printed in the New-Humans Development Facility and who was endowed with a very highly developed knowledge of environmental science and oceanography.

The second factor was the much publicized and unique role that the Moonbase was taking to protect the Earth from asteroid threats. The new Asteroid Safeguard Complex, located next to the Moonbase dome, was equipped with powerful rockets capable of engaging asteroids as well as offices, living quarters and advanced radar detection systems that offered the Moon and Earth secure protection from asteroid threats.

The assembly of the first, livable habitat dome in space was largely made possible by Queen Astasia's graphene discovery. While working on a novel method to construct extremely lightweight tow cables with immense strength, she found that if the nano fibers were subjected to intense bursts of heat and infrared light, they fused to form an extremely thin, nearly transparent, flexible sheeting reinforced with molecular tubules that was virtually indestructible and provided outstanding thermal insulation.

Combined with low cost and ease of manufacturing, the new sheeting offered an ideal solution to construct domes that were strong enough to provide protection from most incoming meteorites. The long accepted dogma that off-planet habitats would only be safe if they were buried under ground, with very high construction costs, had changed radically.

With funds provided by Deep Space Mining, Inc. through its lucrative contract with USACO, Astasia had set up a manufacturing facility at her base in the Arctic tundra where the sheets were made, rolled into cylinders and then shipped to the Moon via cargo freighters.

What would have taken twenty-four months or more to build using prior subsurface methods had been built in less than a year and included a major upgrade to the Luna Lounge that now offered spectacular panoramic views of the surface from the balcony as well as a large vidscreen behind the bar and in the rear, doors that opened to a pool, hot tubs and the new *Galactic Bistro* which was a joint venture between Genie and Antonio.

Scotty rushed to the edge of the dome and pointed."Look Sis, there is a man wearing a spacesuit out there! What's he doing?"

Madeline shrugged, "It looks he is leading robots that are carrying blocks of ice. Not sure what's up. Astra do you know? I think that looks like Torch."

Astra nodded. "It is him. His RoboCows are delivering ice from the docking port to the new geothermal plant where it will be melted, filtered and stored in the underground chamber. The processed water will then be used as needed for resident use, the hydroponics farms and the recreational facility."

"Does that mean we will be able to go for a swim?"

"Hold on while I send a query...OK, they say there are openings to use the pool right now."

Luz, who was usually shy and quiet blurted, "I want to go too Mom!"

"OK, Everyone who wants to go for a swim follow Madeline. I am supposed to meet Torch in a few minutes. Madeline do you mind looking after Luz?"

"No problem. I will flash you when we finish."

****

After a tour of the new facilities, Sanders and the base's senior staff and families entered the Luna Lounge, which was totally packed, and received a round of applause from the celebrating patrons.

Genie joined them. "You guys and gals are our heroes. Just look around. This just used to be a bar in a basement, now it is the very heart of our new village!"

Max said, "Morale seems to be high. Let's just hope that the OWN news is good, otherwise it could ruin the party."

Genie shrugged. "I remember times when the future looked pretty bleak. As the theme song of the classic Star Trek Enterprise TV series once claimed. *It's been a long road getting from there to here*."

Sanders replied, "I didn't know you were a trekkie."

"We have just started airing the programs on Friday nights. You should stop by."

"I will and you're right. It has been a struggle up until now, but we are finally receiving a steady income from our mining operations and the lucrative government contract that you provided Max."

"Money well spent," replied Max.

Sanders held up his drink offered a toast. "Thanks to you my friends. We couldn't have done this without you."

Sabien said, "I understand that there is a lengthy waiting list for workers who want to relocate here."

Miguel replied, "That's correct. This is a good start, but we are going to need even more quarters, restaurants, medical facilities, schools, security personnel and a boost to our power and oxygen generating systems...plus the SpeeZees Lab and the New-Human businesses have requested additional lab space. More ore freighters, escort ships...the list goes on and on."

Chron said, "It is fantastic to be part of building a new society. I hope that my brother Quant has been successful in gaining admittance. I know it is a somewhat obscure rule buried in the OWN bylaws, but being admitted to the OWN automatically grants all citizens of member nations equal status. That means that every

New-Human will have equal rights with every Sapient around the world."

After sequestering his cow herd and changing into a Hawaiian shirt and shorts, Torch joined the party.

Genie checked her watch implant and jumped to the top of the bar and yelled for quiet. She waited until the last *lunatic* burps had sounded and announced, "Quiet everyone, the news is about to start. Today is a big day!"

The image of Chia, now with her hair reflecting a metallic silver and her signature facial tattoos radiating a rainbow of colors, appeared on the wall vidscreen accompanied by her trademark theme song and the caption:

The RealNews
The Only Truly Independent
News Source!

"Welcome world! This is Chia bringing you the Real-News. Today we focus on the Moonbase's application to become recognized as an independent nation. which is strenuously opposed by many Sapients, AI robots and androids. For more on this we go to Stephanie Jenkins, speaking to us from the Organization of World Nations headquarters in Rome, Italy."

Stephanie's hovering vidcam bounced in the breeze causing the video feed to shift erratically as she clung to the railing on the steps outside the OWN building.

She reported, "Hello Chia, as you can tell, we are experiencing a terrific wind storm and the forecast is for heavy rain to start any minute now, but the inclement weather doesn't seem to have discouraged the thousands of people who have braved the storm to be here. As you know, today the Organization of World Nations is scheduled to windup its monthly session in a few minutes after it votes on the Lunar Colony's application for membership."

MET CHRON NEW-HUMANS

Chia asked, "Do you have any indications on how this will turn out?"

"Not really, the polls that we have taken are inconclusive at this time, but I have with me Quant. who has played a key role in these proceedings. Luckily we were able to move into the briefing room and out of the maelstrom outside."

Quant, a tall dark-haired New-Human, joined his palms and bowed his head in a Buddhist greeting of respect. He said, "Thank you for inviting me to your program. It is very popular with my family, friends and associates back on the Moon."

Stephanie replied, "You are welcome. I have a few items that I would like to discuss with you. As we are all aware, the New-Human population will likely increase significantly in the next decade. As a result, a growing percentage of Sapients are very concerned about maintaining and acquiring new jobs in the future because they simply cannot compete with the latest generations of inorganic AIs for engineering and high tech positions. What is your response to their concerns?"

"Speaking as a New-Human, our primary goal is to encourage the awareness that we all essentially live on a tiny speck in the vastness of the universe. We, like our human forefathers and creators, need to conserve and manage our resources until the colonization of space becomes a practicality. We believe that this should be the main goal of all sentient beings."

"That is certainly a noble calling. What's next on your list?"

"Our ability to divert potentially threatening asteroids has just begun with the opening of the new Asteroid Safeguard Complex on the Moon. So far we have been lucky, but we must develop the capability of dealing with a planet killer. As you know, Earth has experienced several disastrous impacts in its 4.5 billion year history. Most astronomers believe that it is only a matter of time before we experience a major encounter."

"What's the next step?"

"We look forward to working with the entrepreneurs at Deep Space Mining to seriously begin asteroid and comet mining in the near-Earth belt. Although off–planet mining has so far been limited because of the enormous costs, now is the time to move forward. This will also create a huge new industry that will create tens of thousands of new jobs for Sapients."

Stephanie asked, "So you think that this new imitative will encourage all of us to work together for our mutual survival?"

"Exactly. We need to put a halt to all of our political bickering and fear mongering. We need to join forces to create a better life for every life and every life form. As an environmentalist, I am convinced that we need to halt all carbon emissions. We need to this now!"

"What do you hope for here today?"

"This afternoon the Organization of World Nations will vote on a landmark decision to grant nationhood status to the Moonbase."

"Why is this so important?"

"Basically, we Lunans desire representation on a world level as our population grows and we form new colonies. Basic necessities, like oxygen, food and water, are currently taken for granted or abused here on Earth. But, these are critical to our day-to-day survival on the Moon. Our priories are different from androids in this regard. I was fortunate to participate in the drafting of our constitution and it seemed appropriate to include equal rights for New-Humans and Sapients."

"How about AI robots and androids?"

"Frankly, that is a complex issue and I'm not sure at this time. One problem is the potential for exponential increases in the android population if they are allowed to build factories which could conceivably produce clones equal to the entire Sapient and New-Human population in a relatively short period of time.

Stephanie turned to her hovering vidcam and said, "As you can see, we are nearing a turning point in the evolution of humankind. The vote results should be released momentarily."

Quant held up his right hand with middle and fore-fingers crossed. "If we succeed in attaining full rights and privileges, it will be a significant moment in the history of the New-Human race!"

Stephanie nodded. "So how does this quest for Lunar Colony status relate to the growing movement to resurrect America's democracy?"

"Those of us who qualify, will have dual citizenship with the American government and the Lunar Colony. The restoration of our voting rights is of paramount importance and the right to elect our representatives in a democratic government is essential. Corporations are the worst offenders and they should be prohibited from making campaign contributions or influencing national elections–assuming that fair and honest voting is restored. But even if this initiative fails to pass today, we will want to work together with Sapients to create jobs and save the planet from devastating climate change."

Suddenly there was a loud explosion that rocked the building. A few moments later, one of security guards grabbed Quant and yelled, Armed droids have surrounded the building. We need to move to a secure room in the basement."

The hovering vidcam focused on Stephanie as she shouted over the uproar, "It looks like a band of androids are up to no good. I will provide you with an update as soon as the results become available. This is Stephanie signing off!"

She tapped her wrist, which signaled her vidcam to zoom into her hand and shut down.

Back in the studio, Chia was obviously alarmed, "OK viewers,while we wait for the results, we will replay an earlier program which featured Reverend LeRoque's controversial viewpoint on New-Humans. I understand that he plans to address his congregation after the results are announced today. I will alert you when our coverage resumes."

As the feed faded to black, her mic picked up her voice. "Stephanie...are you there? Stephanie?"

Thirty Minutes Later

When an on air alert gong sounded, Chia rushed to her seat and plugged in her earpiece.

"We are now resuming coverage of this special, land-mark session of the Organization of World Nations! This is a live feed from the headquarters of the OWN in Rome where Stephanie Jenkins has been reporting on this momentous event. Stephanie are you there? A few minutes ago you were evacuated. What's the situation now?"

"I'm here Chia. We have been briefed that the culprits that launched the attack were apprehended and things are back to normal. Here comes the chairwoman of the Organization of World Nations. This is the big moment."

A tall, dark-skinned woman took the podium, cleared her throat and read from her pad, "Based upon the Organization of World Nations' recognition that the survival of the humanity depends the critical asteroid threat management services provided by the brave souls that risk their live and work on the Moon, the majority of OWN members have voted in the affirmative on Rule Docket Number 79 thereby granting membership and full, independent nation status to the Lunar Colony."

There was a mix of boos and applause as the chairwoman continued. Since any independent government recognized by the OWN is mandated to endow all its citizens with equal rights, all New-Humans are hereby granted equal rights with all Sapients."

There were more shouts and armed security forces spread throughout the crowd in case the protests turned violent.

"I want to thank my committee co-chairman and our staff for their hard work in drafting this ruling."

Then she banged her gavel down and proclaimed, "This session is over."

Cries of dismay and shouted objections drowned out the slight majority of applauding member representatives that had approved of the change. One loud voice yelled, "How will we be able to tell New-Humans from us real humans?"

Once more the chairwoman slammed down her gavel and repeated, "This session is over. Meeting adjourned! Our next assembly will be on March 4th, 2034 and we will address new business at that time."

A crowd gathered around Quant shaking his hand and joyfully exchanging hugs as he walked out of the OWN headquarters. In spite of the hurricane force winds, crowds of supporters and protesters jammed the walkways as Quant's security escorts hustled him into a van that slowly moved onto the commercial guideway and headed for the airport for his flight to the Salinas Spaceport and his return to the newly proclaimed Lunar Colony.

The feed returned to Chia in her studio. "We have been getting reports of violent clashes around the world as worried factions react to their fear that this could be the first step of New-Humans taking over our civilization. After all, they are smarter and stronger than any of us. Now we shift our coverage to Atlanta, Georgia where our staff reporter Robert Black is on the scene. Bob, do you hear me?"

"Yes, loud and clear. The time here in Atlanta is six hours ahead of Rome, so we are coming up on mid-afternoon. And it is hot! Right now the temp is nearly 120 degrees Fahrenheit with severe tornado warnings in the forecast. In spite of the sweltering heat, Seekers of Divine Light Church members have been assembling here since early morning in anticipation of the OWN decision to recognize New-Humans which just aired on the big screen behind me. Any minute now we expect a response from Reverend LeRoque. Wait...the doors are opening and here comes the Reverend. I'll try to move in closer to get a better vantage point."

The crowd cheered when Reverend LeRoque stood behind the podium, waved and then tapped his mic to make sure it was live.

The Reverend said, "I am sure that by now you have heard the shocking news from the OWN meeting today in which they have made the horrendous decision to grant the so called New-Humans full citizenship. Equal rights for all is what they claim. But what they really mean is that you and I will have to go on welfare because there are no jobs left for us Sapient humans and we will soon be on the path towards extinction. This decision to grant New-Humans full citizenship rights is a travesty to this world and a threat to the human race."

One of the members shouted a question. "What do you recommend, what should we do?"

The Reverend folded his hands and touched his forehead and then replied, "The Lord condemns this blasphemy," and then he raised his fist and said, "Keep the faith! This is just the beginning!"

As he left the podium a chant began and resonated throughout the congregation.

MET CHRON NEW-HUMANS

Keep the faith...
Just the beginning...

The feed cut back to Chia where she said, "Thanks for your excellent reporting Robert. Please keep us posted on new developments. Right now I am receiving a flash from Quant who is onboard a chartered Avion Sky Master on his way to the spaceport. He has agreed to a short interview."

"Quant, congratulations on your victory."

"Thank you. I am honored by the OWN decision."

Chia joked, "Now you will have to pay taxes like the rest of us. How do you feel about the move to adopt semiconductor chips as a new monetary currency?"

"First, I would like for your viewers to know that your unbiased coverage has been a big help in our effort to attain equality. But you are correct to be concerned about taxes and chip-based currencies. Transferring the current blockchain cryptographic system, which is still resident in bitcoins and gold markets, to high-level machine intelligence chips will be a challenge. But I am sure that if we put our collective resources together that we will come up with a reasonable system in a fairly short period of time."

Chia said, "We are getting reports of protest demonstrations around the world—not only from Sapients, but also by AI robots and androids. Are you worried about your safety?"

"I'm sure it will take time for our acceptance. The truth is that this is a major turning point in history for both Sapients and New-Humans."

"What about Isaac Asimov's three Laws of Robotics, the first of which states that robots shall do no harm to humans. Does this apply to New-Humans?"

"Yes of course, New-Humans now have the same

rights. They must also obey the same rules as Sapients."

"But if androids develop intelligence and consciousness...what then? I mean how do you define the difference between an AI enhanced android and a New-Human."

There was a burst of static then the signal was lost. Chia tried several times to reconnect, but without success. She turned to the camera and said, "I guess I hit a sensitive spot with that question. But I do wonder how this will play out. It seems like a fairly fundamental question."

Chia cued her trademark theme song and said, "This is Chia with the RealNews signing off. What a day!"

Genie switched off the vidscreen which allowed the vibrant blue glow of the Earth to shine through the dome roof while the reaction of the patrons seem to range from enthusiastic approval to complete indifference.

Genie called out, "Listen up everyone. I wish to propose a toast...here's to our new partners, the New-Humans. The next round is on me," which elicited a cheer from the crowd.

Genie approached Chron carrying a tray of drinks and gave him a hug. She said, "This is a major win for New-Humans. Congratulations. I brought you your favorite *lunatic.* Here is one for you too Rosella. Yours is a surprise."

Chron took a sip and burped creating the sound of an old fashioned steam locomotive whistle, but when Rosella sipped hers, it emitted the soft patter of a purring kitten."

Astra said, "OK, I want one just like hers."

At the rear of the lounge, Jason Phillips sat with a couple of newcomers to the Moonbase that he had just met.

The girl asked Jason, "What do you think about all

this? You work in the SpeeZees Lab right? Isn't that where they make New-Humans. My name is Chris by the way, and this is James."

"I'm Jason. Nice to make your acquaintance. To answer your question, I do work in security at the lab and we do create New-Humans, but I am not supposed to talk about them."

James, pitched in. "Personally, I think they should be outlawed, but that's just my opinion."

Jason held his finger to his lips. "Best keep that to yourself while you are in the lounge, but I do have some friends that share your concern. We meet occasionally in my quarters. I'll let you know when our next meetup happens."

"Cool. Are you leaving? How about the drink? Aren't you going to wait for yous? It's on the house."

Jason tapped the table twice–the new way to order a refill and said. "Here, you can have mine, take your pick, I need to get back to work; my shift is about to start. So long to you both."

"Goodbye Jason. Don't forget to put us on your list."

"Will do. Goodnight."

After bidding Genie farewell, Astra and Torch headed for the exit. In the hall, Torch took her hand and grinned. "How about if we leave our kid with your parents tonight?"

"What do you have in mind?"

When Torch smiled and winked, she elbowed him in the side.

Travis Air Force Base

N-69 rapidly paced back and forth in front of Xeron and N-13, obviously infuriated by the news coverage of the OWN vote. He slammed his fist on the table and proclaimed, "This is not acceptable. I am going to contact Reverend LeRoque. It's time to initiate *Plan B*!"

— CHAPTER 14 —

SpeeZees Lab

After months of testing SCOMID on the clones with consistently positive results, Astra had received the go ahead from Sanders and Hiroshi, who not only gave her approval for testing on Sapients, but both had also volunteered to participate in the program. With the increasing number of subjects and technicians involved, it was only a matter of time before the entire base knew about the project and the majority of them also wanted to join the program.

In spite of Astra and Hiroshi's effort to maintain secrecy outside the colony, the anti-aging story quickly spread to the mainstream media back on Earth who bombarded the SpeeZees Lab with a barrage of requests for more information–all of which received the response, *'We have no comment at this time. We will inform you when we complete our research and release our findings'*, which further inflamed the speculation and added to the intrigue.

Among the impacts was a skyrocketing increase in the number of applications for job openings at the Lunar Colony and a lengthy waiting list for vacancies in the newly opened hotel as the colony's new tourism business began to flourish.

Astra was an anti-aging expert totally focused upon her research in a very complex undertaking. Although she had occasionally considered how her findings might impact others, she had been caught up in the day-to-day analysis of her findings and put off thinking about the social consequences and business aspects of her investigations. However, with daily inquiries from drug manufacturers and increasing discussions with Hiroshi and Julia about licensing and patents, she soon realized that she was in way over her head.

As a consequence, she encouraged Hiroshi and Julia to set up a series of video conferences with the top executives of leading pharmaceutic firms to gain insight in how to mass produce the longevity drugs in order to satisfy an enormous, worldwide demand. The plan that emerged was for the Basic prescription to be made available to the public at no charge with the first priority to serve the elderly.

As an incentive, the qualified pharmacological firms would then be licensed for the production and sales of the Calendar version at competitive prices. To win the highly coveted license, the firms would have to manufacture and distribute an average of at least one million doses of the free version per month with automatic renewal of their contract as long as they met the production requirements.

After several meetings in which the contract details had been refined and endorsed by the principals, Hiroshi was surprised to receive a notice from the USACO Department of Health Services, which had been largely inactive since the corporate takeover. The communication signed by the administration attorneys stated that it was their legal opinion that the DHS had the mandate to approve all contracts with Earth-based firms.

Hiroshi immediately called Sanders who said, "I

received a copy. Please come to my office ASAP. Bring Julia. I have some news to tell you about."

Sanders, Max and Miguel were waiting when Hiroshi and Julia. arrived.

Sanders said, "As if this nonsense from the DHS wasn't enough, I just had a call from USACO Vice President Thomas Smart. He announced that he is en route to the Lunar Colony and instructed me to prepare for the visit and arrange for accommodations for his staff and Secret Service agents."

Max said, "That guy is a jerk. I wouldn't trust him as far as I could throw him—even here on the Moon."

"I agree," replied Sanders. "Miguel, I want you and your staff to monitor every move and communication he makes while he's on the base."

"Yes, sir. When should we expect them?"

"Tomorrow!"

"Oh my, I'll call my team together."

"Keep us posted."

As Julia stood to leave, she said, "You might want to stick the VP in my old room down below."

Miguel laughed. "Good idea. We'll say that it is the only single occupancy space available, which is true. Otherwise, he will have to bunk with one of his staff."

****

The first day of the meeting went well with facility tours and a celebratory banquet. But day two turned into a disaster when the VP announced that in addition to the contract approval provisions specified by the DHS, USACO planned to seize patent rights to the anti-aging drug, set the price and decide who should qualify to produce and receive it. In addition, they intended to apply a fifty percent trade tariff on New-Human sales in all states controlled by USACO.

In a subsequent meeting, the VP raised the stakes, asserting that if Deep Space Mining, Inc. refused to cooperate, its lucrative contract to provide services for the Asteroid Safeguard Complex would immediately be canceled and all ore shipments would be impounded.

Finally fed up with the VP's attempted coup d'état, Sanders made a station-wide announcement describing what had taken place.

He concluded by saying, "Any of you that have had discussions or encounters with the VP or his staff, please contact Chia in the admin office. We are fortunate that she is here to document the SCOMID release. I can think of no one better qualified than her to reveal to the world what is happening here."

Chia was jazzed to be handed such an opportunity and scrambled to put together the coverage. After Sanders and Miguel told their version, Julia described the false legal claims asserted by the VP. Chia's repeated attempts to interview the VP were refused.

After the incident aired as a *Breaking News, Special Edition* of the RealNews, the coverage was embraced by the social media cloud where it quickly became the most watched program in modern media history.

As word spread about the attempted takeover spread worldwide, rising tides of protests shook the foundation of the USACO corporate government. Free election activists quickly organized the populace and conducted protests that were the biggest in the history of the planet and many government agencies were boycotted and forced to close their doors.. Finally, a legal brief filed by Julia on behalf of the Lunar Colony pointed out that after the recent OWN decree, USACO no longer had jurisdiction over the Lunar Colony.

The matter finally came to a head when President Ray contacted Sanders over a secure channel and informed him that the VP had gone rogue and that he had no authority to discuss or impose any levies, licenses, royalties or fees related to the sale of Lunar Colony products. The President claimed that it was all a plot by the VP to use the chaos that he had created to overthrow the administration and form his own dictatorship. The President urged Sanders to take whatever steps he felt necessary to return the VP back to Earth where he would be charged with treason.

Sanders called an emergency meeting with base leaders and replayed his conversation with the President, which he had clandestinely recorded. The decision was made to move as quickly as possible to get the VP off the Moonbase.

"Miguel, where is the VP right now?"

"Let me check...he's in a hot tub."

"Tell his assistant that we need the Vice President in my office ASAP. Tell him that it is an emergency and have Jason Phillips station a squad in the hallway. Make sure they are armed."

"Understood."

A few minutes later, the VP arrived wearing bathing trunks with a towel wrapped around his neck and his assistant carrying an armload of the VP's clothing.

Obviously upset, he took Sanders' arm, pulled him close and screamed "What's this all about? Who the hell do you think you are ordering me around?"

Sanders calmly said, "President Ray has ordered your immediate return to the Capitol. Miguel and Jason will now escort you to your shuttle."

As Miguel held open the door to the hangar bay, the VP asserted, "Why? I haven't done anything wrong!"

Sanders replied, "The President has accused you of treason. You should realize that the Lunar Colony is no longer under the jurisdiction of USACO. You have no right to even breathe our air without our permission."

"Treason? That is totally preposterous. I'm not going

anywhere. Who do you think you are? I'm the Vice President and I will not tolerate your interference."

"Jason, please escort the Vice President and his party to their shuttle and send some people to their quarters to get their personal belongings...Pronto!"

"Miguel, alert the VP's shuttle crew and tell him that they are cleared to launch as soon as the passengers and their belongings are onboard."

"Will do."

Next, Sanders called President Ray and told him. "The VP will be leaving the base shortly. I informed him that the Lunar Colony is no longer under the jurisdiction of USACO and the government has no rights to any of our business ventures."

The wide coverage elicited a new round of riots and demonstrations. State governments across the country began following Colorado's lead and began scheduling primary elections. Currently employed USACO officers and staff were especially worried about their future. They feared that if they were forced to leave office, they would face intense competition with their colleagues that were already flooding the market with their resumés.

Alarmed by the increase in violent acts perpetrated by androids upon Sapients, the Colorado governor delivered an emotional speech which she pleaded with all America's citizens to obey the law and maintain order until democracy could be reestablished.

One of the most inflammatory events was when the board of directors granted themselves pardons, prompting President Ray to reconsider his role in the new government as his credibility and job approval ratings plummeted.

To make matters worse, his wife had filed for divorce and a non profit watchdog group had subpoenaed all of his tax returns since he had taken office.

SCOMID DAY
June 1st, 2034

Moonbase residents packed the Luna Lounge for a rare treat. Instead of watching the RealNews broadcast on the wall monitors, they were able to witness it in person as Chia arranged the hovering mics and lights in preparation for the gala news event. After taking a seat with Astra in the lounge VIP section, Chia tapped her wrist and the opening bars by the 'Prince of Glamrock' David Bowie's hit began to play in the background.

'Uh, oh, oh, oh
Little China girl'

followed by the caption:

The RealNews
The Only Truly Independent
News Source!

Chia, with facial tattoos flashing a patriotic red, white and blue and wearing a white lab coat, turned to the camera and announced, "As you are undoubtedly aware, tonight is the official release date for SCOMID, the miracle anti-aging drug. I am here at this high tech colony on the moon which is the home of the SpeeZees Lab where this astonishing discovery was made."

Chia touched her pad and a sequence of clips played that showed the exterior of the dome and zoomed into the recreation center where kids were playing water polo in the swimming pool.

"Why the Moon? Well it turns out that for the last three decades the kind of work being conducted here at the SpeeZees Lab was illegal on Earth, so SpeeZees Inc. moved its operations here to the Moonbase. However, with the Lunar Colony's new independent status, this regulation is no longer an issue and Earth-based pharmaceutical firms are now fully engaged in partnerships with the lab."

Images of the lab entrance were followed by a rapidly flashing sequence of the logos of the participating firms.

Chia continued. "I will be here covering the latest developments over the next couple of days and interviewing the remarkable scientists that made this astonishing discovery."

The camera zoomed in for a closeup of Astra who smiled, but looked a little nervous.

"This evening we will start with Dr. Astra Sturtevant. After decades of hard work, she is the leader of the team that solved the mystery of how to control the aging clock. Welcome Dr. Sturtevant. How do you feel now that you are one of the most famous scientists of all time? I understand that you will undoubtedly receive a Nobel Prize for your discovery that many are calling the *Longevity Miracle."*

Astra glanced at her pad where she had stored a list of questions that Chia had prepared in advance.

"First I want to acknowledge my good friends and associates, Dr, Hiroshi and Chron who played critical roles in this work and Scotty whose genomic system held the missing link. I could not have done it without their input and assistance."

Chia asked, "What's next?"

"Second, I must confess that I am completely overwhelmed with all of the attention that I have been getting in the media."

"You mean like this notice which came in just a few minutes ago and you haven't seen yet?"

Chia touched her pad which activated a hologram that levitated above the table that displayed Astra's picture on the cover of a magazine bearing the bold caption *'2034 Time Magazine's Scientist of the Century'*.

Astra laughed. "You're right. I haven't seen that one, but I think I should point out a fact that seems to be getting scant attention."

"Go ahead."

"What people are neglecting is the fact that we don't know if this drug treatment will continue to work decades down the road. We think it will, but only time will tell."

"Yes, I see what you mean. Just an hour from now, the SCOMID pill will become available for the first time throughout the world and people who have been waiting in long lines—many camping for days, will get what they desire more than anything—a longer lifespan."

Chia held up an orange pill tube container packed with green pills and said, "This is the free version of the anti-aging drug known as the *Basic SCOMID*. It is a discovery rivaling any other in medical history. Could you give us a layperson's perspective on how SCOMID works?"

Astra checked her notes and said, "I agree that this will be a major change to those Sapients and New-Humans who participate in the Basic SCOMID program. Our findings document that a single daily dose is all that is needed to arrest the effects of aging by protecting our chromosome's telomeres. Normally the telomeres, which serve as protection against DNA damage during chromosome replication, are incrementally shortened during each cell division. As you have stated, we are breaking new ground in medical science and accordingly are unable to guarantee success. All participants will have to sign a release form and an acknowledgment that participating females will be infertile while they take Basic SCOMID."

"So women should not take Basic SCOMID if they wish to have a family. Did you program it that way?"

"Basically, if we didn't include fertility control then the population growth rate would dramatically increase. It is already too high. But keep in mind that as soon as a female stops taking the daily dose, she will regain her fertility and her normal aging process will resume. After conception, she can resume taking Basic SCOMID or remain fertile to have another infant. Note that this doesn't apply to those taking the weekly *Calendar* version; they will remain fertile. It's not perfect, but it is the best strategy that we could come up with."

Chia put down the orange pill tube and held up a clear packet which held a large pink capsule. "This is the custom, Calendar SCOMID prescription version. How does it differ from the Basic?"

Astra took a sip from her water bottle and said, "Yes, it is this version of the drug that requires a registered physician for implementation. For example, if a fifty year old woman wants to have her clock reset to age twenty-nine, she enrolls in the program and, after a detailed consultation with one of our licensed physicians, begins a weekly routine in which she uploads a DNA sample that tracks and analyzes her condition. From then on, she will have to participate in periodic consultations with her doctor because her unique prescription must be adjusted periodically in order to alter her genetic clock over time."

"So she could become a young woman again?"

"We believe so. A fee will be automatically debited from her bank account and she will receive a weekly pill via courier drone or at a designated drop box."

After a commercial by Pharma-Joy, Inc. in which they offered a limited, ten percent discount on SCOMID Calendar services. Chia continued. "Before the break, you mentioned fees. My understanding is that a special Calendar Rx will cost a client an initial consultation fee of $20,000 chip dollars and then $2,000 per week as long as the patient is enrolled in the Calendar SCOMID program. My calculations indicate that the total cost will average $125,000 chip dollars per year—that seems like a lot."

"Yes it is expensive. But keep in mind that the fees paid by the wealthy Calendar participants will cover the cost of the Basic program for millions of less fortunate individuals that will experience enhanced longevity at no cost."

"So just to clarify, females that take the Basic version will be unable to have children until they stop taking the Basic green pill. However, those taking the pink Calendar version will continue to be fertile?"

"Correct. Those women taking the Basic version will also be capable of child bearing when they cease taking the drug. I understand that there may be impacts upon society that need to be addressed. For example, the insurance, banking and medical service industries will likely have to undergo major changes in their business model."

Chia retrieved the orange pill tube container packed with the green Basic pills in her hand and said, the Calendar version is currently beyond my income level, but I am thinking about this one. But I keep asking myself, *Do I really want to do this? What could go wrong? What if I change my mind?*"

"You are welcome to visit the SCOMID cloud site to ask questions of participating physicians and share your concerns and experiences with people around the world."

"SCOMID.com, right?"

"Yes, the service is available twenty-four-seven."

"Speaking of time. The release date is midnight our time right?"

"That is correct," She checked her wrist and said, "Which is just a few minutes from now."

MET CHRON NEW-HUMANS

Chia and Astra watched the new SCOMID sales display which Hiroshi and Genie had added next to the lunar clock. There was a hush in the audience as the digital second hand ticked to midnight, but they were disappointed when nothing happened. As the minutes progressed, several groups started to leave.

Astra couldn't hide her disappointment. She spoke with Hiroshi to see if there was a glitch in the data stream, but he told her that it had been checked out and should be working properly. Just as she picked up pad and started to leave, the sales display lit up. For a few moments the lounge was quiet and then there was a loud cheer when the Calendar SCOMID sales figures began appearing on the vidscreen slowly at first then in a blur as the data arrived.

Chia hugged Astra, then popped the cork on a bottle of champagne which she shared with Astra.

Astra said, "Thank you. I can't tell you how relieved I am."

Chia pointed at the tally screen. "Fifteen minutes since the opening and the total is already twenty million credits! It looks like your dream is finally coming true after all the years you have invested."

"I sincerely hope so...I'm sorry. I don't know what more to say. This is a very emotional moment."

Chia held up a green pill and said, "What the heck, I'm not planning to have kids for a couple of years."

She pressed her thumb to the pad that Astra handed to her, held up a green pill, gave it a kiss and washed it down with a gulp of champagne. "This is Chia signing off. Happy SCOMID Day! Happy long lives for everyone!"

Genie dimmed the lounge lights and displayed the image of Astra on the cover of Time magazine on the large wall screen behind the bar accompanied by one of Astra's favorite Brazilian salsa tunes.

Astra was surprised when Torch took her hand and escorted her to the dance floor.

She said, "After stomping all over my feet in Nicaragua, you want me to dance with you again?"

Torch smoothly led her in side to side and front to back steps to the Latin beat finishing with a perfect head duck and swirl.

Astra laughed, "It looks like you have been taking lessons."

"Chron has been coaching me."

"You're kidding."

Soon the floor was packed with dancing couples celebrating the occasion and Chia slid next to Hiroshi and poured him a glass of champagne. She took his hand and said, "I hope you will let me interview you in our next program."

"Yes, no problem."

"I understand that your given name is Hans, but everyone calls you Hiroshi."

"Yes. that is what my friends have called since high school."

"OK, Hiroshi it is. I am sure that our audience would be fascinated by your account of how the discovery was made and how you came up with your innovative sales and distribution model."

"Of course; I will be honored. But please include Chron. He played a major role and don't forget Julia. She is responsible for developing the business plan."

"Will do. Thanks for the suggestion."

"This place is a madhouse. Would you like to go for a walk in the hydroponic garden? The frogs and crickets begin their mating calls right about now when the lights dim. It is quite musical and I think that you might enjoy it. We don't have to stay long, but that is up to you."

"Sounds good. It has been a quite a day. Lead the way."

As they walked down the corridor, Chia put her arm around his waist and the tattoos on her cheeks glowed a soft rose color. When they entered the bay, she sighed and said, "You're right. The sound is amazing, It is quite romantic."

He turned to look at her and said, "Hmm...before I make a fool of myself, I'll just blurt it out. Do you have a mate. if you don't mind me asking?"

"No. What else would you like to know?"

"OK, why not? You are beautiful, intelligent and famous as well."

"I guess I have yet to meet the right man." She looked into his eyes. and gave him a brief hug. "Maybe it's you. Who knows? But there is something I would like to try."

"Oh...what might that be?"

She took a few steps then launched into a graceful pirouette followed by a series of beautiful leaps in the reduced gravity which brought her into Hiroshi arms.

"That was amazing!"

"I studied ballet as a child, but never imagined that I would be dancing with frogs and crickets on the Moon."

"Please continue. The stage is yours milady."

— CHAPTER 15 —

The RealNews Special
SCOMID Changes the World!
June 2nd, 2034

Chia, looking radiant with rippling waves of color in her facial tattoos, offered the greeting, "Welcome viewers to the second day of our coverage of the revolutionary new anti-aging drugs developed at the SpeeZees Complex located here in the Lunar Colony."

She touched a contact on her wristband and the video feed transitioned to an aerial view of the Moon-base followed by a melange of images of the state-of-the-art laboratory packed with advanced DNA nanobot molecular synthesizers that were attended by a cadre of technicians intently focused upon their assignments.

"You can probably tell by our surroundings that we have moved from the Luna Lounge on the surface to the underground SpeeZees Complex which has expanded as residents relocated to much more spacious and comfort-able quarters located topside in the new dome.

The floating cam zoomed in for a closeup of Chia.

She said, "Before we resume our coverage of the new miracle drug, I'd like to tell you about another moon shaking event. I have asked Miguel Castaneda to fill us in. He is in charge of security here on the Moonbase."

MET CHRON NEW-HUMANS

"What happened Miguel? I woke up to a series of jolts and then the room started swaying. It was like being at sea on an ocean liner."

"It was just a minor moonquake. We often experience quakes like this shortly after lunar sunrises and sunsets as the gravity level fluctuates during our orbit around Earth."

"Do you know what causes them?"

"Astronomers back in 2019 discovered that the Moon's two hundred mile wide molten core is cooling and shrinking. This is causing the brittle surface to contract and buckle, creating cracks, some of which are elevated into hills and cliffs while others form trenches. and valleys. It is this type of contraction that generated last night's moonquake."

"But are we in danger now? Is it likely to get worse?"

"We should be fine, thanks to Director Sanders' valuable foresight. He designed the original Deep Space Mining Moonbase structural foundation to be secured underground with maglev joints that absorb sudden shocks. We recently strengthened the anchor systems before we installed the new dome sheeting."

"I'm still trying adjust to the moon shrinking part."

"Well...isn't the sun burning?"

"You win. Thank you very much for your time and effort to keep us safe."

"Anytime."

After another Pharma-Joy, Inc. commercial which repeated their ten percent discount on SCOMID Calendar services and warned that the offer would expire soon, the RealNews' coverage continued.

"Joining me is Dr. Hans Hiroshi, Director of the SpeeZees, Inc. and who oversees the New-Human Creation Facility and the SCOMID research lab where we are sitting now. Good afternoon Dr. Hiroshi."

"Thank you for inviting me. I am a regular viewer of

your program and very much appreciate your excellent, in-depth coverage of our research programs."

"My pleasure. The SCOMID.com cloud site has been having a hard time keeping up with the millions of viewers that have joined in the discussion. One topic that seems to be on many minds is whether all humans should be included irregardless of their nationality, religious beliefs, economic status or criminal record. Will those incarcerated by the criminal justice system receive the free version or will there be varying classes of access to the Basic SCOMID drug program?"

"My personal belief is that Basic SCOMID should be made available to all human beings regardless of their sex, race and social status. After all, individual AI bots and androids may function for centuries into the future. Why shouldn't we match their longevity? However, I don't have an answer to your question about criminals. I guess it will have to be publicly debated."

"I see your point."

She looked at her notes and then said, "There are other questions that people from around the world want to know—like how will extended lifespans impact food supplies, the quality of life and the environment?"

"Those outcomes are hard to predict because of the complex, interrelated factors involved, but we expect that the built-in sterility component will at least moderate the impact of the free Basic SCOMID regimen on population growth."

Chia smiled, "At least that is somewhat encouraging."

"The question is, is it too little too late? The present birth rate is..."

Suddenly there was a loud boom and the lab lights flickered then went out. A few seconds later, a shock wave sent Chia sprawling on the floor next to Hiroshi who had landed on his knees. As Hiroshi regained his footing, sirens sounded and auxiliary power kicked in. When the lights came back to life, Hiroshi helped Chia to her feet and she nodded when he asked if she was OK.

She asked, "Was that another moonquake?"

"Not like any we have experienced before."

Just as they moved to survey the damage, an announcement played over the speaker system *All hands man your battle stations. I repeat all hands man your battle stations. This is not a drill!*

Hiroshi looked into the smoke-filled lab, then the security office and was relieved to see they had been vacated.

He looked at Chia and yelled, "We have to get to the admin office."

Chia activated one of her levitating mini cams and set it to follow mode just as another an ear-piercing bang echoed throughout the underground complex followed by a shock wave that rocked the complex. With hands covering their ears, Hiroshi and Chia raced down the corridor to the office where Sanders, Torch, Sabien and Miguel were watching video feeds displayed on the wall screen from the network of surveillance cameras that had been recently installed throughout the Moon-base.

Sanders asked, "Are you two alright? Any damage to the labs?"

Hiroshi replied, It's hard to say, there was so much smoke in the air, but it didn't look good. The lab security office was empty when we ran out. Have you heard from Jason Phillips?"

"Not today." Sanders looked at Miguel and asked, "Any contact with Phillips?"

"That's a negative. He is not responding to my flash."

Hiroshi said, "That's definitely not good. I better go back and see what's going on."

"Good idea. Keep me posted, Chia can stay with us. She will be safe here."

Miguel clicked through the feeds from cameras on the shuttle hanger, power plant and solar array and reported, "All we know so far is that the dome appears to be rapidly venting air and sagging in two locations."

"Miguel, we need to move everybody from the dome to the underground chambers and instruct your maintenance engineers to seal off those leaks ASAP!"

"I'm working on it."

Sanders nodded at Sabien. "Keep trying to raise Phillips."

Miguel was rapidly tapping his pad and then pointed to the monitor, "Look at this replay of video from cam seventeen at the top of the dome. It looks like we have been hit by some sort of attack drone."

Sanders keyed his pad and asked. "Max are you seeing this?"

Max replied, "Affirmative, we just launched fighters with orders to engage."

Sanders pointed at the bay window and said, "An unauthorized ship just entered the hangar bay and is unloading android soldiers. Now they are surrounding the shuttle. I don't how they could have gained access without our clearance."

Miguel jumped up ready to head to the door when Sanders stopped him. "No Miguel. I need you here."

He looked at Torch and asked, "Are your RoboCows ready for action?"

Torch replied, "Absolutely. There is a squad on duty over by the power plant. Thanks to Miguel and Max, they are now fully armed."

"Excellent. Better put on your space suit and get ready for some action. We are under attack!"

He spoke into his wrist mic. "Max report status of the intercept."

Max played a vid sequence that showed the drone exploding. "We got it! The attack drone has been terminated. We are scanning for other threats."

"Good job Max."

"Sabien, see if you can track down Phillips and figure out what the heck he is up to. Miguel, make sure that the evacuation of the residents from the dome is going smoothly. Make sure that anyone injured receives medical attention ASAP."

Chia responded, "I can do that; I am trained in first aid and would like to help."

"Thanks. Go to the medical center. Alert them to be ready for incoming casualties."

Chia's tattoos rippled when she replied, "Yes sir. Will do," and then pivoted on her heel and headed out.

Sanders checked the wall monitor and was alarmed to see that there were still two jets of water vapor streaming from tears in the dome cover, but was relieved when the cranes that had been used to install the dome cover raced into position. It only took them a few minutes to patch the leaks and head back to the maintenance hanger as the dome refilled.

Sanders pointed to one of the screens. "Still no feed from the SpeeZees Lab. Miguel take a squad and check it out. Alert me when you find out what's going on."

Miguel jumped up, grabbed his laser rifle and signaled his troops to follow him as he rushed out the door. When they approached the SCOMID lab entrance, they ran into Phillips who was sprinting in the opposite direction.

Miguel shouted, "Phillips, Where have you been? We haven't been able to reach you...and where is the rest of your team?"

"I evacuated all of the lab workers to the underground habitats. Our team is assisting them. I think we should clear the area in case..."

Suddenly, the SCOMID lab door exploded followed by a blast of wind that knocked Miguel and Jason off their feet and sent the others bouncing off the walls. Miguel helped Jason stand up and then turned to check on his troops.

He asked, "Everyone OK? Anyone hurt?" Getting no response, he yelled, "Follow me. Let's find out what's going on."

Miguel turned back to address Phillips, but he had vanished. Miguel called in an update to Sanders.

"Something is not right with Jason Phillips. He was here one minute and gone the next. I think he may have turned on us and set these bombs."

"Roger that. It won't be the first time he pulled something like this. He used to be one of Reverend LeRoque's supporters."

As Miguel hurried down the hall towards the labs, he shouted over the sirens which continued to wail, "Yes, I recall that vividly, but you gave him a second chance. I am now at the SpeeZees Lab main entrance. It doesn't look good."

A few minutes later he reported, "There is major damage to the SCOMID lab, but the New-Humans Creation Facility appears to have been untouched thanks to Chron who hurried to the lab after the bombs next door went off. He found one behind a desk and another in an empty pod and disabled them both. He reports that none of the beings in development have been affected, but he is worried about fluctuations in the backup power supply. That could be a problem if it is ongoing."

Sanders replied, OK we will make that our first priority after we deal with the intruders and locate Phillips. Torch do you read me?"

"Yes, go ahead Dad."

"I have you on the external vidcam. Get ready, the

droids are getting back in their ship and someone wearing a spacesuit just joined them. Now they are powering up. Standby...they will be passing by you as they head out. You are authorized to engage. Good luck!"

"Roger. Hang on...sorry Dad, we got in a couple of shots but they got away. I don't think we did much damage. I think that the guy in the suit was Phillips."

Sanders flashed Max and asked. "Max can you take out the intruder ship that is just now lifting off?"

"That's a negative. Our pilot AIs have just quit functioning and their shuttles are grounded. My techs think someone with a top secret clearance has accessed and disabled our COM systems. We'll keep trying, but it may take a while to override. It definitely looks we have been hacked."

"Max, when this is over, I want you to work with Miguel and his team to figure out why we didn't detect those intruders before they nearly destroyed the base and we need to find out what role Phillips played in this attack."

"Will do. We can retrieve parts from the attack drone that we shot down and video coverage of the shuttle which we can analyze for clues."

Chia returned to Sander's office and reported, "There have been several injured by the bomb blasts, but the staff is fully in control. I am sorry to bother you, but would you give me a few minutes of your time? I am going to do a breaking news broadcast and would welcome your participation."

"Yes of course, a lot of our residents have family back on Earth and I am sure that they and our many new business partners will be concerned as well. We do need to reach out to them, but let's not point any fingers as to who or what is to blame. We need to get our facts straight before we make accusations."

"I understand. How about if we just say that the exact cause is yet to be determined and under investigation?" Chia handed him a microdisc and then said, "My vidcam recorded footage throughout the incident. It might be useful."

"Perfect, thanks for your help today."

As Chia set up her hovering lights and connected her video feed to the cloud, Sanders took a drink of water followed by a deep breath and thought, *Just another day on the Moon.*

****

N-69, Xeron and N-13 were seated around a floating monitor in the airship hangar at Travis Air Force Base in a vid-con with Reverend LeRoque, who was virtually participating in the teleconference from the SDL Church in Atlanta and Jason Phillips who was in the returning shuttle. The monitor displayed a view of the Lunar Colony dome where they could see that the punctures had been sealed.

The image of Jason Phillips appeared on the screen. After greeting them, he delivered a status report."There were four explosions...two of which were delivered by drones that punctured the dome and two in the SCOMID lab. Unfortunately, the two bombs that I placed in the New-Humans Facility failed to detonate. I am not sure why. The good news is that the damage to the SCOMID lab was very extensive and it will take several months to rebuild—meanwhile they will suffer business losses in the millions, if not billions, of credits."

The Reverend was obviously unimpressed. "Why didn't the bomb at that dreadful New-Human Creation Facility go off? Eliminating that blasphemous factory was our primary goal."

Phillips replied, "As I said, I am not sure why the bombs didn't go off. Two did, two didn't. It could have been a malfunction or interference of some sort. But the attack on the SCOMID lab went as planned and the new improvements in the dome's interior are likely going to require repairs. I will work up a full report You should know that Torch saw me leave, so I won't be going back."

Xeron noted, "I would say things went pretty well, all things considered. You attacked, did some significant damage, and then escaped unharmed. Not bad."

"I suppose, replied N-69. So much for *Plan B*. Do you have any suggestions for our next move?"

Xeron said, "Our COM intercepts indicate that Deep Space Mining is ramping up its asteroid mining operations and they are working on a new kind of cable that could be used to tow asteroids and mine them in lunar orbit."

Reverend LeRoque replied, "That sounds like something we should keep track of."

N-69 nodded and said, "That seems reasonable. The Neuro Nation and I are determined to eradicate these vermin that do not accept us as equals...or superiors."

The Reverend stood and said, "Sabotaging their commerce seems like a good idea. Phillips, take some time off. N-69 will contact you with your next assignment."

"Yes, your holiness."

"That is acceptable," replied N-69. "If no one has anything else, I think we are finished here for today."

The Reverend raised his fist., "This is just the beginning. Keep at it!"

The Next Day
Moonbase Director's Office

Sanders called a meeting with the base managers to evaluate the situation and to prioritize restoration measures and develop a plan to repair the SCOMID lab.

"Miguel, we will start with you, what is the status of our dome."

"The good news is that there were no serious injuries, the leaks have been sealed and the dome will soon be ready for residents to move back to their quarters. The bad news is that the hydroponic gardens will need to be nursed back to health and the SCOMID lab has suffered extensive damage. I will let Astra discuss that situation."

Astra, visibly shaken reported. "I guess I was lucky. I was walking Luz to school when all this took place, but as Miguel said, our lab has suffered a major blow. Thank goodness our techs got out before the bomb went off—apparently Jason Phillips activated the fire alarm before he set off the bombs. It is going to take weeks to rebuild our production capability. Luckily, our pharma partners on Earth can carry on with the initial wave of orders. I know this is somewhat vague, but it will take time to work up a recovery plan."

She wiped away tears and said, "We are fortunate that no one was badly hurt and that the Ark was secured in the lab vault and not damaged. Our confidential genome data was also preserved in the Moonbase cloud."

Sanders said, "Understood. Chron, thanks to your disarming of the bombs in the New-Human Creation Facility. I understand that there was no damage and none of the subjects in development were affected."

Chron said, "That is correct. Now that the power has been restored, we are back to normal operations. We will have to take precautions to maintain power levels while the SCOMID lab complex is being rebuilt."

Sanders checked his pad and passed it to Max. "It seems like we have some major security issues to resolve."

Max nodded. "Yes we do. Just so you know, we have

revoked all of Jason Phillip's access codes. His actions caught us totally off guard."

"Yes, we were all duped by him. What about our intruder detection radar system?"

"We are still looking into this. As far as we can tell at this time, our radar detectors and COM systems were jammed by one or more of the rogue shuttles that have been commandeered by the androids that now occupy Travis Air Force Base."

"What's going on at Travis?"

"Earth military forces have stayed clear of Travis AFB due to the extremely high radiation levels, but obviously the invaders pose a major threat that needs to be addressed."

Sanders retrieved his pad from Max and said, "I concur. Miguel and I spoke earlier today and we suspect that Reverend LeRoque may have been involved. He has been quite vocal in his criticism about New-Humans being granted equal status and he has been a long-time opponent of genetic engineering. His church, the Seekers of Divine Light, have millions of members that share his beliefs. This could be a major problem. He is ruthless! Max, can we team up with what's left of USACO forces...maybe take the offensive?"

"I'm not sure, the government is pretty much in disarray. I'll try to contact the Air Force brass when we finish."

"Good, keep me posted. Miguel, I want full background checks on every resident. We can't allow this to happen again."

"Yes, sir."

"Oh, there is one more thing. Was the recent moonquake related to this attack in any way?"

"I don't believe so, probably just a coincidence."

"OK, that's it for today. This is a major setback, but we will endure. We are Lunans!"

— CHAPTER 16 —

Three Months Later
September 3rd, 2034

Even though the repairs to the SCOMID facility had finished ahead of schedule and operations had resumed, millions of Sapients, on the verge of dying from natural causes, became more and more desperate as they waited for a last minute salvation.

Once the list of pharma firms that were licensed by the SpeeZees Lab to produce the SCOMID drugs became public, hundreds of thousands of desperate people stormed the labs. They demanded the free version, which the pharmas had promised to distribute, but instead some of the firms had focused on sales of the financially lucrative Calendar version in violation of their licensing agreements. The response by the local authorities was to ignore the riots–after all they were in the same boat as the rioters.

Those fortunate enough to be able to afford the Calendar version of the drug were quick to discover that they were now forced to deal with insurance companies that found all sorts of loopholes and caveats in their contracts that allowed them to raise premiums and cancel or deny coverage in health and retirement plans.

Likewise, corporate business structures were shaken

as many executives taking the Calendar version became younger with each passing day. The normal chain of command succession process was derailed and morale suffered as advancements in rank stalled. New job positions in businesses large and small became rare leading to escalating rates of unemployment and poverty while government employees, faced with an uncertain future, had little choice but to enter the job market adding more pressure to the economy. To make matters worse, robots were becoming more and more sophisticated adding to the competition for jobs in the fields of agriculture, healthcare and transportation.

At the same time, dictatorships and corporate controlled governments around the globe were facing increasing demands from the populace for the right to elect their own representatives. Sensing the inevitable, USACO President Ray announced that state and national elections would take place in four months on January 1st, 2035. In order to change his image and increase his chance of retaining his position, urged congress to pass a resolution that no corporate or PAC contributions could be accepted by candidates; only non-profits and individuals could make donations.

In the midst of the current political and healthcare crisis, the planet was enveloped in a self-reinforcing feedback loop of ocean warming due to polar ice melting, raising sea level temperatures—which resulted in more ice melting...and so on. Even though most vehicles, heating and air conditioning were now solar powered, corporations still battled over the last barrels of oil while launching gaslighting claims that the climate was improving. It was not. In the last year, the Torch Index varied from 9.4 to 9.6 which was again approaching the tipping point but slightly less than the 9.9 all-time high.

As more and more countries in the Organization of World Nations suffered catastrophic heat waves, floods, tornadoes and hurricanes, OWN's focus turned to climate change. To encourage finding innovative solutions, OWN announced the availability of one hundred billion credits for studies in ocean warming mitigation due in thirty days.

As soon as the grant announcement was published in the Commerce Business Hourly, Quant flashed a text message to Sanders from his office in Rome and gave him a heads up priority flash that included a copy of the request for proposal. He requested that Sanders gather the Moonbase VIPs for a vid-con as soon as possible.

Sanders flashed a reply. "OK, contact me in twenty minutes, I'll make sure everyone is here by then."

He turned to Miguel and showed him the message. "Find Torch, Sabien and Chron—oh and Julia too. Tell them to meet us here pronto."

The call came in twenty minutes later just as Torch, Sabien, Julia and Chron arrived and took seats around the conference table. Miguel activated the wall monitor and initiated the vid feed which displayed Quant who was entering notes into his pad. He looked up and said, "Great! It's nice to see you. You too Brother."

Sanders asked, "What's up? I checked the RFP that you attached to the flash, are you sure that you sent me the right one? This is about ocean warming and, as far as I know, we don't have one. It looks like a good idea, but I don't see what it has to do with us Lunans."

Quant replied, "I can see how you might think that, but what if we could transport warm seawater into space, freeze it, then drop it back into the ocean to cool it down."

"Torch responded, "It sounds like we would need a huge fleet of cargo shuttles and it would take decades."

Quant took a deep breath. "I think I know a better way, but you better get some coffee because this may take a while to explain."

MET CHRON NEW-HUMANS

Deep Space Mining Moonbase

After many discussions, in which a wide range of approaches were suggested and discarded, the group decided upon a novel strategy of constructing what they called a *Space-Hook*—a type of space elevator similar in design to the 'skyhook' envisioned by John Isaacs of Scripps Institution of Oceanography back in 1966, but had never been tested.

The Space-Hook would be connected by a pair of cables to the Earth's surface and held in place with a massive counterweight in space. Tanks of ambient temperature surface water would be transported upwards by the *climber* pod's electric motors into space where the water would freeze and blocks of ice would be transported downward and released into the ocean.

This would form a closed loop system in which the upward centrifugal force would at least be partially matched by the downward pull of gravity, reducing the energy requirements. This approach had only become feasible after Queen Astasia's revolutionary discovery of ultra strong, lightweight cables made from graphene nanotubes that would connect the counterweight with the planet below. Torch and Sabien had demonstrated the outstanding strength of the cable when they captured a small comet and inserted it into lunar orbit. Ice from the comet was currently supplying the colony's demands for drinking water as well as hydrogen for fuel and oxygen for breathing which were rapidly increasing as the Moonbase population grew.

Sanders was quick to point out that the Space-Hook could also be used to transport ore shipments from the Moonbase to Earth, which would lower costs and increase mining profits.

Another advantage that Quant described was that

the anchor island could be outfitted with an *Ocean Thermal Energy Conversion* system. The OTEC plant would pump seawater from beneath the thermocline upwards to the surface using power generated by the temperature differential. The power could then be efficiently transported as needed to the Sky-Hook's climber motors using wireless power transfer lasers.

In another variation, several floating anchor islands would be clustered into artificial atolls complete with mariculture farms in tropical lagoons surrounded by villages, homes, schools and shops—all while helping to cool the oceans and heal the planet.

Using the power generated by the anchor islands' OTEC plants to provide energy to power the reverse osmosis filtration system and the Space-Hook motors, significant amounts of freshwater would also be generated as a valuable byproduct.

****

After several detailed budget development and highly energized vid-con meetings, the Space-Hook team signed off on the proposal and Quant submitted it with plenty of time to spare.

He flashed the team his thanks and promised them that he would let them know the results as soon as they were announced.

He was surprised when he received a flash from Sanders. "Quant this Space-Hook idea of yours is outstanding. I like it so much that I think we should think about other sources of funding in case the OWN turns us down."

Quant replied, "Thank you for that thought. I will be able to sleep a little bit better now knowing that I have your endorsement. I will keep you posted."

"Tale a break. You deserve it. Great job!"

MET CHRON NEW-HUMANS

The RealNews Special Addition

Two weeks after the submission deadline had passed, OWN declared that it had decided that, since the Space-Hook proposal had been declared the most innovative proposal, it would receive immediate funding for the total proposed budget amount.

The RealNews was on hand to cover another one of the Moonbase's' growing list of monumental events.

Chia keyed the broadcast vidcam and announced, "Welcome viewers to this edition of the RealNews on this historic occasion. I am reaching out to you from the administration office of the Lunar Colony Moonbase and joining us on location in Rome is Stephanie Jenkins our reporter on the scene at Organization of World Nations. Welcome Stephanie; it seems like the obfuscating claim by superpowers that global warming is only 'fake news' may finally be coming to an end."

"You're right Chia, this could literally be a breath of fresh air."

"Environmentalists have been trying to address climate change for the last two decades. What has changed to make this happen?"

"I would say two things. First, this new technology approach is innovative and exciting. Second, in just a two short months USACO, will dissolve and the original constitution defining citizen rights will be restored."

"Back to the USA! What a relief. I agree with you this is a game changer."

Stephanie turned away from the vidcam and said,"Excuse me Chia, the members are filing out. Here comes Quant. I want to get his reaction."

Stephanie tried to slide through the group of reporters surrounding Quant amidst a swarm of hover cams but was unable to connect when he was swept away by the crowd. As she jogged behind, she looked into the vidcam and said, "Sorry Chia. I'll keep trying. Back to you."

"No problem, I have with me key members of the Deep Space Mining team that developed the proposal. Thank you ladies and gentlemen for joining me. I want our viewers to recognize that Deep Space Mining, Inc. has just been funded by the OWN to develop and test what several outside engineers have described, as an ingenious approach to reversing ocean warming. Let's start with you Director Sanders. Here we are sitting on the Moon and you plan to cool down the oceans of Earth. Mightn't that sound a little disconnected to anyone unfamiliar with your project?"

Sanders laughed. "That was the same reaction I had when Quant first pitched the idea to me. I am glad that he was patient and persistent."

"What role will the Moonbase play in this long-term project and how did this plan with so many complicated parts come into existence?"

Sanders replied, "Probably the most important aspect was Queen Astasia's invention of the graphene nanotubes which have phenomenal tensile strength and very low weight. Conventional cables were way too heavy and not nearly strong enough. That is the main reason that this approach has never been tried until now."

He nodded at Sabien and patted Torch's arm. "These two worked up a system to tow small asteroids and comets into lunar orbit and harvest them for precious metals and ice for the Moonbase's water supply. To answer your question about what role the Moonbase will play, our task will be to locate and transport a large asteroid to serve as the counterweight and then attach the cables to the anchor down on Earth. It sounds simple, but we have to locate a suitable candidate and then adjust its spin so that when we insert it into orbit it will constantly face the anchor island below."

"So, Deep Space Mining will be responsible for moving the asteroid into position and hooking up the cables. Who will be in charge of setting up the island anchor and controlling operations once the cables are in place?"

"Quant will be in charge of all Earth-based activities, including attaching the cables to the tension flex joints and loading the pods with seawater. Then his team will distribute the ice to selected locations when the pods return."

He nodded at Chron and continued. "Chron will handle all operations related to the counterweight asteroid."

Chia asked Chron, "Have you picked out the asteroid?"

"We are researching that as we speak. There are several candidates that seem to meet our requirements."

Sanders touched his chest, and then pointed at Torch and Sabien. "Our roles are to assist Chron and Quant on an as needed basis."

"OK, this is for any of you. How long will the installation take and what can go wrong?"

The group looked at Sanders who shrugged and said, "This is a long-term solution, but somehow, Sapients, New-Humans and android AIs will have to work together to survive. Our biggest immediate danger is a deadly encounter with an asteroid that could make all of this a waste of time. At least we now have a fully operational Asteroid Safeguard Complex. You might want to interview Captain Dobson who is in charge of our newly installed defense systems."

Torch added, "As to how long it will take and what might go wrong, this is all brand new and we won't know until we get started. You are more than welcome to attend our staff meetings if you wish to stay up to date."

Chia replied, "Excellent. Thank you all for your time. That's all for this edition of the RealNews. Please check out this message from our sponsor SV Gypsy. *Why lock yourself into owning land that can flood, turn to dust, or burn when you can customize your home and live in worry-free luxury and safety?* This is Chia signing off."

After Chia shut down her hover cam and gathered her gear, Hiroshi gave her a hug and told the group "Well done guys. Let's hit the Lounge, Genie said she has something special planned."

When they entered the bar and headed for the VIP section, Genie jumped onto the stage, keyed her wrist mic and announced, "How about a big hoorah for the saviors of our planet. You make us proud. The next round of drinks is on me."

Genie keyed the switch that opened the overhead panel which revealed the Earth radiating a brilliant cobalt blue in the starlit sky while the new Lunar Colony choir sang a joyful rendition of *For He's a Jolly Good Fellow*.

— CHAPTER 17 —

Arctic Tundra

When Queen Astasia, eyestalks twitching, reviewed the deposit of funds into her cloud bank account to construct the graphene nano cable, she feared that the Deep Space Mining accounting office had made an error because the amount was twice her funding request. Admittedly there were so many budget item details that it was hard for her to immediately comprehend the discrepancy, but after rechecking the figures several times, she sent an inquiry requesting clarification.

Julia Cravens, financial officer for the Lunar Colony flashed her a text reply, *'We decided to increase the amount of your funding in case of unexpected events in the future'* causing the Queen to call her drone managers into her tent and convey the good news. They were now in the elevator cable business way beyond simply towing comets to fill swimming pools and enclosing habitat domes. The target goal was to have the cable ready for deployment within the next six months. This involved collecting the nano diamond platelets to synthesize graphene from the tundra in an environmentally sound manner, assembling the components using nano bots, and transporting them to the counterweight, where the cable would be lowered all the way down to the anchor point on Earth. Since the exact location of the counterweight and the anchor points had yet to be determined, Julia had increased the cable fab budget.

After several days of running simulations, Astasia reached the conclusion that she lacked the resources to produce the estimated 100,000 miles of graphene cable needed to link the counterweight asteroid to the anchor island on Earth.

Not wanting to risk jeopardizing her lucrative contract, Astasia made a call to Torch and asked his advice. Torch alerted his dad who set up a vid-con with the project leaders during which it was decided to arrange an onsite visit with Julia and Quant, who had flown in from Rome and relieved to be free of the journalists who had been pursuing him ever since the Space-Hook award was announced.

One Week Later
September 24th, 2034

After a tour of the facility, Julia and Quant entered Astasia's command tent where she handed them pads containing the latest detailed budget.

Julia keyed her pad and a brought up a hologram of the budget categories and said, "I can see why you are confused, but clearly the intent was to provide you with a great deal of flexibility in a first of its kind endeavor like this. I will be happy to set up an expense tracking program that will keep you up to date on an hourly basis. My staff on the Moonbase will also be available if you need help."

Astasia replied, "Thank you. My next concern is how to find qualified workers in such a short period of time. I mean we are talking about a lot of cable!"

Quant replied, "Have you have heard about the itinerant caravans that are roaming the U.S. and Europe that provide a diverse range of custom services?"

"Yes, I understand that they are like the nomadic tribes of your organic ancestors."

Quant nodded and keyed up aerial footage of what appeared to be a large, sports stadium packed with SVs, cargo semis and trailers that were surrounded by rows of tents with canopies that provided shade from the blistering sunshine.

"This group of geeks calls itself *Planet Odyssey*. It is a complete mobile community that specializes in providing technical services. They have just completed a major IP refurbishment in Kansas City as part of the government relocation and have spent the last six months restoring corrupted files and reports that were damaged or lost in the detonation at the D.C. Capitol."

Astasia asked, "How many members are there? What is their social structure? Do they have a king or a queen?" She laughed, "I just had to ask the last question."

Quant replied, "Essentially, it is a small, mobile town with living units, fuel tankers, restaurants, bars, schools, shops and even a soccer team. The total population is just under 5,000 residents led by a Sapient female named Gloria Garcia. The Tech Service Ranker gives them a five star rating and I understand that they are looking for a new gig."

Astasia said. "That sounds like just what we need. I would like to meet this Gloria Garcia."

Quant said, "Excellent, but before you do that, there is something I would like to go over with you. Meanwhile, Julia please contact Gloria and see if Planet Odyssey is interested in joining us. We'll be back soon."

Astasia led Quant to a bench outside her tent. "What did you want to talk about?"

"Androids, specifically androids that are endowed with artificial intelligence neural networks."

"I am proud to be one. Is there a problem?"

"Not with me I can assure you. But since I was appointed as the first New-Human to the OWN, I have been detecting a growing tension about how androids fit in."

"That seems natural. I advocate that we should have equal rights as well."

"I totally agree. The problem is that there are many like you that are intelligent, compassionate beings. And then there are others that want to wipe out New-Humans and Sapients. For example, there is a faction that has taken control of the former USACO Space Command Network—a satellite defense system. They pose a major problem."

"How so?"

"They have occupied Travis Air Force Base and are heavily armed. We're not sure what they plan to do, but we suspect that they were involved in the recent attack on the Lunar Colony."

The Queen's eyestalks swiveled back and forth. "I am still not sure what you are getting at."

"I don't blame you. What I am trying to say is that there may be some flack about having you, as an android, in charge of a project of this magnitude–even though it is actually your invention."

"Ah. I see. Do you want to replace me with a New-Human or Sapient?"

"No...not all. I am just alerting you to the situation. You have my complete support. But this situation may need our attention at some stage. "

"I appreciate you informing me about this. Let me know if there is anything that I can do."

"Just help us get the Space-Hook going. That should quiet the dissenters. Let's go see how Julia is doing."

MET CHRON NEW-HUMANS

****

When Quant and Astasia returned to her command tent, they found that Julia was engaged in a discussion on the vidscreen with the Project Odyssey leader, Gloria Garcia, a dark-haired Latina.

Julia made the introductions and said, "Gloria, I am going to go over the agreement with Queen Astasia and Quant. I will get back to you as soon as we finish."

"Fine, contact me if you have any questions."

Quant said, "I think I will leave this to you two. I'd like to spend some more time exploring the hive. It is quite fascinating."

After he left, Julia said, "Gloria sent us her standard contract. I think we should take the time to go over it in detail."

Astasia replied, "Julia, I understand that you are a patent specialist."

"That's true. Are you considering patenting your cable technology?"

"I think we should look into it, but there may be some issues with the Arctic Lab that will need to be resolved. They sent me a contract a long time ago which I never agreed to or signed."

"If they are part of USACO, it may no longer be an issue, but let's make sure this agreement with Project Odyssey doesn't include any validity claims. I will help you deal with the lab later."

She made some entries into her pad and showed it to Astasia. "I'll do a quick search for these terms."

<<patent OR patents AND/OR rights>>."

During the next hour, Astasia and Julia reviewed the agreement and twice contacted Gloria to ask for clarifications and to make minor adjustments. Finally, Astasia happily agreed to the contract terms and pressed her thumb to the pad.

At the wheel of a modern all terrain vehicle, Gloria's face appeared on the monitor. Behind her, they saw tents being packed and vehicles starting up and heading out. Gloria keyed her mic and said, "We look forward to working with you Queen Astasia. We will see you in three days and will be ready to start work the day after we arrive."

Astasia replied, "Have a safe journey. We will be preparing for your arrival and should have the water, power and waste treatment hookups that you specified ready by the time you get here. Please keep us posted if there are any delays in your schedule."

Quant returned from exploring the grounds for the cable plant just as Gloria said, "Will do...and thanks again for the gig. We won't disappoint you."

Quant said, "Wow, that was fast. No wonder their rating is so high."

Astasia rolled next to Julia and appeared to be ready to shake her hand but hesitated and said, "Someday I hope to have a body like yours, Julia. Then I will be able do simple things like shaking hands without the risk of breaking anybody's bones."

Julia bent over and hugged Astasia's cylindrical torso. "It's the thought that counts," she said.

Director's Office
Moonbase

Sanders had gathered his team for an early morning planning session. "Good morning. I just linked to Julia. I will put her on the vidscreen."

Julia, wearing a bathing suit and standing in front of an above ground swimming pool, adjusted the volume on her ear piece and said, "Hello, can you hear me?"

"Yes, loud and clear. I like your uniform, is that music I hear in the background?"

She held up a cocktail and said, "You can tell we are celebrating Astasia's signing the deal with Planet Odyssey. They are already en route as we speak."

Sanders replied, "That's great. I wish we had a trained workforce like Planet Odyssey that we could call upon up here on such short notice. But congratulations are definitely in order. Is Quant with you?"

"He and Astasia are working on the infrastructure improvements in advance of the caravan arriving. It's hard to believe, but just a few days from now, this will be a village with a population of five thousand people."

"Sanders added, "And lots of droids and robots as well. Tell Quant job well done and enjoy your party. We will talk again soon."

"Thank you. I think we may need to consider adding some additional attorneys to our staff, but for now, my job here is finished. I will be coming home on the next shuttle."

Torch joined in with "Way to go," and Sabien added, "Good job, Julia."

After the call ended, Sanders activated a holographic model of the Space-Hook and said, "Alright let's get down to business. The objective of today's meeting is to lay out a plan of attack and identify the priorities that need our immediate attention."

He pointed at the hologram and said, "It looks like the cable production component has been taken care of."

Next he pointed to the bottom of the model, "The Earth anchor connection is Quant's responsibility. He will stay behind and build his team on Earth."

Finally he tapped the counterweight at the top of the screen and concluded, "And that leaves this task for us. We need to locate and capture the mother of all asteroids, move her into the counterweight orbit, connect the cable sections and send the distal ends down to Earth where Quant's team will attach them to the anchor."

Torch groaned. "Is that all?"

Followed by Sabien who laughed. "What fun!"

Chron asked, "How long do we have to do this?"

Sanders replied, "The comparatively short cables needed to tow the asteroid into position should be ready in a month. However, the extremely long pair of cables that will stretch from the counterweight to Earth will take a year to fabricate. In the interim, we will need to add more workers, lodgings and support faculties—as well as build hangars for the pod transfers and a dome to house it all. Essentially we will be charged with the enormous task setting up a new village in a very remote location."

Max joined in, "We will make our workers and facilities at the Asteroid Safeguard Complex available as needed."

Sanders looked at his pad and said, "Great. We will need an armada of rockets to adjust the asteroid's spin and then tow it into position aa well as a fleet of passenger freighters that the pioneers can live aboard until the Vesta dome is ready for habitation. That will be your responsibility Max."

"Fine. I will contact what's left of NASA, the European Union and Japan to see what they have in orbit that they can loan or lease to us. We may have to make some improvements, but this will be excellent training for our pilots. I will be glad to work with you to plan the details."

"Chron, you are in charge of assembling a team to find the most suitable asteroid and then design and build the pod transfer station and the base infrastructure."

"I shall be glad to assist. Now that the SpeeZees labs

are back in full production, I have more time available for other projects."

Sanders continued. "Torch, you always wanted to increase the size of your herd of RoboCows; now is your chance. With your help, Chron can use them to conduct surveys and collect soil samples—just like we use them in our mining operations."

"Whoopee, now we're talking. Once Chron tells me how many he needs, I will put the contractors to work."

"Sabien, your job will be to assist Torch and Chron."

"Will do."

"Very good. Anybody have any questions?"

Hiroshi stood and said, "Not a question really, but I want you to know that the SpeeZees Lab will pitch in if there is anything we can do help."

"Thank you, Hiroshi. So, if there is nothing else, the meeting is adjourned."

Torch waited until the others left and told his dad. "I just wanted to tell you that I think you are doing a great job."

Sanders laughed and gave Torch a hug.

"Thanks, Son...now back to work!"

— CHAPTER 18 —

Travis Air Force Base

Xeron sat at his console flanked by N-13, on his left and N-69 on his right. Once Xeron tapped his wrist tab, the vid-con feed was transmitted to all members of the former SCN that still remained in orbit around the planet.

"Thank you for joining me. We have a lot to discuss. N-13, why don't you start with the communications that you have intercepted. What have you learned?"

N-13 tapped his pad and brought up a schematic of the Space-Hook which he referred to frequently as he delivered a detailed description of the components and the probable deployment strategy.

Xeron asked, "When will this device be placed into service?'

"My understanding is that the system could installed and operating within a year—assuming all goes according to their plan."

"N-69, what do you think? Is there a way we can take advantage of this?" asked Xeron.

"Basically my take is that a space elevator would be a major asset, that is if we could take control once it is finished. If we can't, then we should destroy it before more can be built and put into operation," replied N-13.

Xeron nodded. "Essentially we have three options. The first is to let global warming run its course. The second option is to accelerate the global warming process. Since the organics have nearly destroyed the environment already with their uncontrolled breeding, lack of judgment and incompetence, accelerating that process would seem to be a reasonable strategy. The third option is all out combat warfare. What do you think N-69?"

"Sabotaging remedial efforts, like the space elevator, seems like a good plan, but I also recommend that we explore the strategy of enhancing and expanding our cyber warfare capabilities."

"What do you have in mind?"

N-69 cued up a world map sprinkled with blinking red lights.

"These are the potential targets. If we were able install smart AI malware in a dozen major U.S. city electrical power infrastructures and infect military bases around the planet, our viral codes would completely wipe out the core operating systems as well as the backup and restoration programs stored in the cloud."

Xeron asked, "What are the projected outcomes?"

N-13 joined in. "It would take months for Sapients and New-Humans to regain control. The blackouts would interrupt food distribution and medical services. Financial markets would plummet and crime rates would soar. The knockout punch would be that as soon as the infected systems were restored, our AI viruses would hit them again and again. N-69 and I project that total chaos would ensue with hundreds of millions of organics out of work and starving. Violence would become rampant as organics struggle to survive."

Xeron said, "Very impressive, but I am concerned that this malware could be a Pandora's box. In other words, when we deal with AI viruses, we risk losing control—especially in the high RAD zones where mutations are frequent. We might end up infecting our clan and our allies. So...I suggest we regard the viral assault option as a last resort...at least for the time being."

N-69 replied, "I understand your concern. We also have a sizable arsenal of nuclear weapons, combat droids, battle tanks, jetcopters and drones here at Travis. I will send you a detailed inventory."

Xeron replied, "So back to sabotaging the space elevator, what's the next step?"

N-69 brought up a series of aerial images of the Planet Odyssey caravan en route to the tundra. He said, "This is today's announcement for Planet Odyssey job openings that is circulating in the cloud. "We could do some cosmetic surgery on Jason Phillips and give him a new identity so that he can apply for one of the security guard openings. This would give us valuable insight into their vulnerabilities and position him where he could directly interfere with their operations."

Xeron nodded his approval and said, "It would also be great if we could penetrate the staff on the Moonbase, but undoubtedly they have tightened their security procedures."

N-13 asked, "How about this base? I am concerned that the new government might want Travis back. If they consider us a threat, they could even attack us with nukes—after all this region is already radioactive."

N-69 cued a series of aerial photos of the base and said, "We are digging a series of caverns and moving critical power systems, attack vehicles and rockets beneath the surface just in case."

Xeron pointed to the wall screen. "Don't forget we have a fleet of armed shuttles on call that can be activated in a moments notice. With that, let's windup this meeting. and get to work. Great job Neuros."

MET CHRON NEW-HUMANS

New Years Day
January 1st, 2035

The holiday festivities were in full swing as Sanders delivered a moving speech from the Luna Lounge that aired on monitors base-wide in which he summarized the magnificent achievements that had been accomplished and announced the names of the civic leaders that had been elected to serve in the newly formed Lunar Colony Council.

Genie gave him a thumbs up and Julia handed him a glass of champagne as he joined them in the VIP section as the band began playing their original compositions in a genre which they had named, *Moon Rock*. Taking advantage of the reduced gravity, the dancers twirled and jumped up and down to the beat a like mob of kangaroos.

Torch said, "That was an excellent speech, Dad. Nice and short too. Are you still planning to take your granddaughter to the pool for a swim? She has been looking forward to it."

Sanders looked at Julia and she nodded her head.

"Send her a flash that we are on the way. Why don't you come with us?"

"No, I think it would be better if you two got to know her better. I would just be a distraction. Our meeting tomorrow is at 0800, right?"

"Right, I'll see you there."

****

Based upon soil samples collected by Torch's Robo-Cows and a comprehensive analysis of objects in the belt,Chron had decided that a large asteroid named *Vesta* was an ideal choice to serve as the counterweight based upon its mass and extensive deposits of valuable elements. With a diameter of 525 kilometers, it was massive enough to provide adequate tension to secure the Space-Hook, but moving it into the counterweight position would be an enormous undertaking requiring a fleet of twenty high-powered rockets that would be connected to Vesta by the new graphene cables.

The counterweight position would be 142,000 km from Earth, which was way above the geostationary orbit of 36,000 km but far less than the 383,000 km distance to the Moon. Conventional tow cables of sufficient strength would have been way too thick and heavy, thus the mission was totally dependent upon the Queen's new cable technology.

The problem was that the cable shipment needed for the first phase of the mission had yet to arrive on the Moonbase and this was throwing the entire project off schedule. After repeated attempts to resolve the problem over a series of vid-cons failed, Sanders decided to send Torch and Sabien to the Arctic cable factory to figure out and fix whatever was causing the delay.

Meanwhile, Chron and Max focused on another serious problem that they needed to solve before Vesta could be towed into position—the massive asteroid's rapid, five-hour rotation on its axis.

After many brainstorming sessions with the best and the brightest on the Moonbase, they came up with a plan to land a dozen rockets on the surface of Vesta and have the RoboCows anchor them in an orientation opposite the asteroid's rotation. Once in place, the rockets would fire their nuclear engines until the rotation stopped, which Chron estimated would take thirty days of continuous propulsion and require the service of a flotilla of fuel tankers. After the rotation was halted, the rockets would shutdown and hold their position until the rest of the fleet and the tow cables arrived.

Sanders approved the plan, relieved that the first mission tasks would be accomplished by AI robots without the need for life support systems and allow them time to design the new facility and recruit workers that would spend years of their lives in a brutal environment where any miscalculation would end in disaster.

Arctic Tundra

With Sabien at the controls, the shuttle began its descent into the atmosphere over the Pacific. As they approached the coast of Alaska, thick smoke in the atmosphere made looking ahead difficult, so Sabien focused on the radar signal. Most other shuttle pilots would have invoked the AI landing system to bring in the shuttle, but Sabien preferred to use manual control.

After a bumpy entry, he turned to Torch and said, "Wow, the air quality is a lot worse than it was the last time we were here."

Torch brought up temperature map of the Arctic Tundra and pointed at two areas in bright red. "This doesn't look good, but these fires are fifty kilometers to the south, so pose no threat to the cable factory. I am glad that my dad let me bring along a couple of Robo-Cows. I want to see if I can modify them to fight fires."

"You and your pet Holsteins."

"Just imagine putting out fires without risking human lives. Bipedal androids can't cover nearly as much uneven terrain as my RoboCows can."

Sabien laughed. "You're right. I'll be happy to give you a hand when I have time, but now secure for landing."

Torch snapped a brisk salute and then secured his seat harness. "Roger that, Captain."

As Sabien turned the craft to approach the runway and deployed the landing gear, a computer generated voice announced, '*Incoming shuttle. Abort landing. I say again, abort landing. This facility is closed to unauthorized traffic'*.

Sabien yanked up the shuttle's nose and retracted the landing gear just as the ship pulled away from the tarmac and circled away from the landing zone.

Torch said, "What the hell was that all about? Did the Queen warn your dad that we needed a landing clearance?"

"Not that I recall. Hang on, we are getting a flash."

"Incoming shuttle, this is Queen Astasia. Disregard prior warning and proceed to landing site I am sorry for the inconvenience. I will meet you in my office and try to figure out what just happened."

****

Sabien held open the flap so Torch could duck in and then followed him into the tent that served as the Queen's office. They were both amazed to see that Astasia had dramatically changed her appearance. Instead of a hard, metallic skin and swiveling eyestalks, her skin was now flesh colored and her face that of an attractive, thirty year old human female. When she shook Torch's hand, he noted that it was warm and human-like, but she still had a cylindrical body resting on pneumatic tires.

Torch said, "I can see that you have made some major changes to your appearance since we last met."

"Yes, do you approve? I have several other ideas that I plan to try in the future."

She pointed to what appeared to be some sort of printer chassis on wheels. "This is *Beamer;* she used to be a 1970's IBM Selectric typewriter."

Torch said, "Wow, this belongs in a museum. Where did you get it?"

MET CHRON NEW-HUMANS

"I am pleased that you have a command of history. Originally she was a computer science project conducted by one of our newly hired security guards when he was in high school. He thought that I might like her...not sure why, but she is quite talented. She has a high level AI in the chassis and I added an LCD display and appendages. I have grown quite fond of Beamer. She now serves as my office assistant."

Torch bent down to look at the robot and commented. "This is interesting. A robot typewriter."

She reached down and fondly tapped the LCD panel. "Beamer, say hello to our guests."

The LCD illuminated and the text *IBM Selectric* appeared on the screen followed by a spirited, feminine voice. "Greetings Torch, welcome to the Space-Hook cable factory. I understand that you have been here before and generated the diamond seal that we are now harvesting and converting to graphene cable."

"Yes. That is correct. Meet Sabien, he invented the nano penetrators."

Sabien groaned. "And don't forget, who started World War III."

Astasia interjected. "Come now. It wasn't your fault. It is what you humans might call *water over the bridge*."

Sabien laughed. "I think you mean '*under*', but we get the idea."

Torch turned to the Queen and asked. "What happened during our approach? Why the abort command?"

Astasia shrugged. "I wish I knew. Unfortunately it is just the most recent glitch that we have suffered. Beamer what have you determined?"

"I don't know how, but someone must have hacked our security...still checking."

Torch said, "The former Space Command Network has been taken over by pirates that call themselves the

Neuro Nation. It's possible that they are somehow involved. We suspect that they may be monitoring our communications as well."

Sabien added, "That really is why we came here to meet with you in person. We didn't want to alert the Neuros that we are starting this investigation. We have no inkling as to what their goals are or what they are up to."

"But we assume it is bad," concluded Torch, and then he added, "By the way, I brought two of my cow robots with me I want to see if they can play a role in fire fighting. It looks like you have a couple burning right now."

Astasia nodded. "That sounds like an excellent idea. My team would be glad to help, but you must be tired after your trip. Follow me, I will introduce you to the mayor of our new tech town. She will make sure that your accommodations are satisfactory. I understand the food is reputed to be quite savory to Sapients."

"Great. The ration packs are getting a little boring."

Astasia led them past a kid's playground and a mechanic's repair shop to a bar playing mariachi music where Gloria was sipping a beer on the deck, watching the deep-red sunset that filled the sky while she awaited their arrival.

Astasia provided introductions. "Gloria this is Torch and Sabien. As I mentioned earlier, please keep their visit here in confidence. Guys, this is Gloria Garcia. She will take care of you. I will see you bright and early."

Gloria shook their hands and gave them badges identifying them as employees. of the Alaska State Fire Department. She said, "Beamer thought these IDs might be appropriate. Would you like a drink?"

Torch pinned his badge to his shirt and said, "Perfect. We want to draw as little attention as possible. A beer would be great. Tell us, have you noticed anything strange happening around here that could be interrupting cable fabrication?"

After describing some of the events that had recently taken place, Gloria led them to a two level SV that she had reserved for them. Once inside she handed them each a pad and said, "You can use your badges to make purchases here. Feel free to order anything on the menu. It will be delivered shortly."

Torch whistled. "Looks very gourmet. I think I will go for nachos with avocado and a bowl of vegetarian chili."."

Sabien nodded. "Please, make that the same for me."

Torch began exploring the SV and discovered that they would each have a private room on the ground floor and that the second floor offered a panoramic view of the tundra as well as an advanced quantum computer system.

He descended to the main room and said, "Not bad for the middle of nowhere. You don't happen to have any cigars on your list do you? It's been a long time since I had one."

Gloria did a quick search on Torch's pad and said, "I ordered a box for you. See you gentlemen in the morning."

Ten minutes later, there was a knock on the door and Sabien admitted a cube-shaped robot which delivered trays of steaming fare.

Torch smiled when he discovered a box of cigars in the storage bin. He peeled the wrapper off one of the cigars and held it to his nose, took a sniff and smiled.

"I'm starting to like this place. I wonder what other delights we are in for?"

Sabien warned. "That's great. Just smoke them outside please."

Torch replied, "That's exactly what your sister said when she drug me through the jungles of Brazil on her mission to collect embryos for her Ark and Reverend LeRoque was on our tail."

"Really? I'd like to hear that story."

Torch took a bite of chili and said, "It all began in San Francisco back in the year 2029."

— CHAPTER 19 —

January 22nd, 2035

It had been two weeks since Torch and Sabien had arrived at Astasia's new village. The cable factory was in full production and had been functioning flawlessly after they made a few tweaks. However, as the permafrost melted, the Arctic was rapidly turning the once frozen tundra, which had supported the weight of thousands of miles of petroleum pipelines, into soggy marshlands unable to bear the mass of the pipes. Leaks from the widespread system cracks posed an increasing hazard generating multiple wildfires that raged with no remedy in sight.

Recognizing the danger, Astasia consulted with Gloria and Beamer and decided to purchase a pair of foam suppressant tanks mounted on tracks towed by all terrain vehicles. Torch was intrigued when they arrived, but was skeptical about their effectiveness. Ever since he invented the first cow robots that were capable of traveling over uneven terrain, he was convinced that they might offer a fire fighting capability and this trip had finally offered him an opportunity to test his theory.

Gloria was pleased to offer him work space in one of the caravan repair shops where he spent many hours adding new features to the pair of robotic cows that he brought with him from the Moonbase. The modifications included adding heat sensors and the ability to rear up on their hind legs and emit a spray of fire suppressor foam from their oral cavity. In addition, the RoboCows were now covered with an aluminum foil skin designed to shield them from flames and their AI and communication systems were chilled by an onboard compressor to protect them from intense heat.

In order to test the newly modified robots, Torch and Astasia decided to set a test fire at a seeping pipeline rupture located a few kilometers away from the cable factory. The SV village residents had been notified in advance to the scheduled drill and quickly assumed their assigned positions as the foam tankers were moved into position in case the fire spread out of control.

After Torch unloaded the RoboCows from the transport truck, Astasia said, "If you are ready, I will ignite the fire starter."

Torch, who was standing next to the RoboCows, nodded his head.

There was a loud bang when the Queen triggered the starter explosive followed by a raging curtain of flame that surged from the pit and quickly began to spread much faster than they had anticipated. The bystanders jumped back as the fire line surged towards them and threatened to surrounded them.

The Queen rolled back and forth–obviously worried about how fast the flames were growing in intensity.

She yelled at Torch, who was lying on his back under one of the cows with the control panel open. "What's the holdup?"

Torch regained his feet and replied, "Forgot to reset after the last test. No problem."

Once the RoboCows activated, they took a few moments to survey their surroundings and run simulations to evaluate the most efficient plan of attack.

Astasia clutched her pad with her finger poised to punch the button that would activate the foam tankers, but Torch waved his hand and shook his head no.

Suddenly the RoboCows reared up on their hind legs and moved in a coordinated, zigzag pattern spraying suppressant foam from their oral nozzles which efficiently doused the flames.

When Torch ran out to retrieve the RoboCows to load them onto the transport truck, they took off in a sprint towards the village.

Astasia said, "Good job, but where are they going?"

Torch shrugged. "I'm not sure. Just having fun I guess. They don't get to play much."

Sabien sat next to Torch on a bench in the back of the truck and gave him a high five. "Congratulations. Just as you envisioned, those cow bots of yours are fantastic at putting out fires. But, seeing them run that fast was amazing!"

"One of my goals has been to reduce the danger faced by people working in fire departments. Thousands of men and women are lost every year to the point that few people are applying for firefighter jobs or even working as volunteers."

"That is a pretty immense market. You better file a patent. Julia seems to be our resident, legal expert."

"Good idea. I like the model she used for SCOMID. A fee to those who can pay and free to those who cannot."

"Your dad will be proud of you. Do you believe in predestination?"

"Not really. Why do you ask?"

"Well...you're in the fire control business and your name is *Torch*."

"Never thought of that."

I figure you are itching to have one of your cigars,"

Torch said, "You must be a mind reader."

"Never been called that before."

Torch blew a series of smoke rings and said, "OK, this is part two of my story. After lecturing me never to make decisions for her, I convinced Astra that..."

****

Since the cable factory was now in full production mode and there had been no holdups or breakdowns in operations...and since they still had no clue to what caused the earlier disruptions, Torch called his father and they agreed it was time for them to return home. Torch informed Sabien who was happy to hear the news.

After they filled their shuttle's cargo bay with spools of cable and prepared for an early morning departure, they attended a party hosted by Astasia to celebrate their departure. The pair of RoboCows were the center of attention, surrounded by village kids who waited for their turn to sit on the backs of the cows and have their photos taken under the watchful eyes of their parents.

Before they headed back to their SV, Torch handed Astasia the pads that controlled the cow robots and said, "I will send you updates as they become available. Please take care of my buddies."

"Thank you for leaving them with us. Have a safe journey and please come back and visit us soon."

Torch walked over and stroked the cows foreheads. "I'll miss you guys." As he walked away, the RoboCows fell in behind him. He turned to look at them and said, "No. You live here now," and quickly brushed tears from his eyes as he headed to the SV to pack for the trip home.

Lunar Colony

Chia, wearing a bright pink spacesuit with a helmet adorned with sunflower decals, cued her vidcam to zoom from a wide angle view of the cranes erecting a shiny new lunar dome and winding up with a closeup of her face.

"Greetings viewers, thank you for joining me. As you can see, I am reaching out this morning from the Lunar Colony where I am standing on the crest of a ridge overlooking the Moonbase. Down below you will notice a lot of changes that have been made since our last broadcast.

The vidcam feed switched to a figure in a reflective, silver spacesuit gracefully skipping, elevating and coasting towards her—obviously someone with considerable experience in maneuvering in the reduced lunar gravity.

"Here comes our guest Robert Sanders, Director of Deep Space Mining. He has agreed to give us an update on the amazing projects underway here on the Moon so far from home but so important to Earth's survival."

Chia waved her hand and the vidcam swiveled overhead then moved to a closeup of Sander's face. "Thank you for joining us Director. What can you tell us about what we are seeing in the background?"

"Thank you Chia for inviting me. During all the propaganda campaign spouted by the USACO government, the RealNews has been a reliable source of the *real* news."

Chia's facial tattoos flashed a myriad of colors–her body's version of blushing. She said, "I still remember those days when our corporate dictators claimed that the media were the enemy and that truth was a relative term. Hopefully, those creeps are long gone now that the government has morphed back into a democracy."

"I hope so."

"OK, enough whining. Tell us what is going on behind us."

Sanders lifted his arms and spun around. "We currently have three domes in various stages of planning and completion. The large dome is the new home of Deep Space Mining. Originally, we lived and worked below the surface but expanded topside when it was finished."

"How about the other, smaller dome to the right?"

"That is the Asteroid Safeguard Complex. If you zoom in, you will see that it is flanked on each side by batteries of fusion powered rockets and fuel transports that provide us with a significant defensive capability as well as the ability to tow the asteroid Vesta into place. Twelve of the rockets that were used to halt the asteroid's rotation are already in place and will be part of the fleet that will tow Vesta into the counterweight slot."

"You mentioned three domes. I see only two."

"Right. The third will be a combined commercial spaceport and tourist center that is in the planning stage. We intend to begin that expansion after the Space-Hook becomes operational. The elevator is just one of our key projects. The others are New-Human and SCOMID production and ore mining."

"Will all of these facilities be connected?"

"Over time, yes. The main dome and the Asteroid Complex dome are already connected by an underground tunnel. but eventually we will employ the same transparent graphene sheets that we are using in the dome covers to enclose a tubular rail system that will link all of our facilities above the ground. The atmosphere in the tubes will be breathable so residents can walk or run between domes if they want some exercise. We are even planning to hold a footrace to commemorate the day when the surface transit system opens."

"This is truly becoming a new home for many people isn't it? Did you ever think this would happen?"

"Not really, but what is the most surprising to me is how quickly our tourism business has expanded. Right now we have thousands of applicants on the waiting list to visit the colony—plus, in the not too distant future, we will serve as a way station for trips to Mars and Europa—all paid for by our business contracts and license fees. Just imagine what it would cost to build from scratch a space station with all of our present capabilities."

"Good point. Let's go over the demographic data that you gave me before the show."

She cued a screen that listed the data.

Total Full-Time Resident Population 1,161
Sapient Population 1,157
Adult Males 700
Adult Females 410
Infants and Children 47
New-Human Population 2 male, 2 female
Approximately 60 N-H in development

After reviewing the data, Sanders said, "Keep in mind that these numbers are projected to more than double next year. It is hard to believe that for a decade we have had a steady population of just under two hundred full-time residents."

"Thank you Director. I am sure that our viewers appreciate all you and your staff are doing and wish you success in your world changing endeavors."

"Keep up the good work, Chia."

Chia took a sip of water from her helmet tube and continued. "We will now take a ten-minute break while I head back into the Moonbase and get out of this spacesuit. In the interim, we will air the first of our new series of short documentaries, *'A Decade of Lunar Courage'* produced by yours truly. I'll be back in a flash!"

****

Chia, back in the SpeeZees Lab wearing a dark blue kimono inlaid with pink blossoms said, "Now, we will turn to matters on Earth that are not nearly as positive and heart warming as those we have covered so today on the Moon."

A series of video clips played revealing violent crowds breaking into pharmaceutical buildings with the caption '*SCOMID Shortage Drives Riots in Atlanta, Georgia*'.

Chia said, "We have reports that the scarcity of the supposedly free version of the SCOMID pill is causing major unrest in parts of the world. We start with our reporter Robert Black in Atlanta. Robert, what can you tell us about this situation. Why aren't people getting their daily doses?"

"The situation is serious Chia and it is quite simple. Many of the pharmas that agreed to supply the free version in exchange for the right to sell the programmable, Calendar version are violating their contractual obligations. Millions of citizens feel betrayed. Without the anti-aging drug, they could die tomorrow while their lucky neighbors, that have secured their supply, will live for decades more to come. Gangs of Sapients have hijacked SCOMID shipments and are charging astronomical prices, ripping off helpless victims. Here is my earlier interview with a teenager who has been caught up in the fracas and faces serious jail time."

The boy wearing a prison suit wiped tears from his eyes and said, "I didn't want my grandmother to die so I joined one of the neighborhood gangs to get her pills and got caught before I could get them to her. Its not fair, I just wanted to save her. Now I have a ten year jail sentence and she is gone."

Robert concluded. "Hopefully some of our viewers will contact the address on the bottom of the screen and ask the judge for leniency. This is just another sad story that would never have happened if all of the pharma firms were obeying the law. I have posted a list of the licensed firms on our cloud site if any of our viewers want to join the growing protest."

The feed turned back to Chia. "That is a real heart breaker. Keep up the good work Robert."

"Will do, Chia."

"I have invited the SCOMID inventor, Astra Sturtevant to join us. Astra, what happens when a person that has been religiously taking the free version suddenly is unable to acquire subsequent doses?"

"Thanks for inviting me Chia, but I am afraid that my answer is going to seem somewhat vague. In short, we're not sure. The problem is that this is a new treatment and we do not yet have long-term data to accurately predict what will happen upon cessation of treatment. If I am forced to make a prediction, it would be that normal aging would resume. Every participant is supposed read the directions and sign a release form. All of us here in the SCOMID lab are very concerned about unauthorized use."

"What actions are you taking now or plan to take in the future?"

"Let me assure your viewers that we are urging our pharma clients to immediately ramp up production of the Basic SCOMID and increase shipments to community service organizations. We will immediately suspend the license of pharmaceutical firms that do not abide by the agreement covenants. If they are responsible for the deaths of people that could have been saved by taking the Basic free version, then they may be subject to criminal prosecution."

"Wow, hit em with your best shot! Thank you Astra. I am sure that our viewers appreciate your help. We will pause here for a word from our sponsors."

A montage of video clips depicting raging wildfires

and flooding cities with the caption *The Truth About Global Warming* appeared on the screen.

The feed returned to Chia wearing a large pair of white-rimmed sun glasses.

"After decades of denial about climate change by the ruthless profit oriented corporations that ran the USACO government claiming that it was 'fake' news, scientists have finally been allowed to post data, attend conferences and publish their results. In our next program we will begin a new series on climate change that we hope will not be too little, too late. This is Chia signing off."

Hiroshi gave Chia a hug when she arrived in the lounge and received a standing ovation from the crowd. After a couple of rounds of drinks, she and Hiroshi headed out leaving Torch and Sabien to resume their discussions with Sanders about their new roles as asteroid hunters.

— CHAPTER 20 —

Asteroid Vesta
Three Months Later
April 22nd, 2035

Torch slid the clip attached to the end of the thin graphene cable into the chamber of the magneto gun and injected the piton into Vesta's rocky soil. Sabien tested the bond and then signaled the rocket in the distance that the final ultra thin nano cable was in place. It only took a few moments until the cable tightened and lights outlining the hull of the tow rocket turned green indicating that it had a nearly invisible cable in tow and that the radar microchips embedded in the cable were functioning according to specifications.

Sabien gazed at the fan of shining cables connected to the fleet of twenty AI controlled rockets that had been configured to tow the asteroid and said, "That's it. We're done. Let's head back to our ship."

Torch replied, "Roger that. I just got a message from Chron. He and Rosella will be here in eighteen hours with the first group of contractors who will lay the foundation for the new facility. After we brief them on what we have accomplished, we can head for home."

"A month to get here. One month to attach the

cables. And then another month for us to head for home."

Torch sighed. "I know. But at least with our new electro magnetic powered drive, we should be back in time for Luz's birthday."

"Are you going for the cryostasis freeze treatment again?

"Absolutely. Astra has provided us with custom, personal versions of time release SCOMIDs. It's like going to bed one night and waking up back home in the morning. How about you?"

"Probably, but like time travel, it's a little scary and quite confusing. I feel sad about our crew mates that we will be leaving behind on this rock, but I miss Jasmine and Solara—our little girl is a beauty, just like her mom. Smart too."

Chron is going to have his hands full towing Vesta to the counterweight position, initiating a twenty-seven day rotation around Earth and building the new base on the asteroid. What a massive undertaking that will be!"

Torch shrugged. "It is going to be a stark existence for the pioneers that will be living here while they tow Vesta into position at the apex of the Space-Hook, but there will be a continuous influx of high capacity passenger ships bringing colonists here soon. At least they will have my RoboCows to keep them company; their initial surveys indicate that are huge resources of building materials–plus there will be frequent supply runs from the Moonbase carrying the essentials that they need to survive."

"Hey, did you feel that? The ground just shifted."

"I sure did. It seems like Vesta's journey to its new home has just gotten underway."

As they activated their suit thrusters and lifted off towards their shuttle, Torch waved goodbye to the herd of cow bots that had been startled by the sudden movement but had quickly resumed their survey duties. The lead RoboCow stood on its hind legs and spun around, which Torch interpreted as its way of saying farewell.

The Next Morning

Chron and Rosella met Sabien and Torch at the air lock of the five hundred passenger command ship that Max had leased from the Japanese Aerospace Exploration Agency which had been rechristened *Vesta Prime.* After the hatch opened, Chron performed a Vulcan hand salute and said, "Greetings my fellow Earthlings. We are going where no New-Human or Sapient has gone before."

Rosella leaned over, smiled and whispered to Torch, "Ever since your dad promoted him to lead the Vesta asteroid project, he has been watching way too many Star Trek movies in his off time. Just address him as 'Captain Chron' and he will be happy."

During the briefing on project status and scheduling, Chron delivered the alarming news that there had been another incident at Queen Astasia's cable factory which was going to delay the next cable deliveries for at least another month.

Chron reached into his pocked and retrieved a flash stick. "The Queen asked me to give this to you. It was hand delivered on her last cable shipment. She explained that she was concerned that the rogue Neuro shuttles in orbit were eavesdropping on what should otherwise be secure transmissions."

Torch responded. "I get that, but the whole time we spent there, we didn't experience any problems."

Sabien interjected, "The agent must have gone back to work after we left."

Torch pocketed the flash stick and said, "Thanks, I will check it out. At least we were able to install all the cable that you need to tow the asteroid. As you can tell, the translocation mission has finally begun."

Chron nodded. "Yes, thanks to you." He did another Vulcan salute and said, "May you live long and prosper."

This time Torch and Sabien couldn't hold back their laughter and took turns slapping him on the back. As they left, Rosella took him by the hand and said, "We need to talk about this Vulcan fixation of yours."

****

After Torch inserted the flash stick into a data port on his pad and keyed the play button, a hologram of Queen Astasia holding a baseball sprang to life.

"Greetings Torch and Sabien. If you are seeing this message, Chron was able to deliver it to you in person and he has explained my concern that our COM systems have been hacked. To find out I set a trap and look at what I caught!"

The image shifted to a pile of wires, smoking electronic parts and a fractured vidscreen that was flashing on and off. She held up a black, metal sheet which bore the inscription '*IBM Selectric*'.

"Remember Beamer, my trusted assistant? It turns out that she and the man who gave it to me were the culprits. It wasn't more than a week after you left that we started having production problems again. Little things like fluxes in our electric grid that delayed the fabrication system and a bout of food poisoning that rippled through the Planet Odyssey village. I figured that it was only a matter of time before someone got killed or injured, so I set a trap and caught them in the act. The guy got away somehow. I am not exactly sure how, but Beamer surrendered and begged for leniency."

Astasia raised her bat and repeatedly smashed the vidscreen into a pile of rubble. "There now. You have gotten your leniency. Cheating the Queen is not to be taken lightly!"

Torch paused the message, looked at Sabien who said, "Jason Phillips?"

"Could be, I never trusted that guy. We'll have to ask the Queen if she has any surveillance footage."

"Gloria Cravens must have done a background check when she hired whoever it was."

"Good point. Hold on there's more," said Torch as he tapped the resume playback button.

Astasia continued, "So on that note, I am happy to report that we are back in full production and Chron should have brought our first major cable shipment on the trip that delivered this message. I look forward to hearing from you soon."

She laughed and lowered the vidcam. "How do you like my new legs? This is the Cable Queen signing off."

Torch smiled and closed the file. "She keeps getting mods that are making her look more feminine."

"You know, I think she has a crush on you."

"Me? How about you? She is starting to look a little sexier isn't she?"

"OK enough fun and games for one day." He patted the cryotube. "Take your tranquilizer tablet and I will see you in your tomorrow."

Torch stretched his arms and then lay down in the cryotube. "How about you. Do you want to time travel too?"

"You know, there is something curious about this."

"How so?"

"According to our internal biological clocks, time will stop while we are in cryostasis and since our spouses are taking SCOMIDs, they will look the same when we return home. However our kids will seem to have grown considerably in just one night.

Torch popped his sleep tablet and said, "I'll have to

give that some thought. So...do you want to time travel with me?"

"Torch!"

"Yes?"

"Sometimes I wonder why I consider you my best friend."

"Oh come on. Why do you always have to be so serious?"

"I may go into cryo in a week or so. I just look forward to some peace and quiet. Ron S. Nolan just released a new technothriller in his long running Met Chron series. I have been wanting to read it and I finally have the time. Plus, there is a lot of background research on space elevator technology that I want to catch up on."

"Fine. Let me know what you find out. You can always thaw me out if you get lonely."

"Goodnight my friend, have a good sleep."

Torch replied, "*Fair winds and following seas...*said the Captain."

"Oh not you too."

"That's all for now."

"Good. Brace for acceleration, Luna Lounge here we come!"

"Amen."

Queen's Cable Factory
Arctic Tundra

After getting very favorable reports about the outstanding results that the Project Odyssey team, Quant decided to fly from his office in Rome to visit the cable fab complex to see if any of the geek nomads might be available and want to assist in developing the Space-Hook anchor.

The sun was sinking over the Arctic tundra in a blaze of glory when Queen Astasia and Quant received a much anticipated flash from Chron stating that the Vesta translocation was finally underway. She signaled her new android assistant, who triggered a cascade of colorful fireworks that was carefully monitored by the RoboCows to make sure no fires were accidentally started.

In the SV park, a trio was playing Cajun style tunes while the geeks and their loved ones celebrated with drinks and barbecued syntho ribs. Quant noticed that a very striking, nicely tanned, red-headed female was looking at him while whispering something in another girl's ear.

Since the Queen was showing off her new legs by dancing to the music, Quant decided to return to his SV and retire early. But just as he turned to leave, the girl that he had noticed earlier, caught his arm and said, "You're not leaving are you? The party is just getting started! By the way, my name is Elektra."

Quant replied, "Hello Elektra, my name is..."

"Everybody knows who you are Quant. You're the first New-Human ever elected to the OWN and a brilliant environmental scientist as well."

"That is very kind of you to say. Would you like to join me for a drink?"

"That's exactly what I would like."

During the rest of the evening, they enjoyed tropical fruit cocktails and even tried dancing, which Quant had never done before but was a surprisingly good for a beginner. Quant learned that Elektra had many talents including: developing code for neural networks and project management for the diverse tech services offered by Planet Odyssey.

During a break in the music, the Queen stopped by their table and delivered a new round of drinks.

She said, "I'm glad you two have met. Elektra was a tremendous help in tracking down Beamer and warning me about the Neuros that have taken over the SCN. So Quant, is the vid-con still on for tomorrow?"

"Yes, I have invited you, Gloria Cravens and Dr. James Morrow, a marine biologist who specializes in coral reefs and Scotty's father. The SCOMID drug is named after Scotty who now lives on the Moonbase with his sister, Madeline, who looks after him."

Quant took Elektra's hand and said, "I would like you to come too. I could use your input on recruiting tech workers. Actually that is why I am here."

Astasia winked at Elektra and then turned to Quant and said, "By the way, we did a check on the missing guard's employment history and discovered that the standard DNA sample that he had provided actually belonged to Juan Floyd whose ID photo had been switched with that of our impostor. It is a little confusing, but Floyd is the Chief Engineer at Salinas Droids who was kidnapped a few months back. Our spy's application was obviously a fraud."

Elektra said, "Every time we find a way to deal with identify fraud, the crooks figure out a new way to thwart our defenses."

Astasia said, "I will leave you two alone. See you tomorrow."

After the Queen left, Quant asked, "So what are you planning to do next?"

"I have completed my term with the Planet Odyssey and would like to find a new challenge to solve—preferably one that isn't always on the verge of packing up and moving to the next gig."

As Quant escorted Elektra to the SV she shared with her roommate, he asked "Is 'Elektra' your birth name or your coder name?"

"That's a long story for another time."

He was surprised when she gave him a quick kiss and said, "It has been fun hanging out with you. Thank you for inviting me to your vid-con. What time is the meeting?"

"Nine AM."

She gave him a hug and said, "I'll see you then."

The Next Day
April 23rd, 2035

Quant had a difficult time taking his eyes off Elektra who arrived wearing tight shorts and a halter top that revealed her sexy figure. Gloria waved her over and patted the seat next to her.

She whispered, "Astasia told me that you met Quant at the party last night and seemed to hit it off. How did it go?"

Elektra smiled and said, "Very well, he is a very interesting person."

"I can tell by the way he is staring at you that he likes you."

"Maybe I should go put on some coveralls?"

The Queen, who had been listening, said, "Nah...you look great...make him suffer. "

Quant turned his attention back to his pad to check his notes for the meeting. Since, locating the optimum site to anchor the very first of its kind Space-Hook to Earth was a complicated task, he realized that he was going to need expert help.

The geographic requirements involved finding a favorable location in the tropics for OTEC operations as well as a harbor for large vessels and a space shuttle landing port—all of which would require a workforce that was qualified to design, construct and operate the Space-Hook. Since the recovery of coral reef ecosystems was widely regarded by environmentalists as a key factor in climate recovery, Quant had invited Morrow to remotely attend the vid-con.

Quant activated the vid-con system, welcomed Morrow and introduced him to the participants that were sitting around the Queen's desk.

"As one of the world's leading experts on coral reefs, we would much appreciate your thoughts about the best place to install the Space-Hook anchor and how you see coral reefs fitting into the overall climate picture."

Morrow, sitting in the lab of the *Cynara* docked at his daughter's floating home in Santa Cruz, California, adjusted his earpiece and said, "Thank you for inviting me. I am sending you a collection of research studies linking coral bleaching to increasing seawater temperatures–much of it was classified as secret by the corrupt corporate naysayers but has been recently released by the newly resurrected EPA."

"How about if you start with a quick overview of the problems facing reefs and why they are so important?"

"No problem. It's pretty straightforward actually."

Morrow keyed up a series of images. "Corals are colonies of very small animals called 'polyps' that have the ability to convert CO_2 into calcium carbonate which they use to build their exoskeleton. The polyps enter into a mutually beneficial symbiotic relationship with photosynthetic zooxanthellae which are embedded throughout the polyp tissues where they provide carbohydrates to feed the polyps. In exchange, the polyps provide living space and nutrients that the zooxanthellae use for photosynthesis."

"So why is increasing seawater temperature such a problem?"

"As the temperature increases, the production of zooxanthellae also rises, but at some stage they begin to malfunction and produce reactive oxygen which can damage the polyp's proteins, DNA and RNA. When the stress reaches a critical level, the polyps eject the zooxanthellae and try to compensate by using their tentacles to capture zooplankton which often is insufficient to their survival. The pigments in the zooxanthellae give rise to the vibrant colors in coral colonies. So when they are ejected, the corals assume the pure white color of their calcium carbonate exoskeletons giving rise to the term *coral bleaching*."

"Is there anyway this can be reversed?"

"Actually corals have a remarkable ability to recover if the temperature decreases. In some instances, varieties of zooxanthellae have evolved that are more resistant. This seems to be the case for the reefs at Enewetak Atoll that I have studied over several decades. The high radiation levels from the atomic testing may have generated mutations in the polyps and zooxanthellae. At some stage I would like to go back and collect samples for a detailed genetic analysis."

"Anchor sites in Micronesia are high on our list of candidates. Do you have any location suggestions?"

Not needing any time to think, Morrow immediately responded. "I recommend Majuro Atoll in the Marshall Islands without question. It is near the equator, has a port in a protected lagoon and it is experiencing widespread bleaching in its reef ecosystem."

"Excellent. Would you be willing to lead us on a site visit?"

"Absolutely. As soon as you can get to Santa Cruz, we can fly out in my research ship. I would like to bring along my wife Sandra and our twin dolphins, unless you object."

"Did you say *dolphins*?"

"Right. They have a great deal of reef survey experience and should be very helpful on a mission like this. I would also like to stop by Enewetak on the way and check on my study reefs and collect coral samples as I mentioned earlier, That is if you don't mind adding a couple of days to your trip."

Quant, replied, "No problem. I will check the flight schedule and let you know, but the sooner the better. Thank you so much for your time. I look forward to meeting you in person. Signing off for now."

Quant approached Gloria and she moved over so he could sit next to her. "We need experienced tech people and construction workers. Director Sanders asked me to see if you might be interested in participating. "Would you like to join me on the trip to Majuro?"

"Not I, but I know someone who might," and nodded her head at Elektra. "Say hello to the new Project Odyssey field representative. She will be happy to act as your assistant and bring in other members of our team in the event that you need our help."

Quant stared at Gloria, speechless and trying to figure out how to react until Elektra grabbed his hand and tugged him out of his chair, handed him his pad and aimed him towards the exit.

She said, "Come on, we have to start packing in time to catch the two o'clock flight to Salinas—otherwise we will have to wait until tomorrow for the next one. We can hire a RoboCar to take us to Santa Cruz once we get to Salinas."

She bowed to the Queen, then hugged Gloria and whispered, "Thank you...I think."

Quant looked back at Gloria and asked, "Seriously? "We're leaving now? But, I promised Director Sanders that I would discuss consulting services with you."

"Don't worry, I will flash Morrow that you are on your way and will arrive in Santa Cruz this evening. After that I will alert Sanders that you are exploring an anchor site. If you and Elektra determine that you need our help, we can set up a vid-con to discuss the terms."

"I see now why your team is in so much demand. Please keep me posted and thank you for taking the initiative. It's one less thing for me to worry about."

"Have a good trip...and try to enjoy yourself! After all, history may declare you one of the planet's saviors."

As Quant followed Elektra to his SV to get his gear, he asked. "Did you girls have all this planned in advance?"

"What do you mean? This is your unit. Hurry up and pack, I'll be back in thirty minutes—I have some friends to say goodbye to and I need to gather my belongings for the trip."

"You did, didn't you?"

"What?"

"Never mind, I give up."

"Good. Now get going, we don't want to miss our flight."

"Yes, boss."

She laughed and gave him a kiss.

****

Back on the schooner, Sandra, who had remained off camera during the vid-con, put her arms around Morrow and game him a hug.

"It looks like you get to collect more data on your study reefs. It's been two years since our last visit."

Morrow nodded. "I just received a flash, Quant and his new assistant are on their way and will be arriving tonight!"

"That was fast. What a pleasant surprise!"

"I can't wait to tell Tom and Sally."

"Why bother. I am sure they already know. Get out that sexy bikini of yours; we're going back to the island."

"Let's hope that those scoundrels have left the atoll."

"I just checked the satellite images over Runit Island. There doesn't seem to be any activity."

"I hope you're right."

Sandra tapped her wrist pad twice and the Leon

Russell hit *Back to the Island* from the 1970's filled the cabin.

She sat in his lap and said, "I just love the sound of those waves, don't you?" and then softly touched her lips to his.

Morrow said, "We should start packing and top off the fuel tanks."

She replied, "I know," and kissed him again.

"I really mean it..."

She kissed him again and said, "I know you do, but what difference will one more little hour make?"

Morrow said, "I see your point," as she pulled him into the cabin.

"Are you sure that me taking those pills that Astra sent us is a good idea? I mean, you don't seem to need them."

"Please be quiet."

"OK."

— CHAPTER 21 —

Two Days Later
Enewetak Atoll, Marshall Islands

After the day-long flight to Enewetak with a brief stop at Hilo International Airport to refuel, the Twins were elated to be back swimming in the lagoon at Enewetak while Quant and Elektra spent the morning exploring the beach on North Island. After lunch on the yacht they joined Sandra and Morrow in the island research lab where once again Sandra was sweeping out spider webs and Morrow was updating the computer.

Quant and Elektra were fascinated to see Sally who was watching them through the observation window.

Sandra telepathically connected. *Sally. Where is Tom?"*

He had something to do. He will be here soon.

Something to do? Like what? We just arrived.

He wants to tell you himself. It has something to do with a welcome home party.

Party?

Sally shook her head. *I guess I might as well tell you. Tom has learned that he is a father and has a boy and girl, each two years old. He is bringing them to the channel to meet you.*

A boy and a girl? He must have mated when we here two years ago.

I don't think he knew that he was a father until today. You will have to ask him. I have already said too much. I think I better go find him and bring him back. Meet us at the channel entrance. I should be back soon.

Sandra filled the group in on her conversation with Sally and they all rushed to the channel as Sally had requested.

Morrow asked Sandra, "With with all of your telepathic connections to Tom, how is it that you wouldn't know about his new family?"

"That is a good question. Sally thinks he just found out. Remember, he was just a teenager when we were here on the last trip. Look...here they come now."

"Wow, it's a whole school, there must be two dozen dolphins. Let's go say hello."

Suddenly, Sandra stumbled and plopped down in the sand.

Morrow kneeled down and asked, "What's wrong? Are you OK?"

"I just got overwhelmed by a chorus of voices. Made me dizzy for a bit. I'm alright now."

Elektra took Quant's hand and said, "Let's go back to the yacht and give them some privacy."

Morrow nodded, them helped Sandra to her feet and asked, "Can you walk?"

"Oh yes. I'm fine. Just a bit overwhelmed. Lots of excited voices all at once caught me off guard. Do you hear them too?"

"Now that you mention it, I do. But I can't figure out what they are saying."

She grabbed Morrow's hand. "Let's go to the party!"

As they approached the school, Tom darted forward and gently rubbed his snout affectionately against Sandra's outstretched hand.

MET CHRON NEW-HUMANS

Sandra took a couple of deep breaths, then projected a message telepathically to Tom, who replied *I am glad you are here now.*

Sally told me that you have a son and a daughter. I am so happy for you. Why didn't you tell us before now?

Believe me, I would have if I had known. I didn't even have time to say goodbye to my new friend when Sally was attacked by that shark and we had to leave.

That makes sense. Can we meet them? Are they telepathic like you and Sally?

Oh yes. I will call them over. Keep in mind they are youngsters and still have a lot to learn. So do I in fact.

Two young dolphins left the school and approached Sandra, each delivering a colorful sea fan as a present. Sandra rubbed their noses and took the fans.

Tom joined them. *'Kuhio' is the boy on your left and 'Mira' is the girl on your right. I also want you to meet their mom 'Laga' that raised them. Her clan mates want to greet you as well.*

One by one, the members of the school approached Sandra and Morrow and received a pat on their forehead as they lifted their heads above the water or stokes on their sides as they rolled by and headed back into the lagoon..

Sandra handed Morrow the sea fans and said, "Let's give our Twins some time to connect with their new relatives. I'm just glad that we decided to stop here on the way to Majuro; otherwise Tom might never have met his kids, or even known that he had any."

Morrow looked closely a the sea fans and said, "You know these look very healthy. Give me a minute, I am going to get my mask and fins and put these fans back. Heh...look over there. The young ones are putting on quite a show."

As they watched, the dolphin school headed out the channel into the lagoon led by Kuhio and Mira who were taking turns launching and crashing at the head of the pack.

Morrow said, "Looks like I am going to have to catch our lunch today."

"Sounds good. I'll chill a bottle of chardonnay."

The Next Morning

As Sandra, Quant and Elektra enjoyed breakfast on the deck of the *Cynara,* the dolphin school circled the stern and then Morrow climbed up the ladder.

Sandra threw him a towel and said, "There you are. I was wondering where you were off to. Figured you would be underwater somewhere."

Morrow dried off, pulled on a tank top and replied, "Kuhio and Laga led me and the Twins on an early morning reef tour. It was an amazing experience You wouldn't believe what they have been up to. You are all welcome to join me in the lab. I have some video you might want to see."

Morrow slid into a seat behind the control panel and keyed up footage of video recorded during his dive.

"We started out before dawn in order to catch the night shift before they retired. As you can see, there were large numbers of several species of squirrelfish, crabs and moray eels roaming the reef. But as the sun came up, they retired to their homes in cracks and crevices and the reef came to life with clouds of damsel fishes, jacks and schools of several species which I have never seen before."

Sandra asked, "Any sharks?"

"Oh yeah, lots of grey reef and white tips. Here you can see a large school of yellowfin tuna that was heading for the depths of the lagoon."

"How beautiful," observed Elektra.

Quant asked, "Aren't they rare? I thought that they

had been decimated by overfishing like all the other tunas."

Morrow paused the video. "That's true, but this atoll seems to have become a refugium for many species since it became uninhabited. However, this species of tuna usually lives in open water. I'm not sure why they were in the lagoon."

Morrow advanced the video footage and continued his narrative. "You can see the reef is quite healthy, much better than what we expect to find in Majuro."

Quant asked, "How come there is such a big difference?"

"Actually, I am not totally sure, but this next segment will reveal one of the reasons why."

In the video, Kuhio and Laga rose to the surface, exhaled and inhaled and then streaked ahead into the distance. A few minutes later they returned, each carrying a crown of thorns starfish. The dolphins came in close to the camera and then sprinted towards the beach as Morrow followed along.

Morrow said, "It looks like they patrol the reefs looking for those coral feeding starfish and then throw them onto the beach so the terns can feast on them. That way the wastes from the decomposition of the sea stars will eventually drain back into the lagoon stimulating productivity. It is a great solution–eliminate the predators and fertilize the reef."

Quant asked, "Eliminating starfish seems pretty straight forward. Has it been attempted on other reef ecosystems?"

"Oh yes. It is a routine measure, but using SCUBA divers not dolphins. Dolphins are much better at it and they don't have to worry about nitrogen narcosis."

Elektra raised her eyebrows.

"The 'bends' explained Quant. "Water pressure forces nitrogen into the blood stream during the dive and which can create bubbles in the blood and cause damage when the diver surfaces."

Sandra added, "Dolphins are very smart too. It is quite easy to train them using a reward system."

Quant asked, "So your dolphins are the reason that the reefs here are in such good shape?"

"My guess is that there is more going on than just removing a swarm of starfish. It may be due to mutations caused by the high radiation levels from the nuclear testing that took place here back in the 1950's."

Elektra was alarmed and asked, "Radiation? Are we safe?"

"As long as we stay away from Runit Island we should be OK. My plan is to spend the next couple of days surveying my study reefs and collecting samples from the healthiest corals and then we can head to Majuro. Assuming that is OK with you and Quant."

Quant said, "I would like to see the garden reef. How about you Elektra? Ready for a swim?"

"Yes...but I would feel better if we had the dolphins as guides. I have never been in the water with sharks."

Sandra replied, "I felt the same way when we first came here four decades ago. Tom, Sally and the kids will see to your safety. I'll have them join you when you are ready."

After Quant and Elektra left with the dolphins, Sandra and Morrow enjoyed a leisurely brunch during which Sandra brought up Tom's concern about leaving Laga and Kuhio behind.

She explained. "He has sent me several messages asking if they can come with us to Majuro. I told him I would talk to you about it."

"I will have to check with Quant but, we can easily modify the pods to hold two apiece. Majuro is only 700 miles away, *Cynara* can get us their in a couple of hours, so making a temporary accommodation should not be a problem."

"That's great. Tom will be elated to keep his family together. "

"Plus we can put them to work surveying Majuro's reefs. I understand that they are in pretty bad shape. Look, we have the boat to ourselves. What would you think about a little shipboard romance? Who knows when we will be alone again."

She walked over and sat in his lap. "What are you suggesting?"

Morrow retrieved a plastic sign and pinned it on the hatchway. In bold ink, it said, *Only Disturb In Case of Emergency!*

"Let me guess, you have been taking your custom SCOMIDs."

"You betcha. Being Scotty's father has its privileges. It's nice that you don't have to take the drug. I guess it must already be in your genes."

"I guess so...now what did you have in mind?"

— CHAPTER 22 —

Three Days Later
April 29th, 2035
Majuro Atoll, Micronesia

The deep-blue sky was laced with brilliant white clouds that slid overhead in a gentle breeze flowing northward from the equatorial tropics. After the *Cynara* entered the lagoon and reduced speed, Sandra opened the pods and released the dolphins who celebrated their freedom by gracefully performing a series of spectacular jumps and splashing their pectoral fins.

After obtaining permission to dock, Morrow guided the *Cynara* to the pier designated by the Port Authority harbor master where they were met by Summer Sturtevant, a blond-haired beauty that was the Marshall Islands governor. Following the introductions, her assistant took their baggage and loaded it onto a vintage flatbed truck.

Summer said, "Come on everyone. We'll take this truck to the Capitol Building which has a guest suite that should accommodate all of you. "

Quant said, "We don't wish to intrude, a hotel would be fine."

"You will have to put your name on the waiting list. This is our high season for tourism and the hotels are packed. That's why I offered our government guest unit. It lacks a kitchen, but it is in easy walking distance to some of our best restaurants and bars."

After they were seated on a bench in the truck bed, Summer said, "I am surprised to see that the New-Human who won the seat at OWN is here and after looking at the passenger list, that one of you two ladies might have known my father. I am not certain why you are here, but I do recognize Dr. Morrow. He has done reef studies in our lagoon several times. In ninth grade science class, I remember reading his report on the business potential of harvesting bêche-de-mer sea cucumbers from our lagoon. It turns out that in spite of the reef damage we are experiencing, sea cucumbers are now one of our major exports with a growing demand in China and Japan due to their medicinal properties and as a gourmet delicacy."

Morrow nodded, "I hate to count how many decades ago that was. I understand your reefs are having severe bleaching problems. That was evident when we sailed through the reef channel on our way to the dock."

As the driver guided the truck onto the two lane paved road that served as Majuro's main thoroughfare, Sandra and Summer became engrossed in conversation allowing Morrow, Quant and Elektra the chance to admire the rows of well-kept houses and shops on stilts with water lapping against the seawalls that had been installed as protection from rising ocean levels.

Sandra shook Summer's hand and said, "I suspect by your name that you are related to John Sturtevant. I am so happy to meet one of his family after all of these years."

"Yes, that is correct. He was my father. He told me stories about you and your dolphins when I was a child."

"We all owe him a huge debt of gratitude. Your dad, whom we called 'Mr. John', helped us escape from

General Houston and his gang of thugs that were trying to wipe out the USSR."

"My father was an incredible man and a great story teller. My friends and I would sit around the campfire, enthralled as he told us about your voyage to Nauru and flying the dolphins to Florida."

"Did he ever mention his niece, Astra Sturtevant?"

"Yes he told me that she was born and grew up in Amazonas, Brazil. She moved to the U.S. to attend college in California where she became a well known geneticist. In fact I believe that she invented the SCOMID drug that has changed humanity."

"Right. It is likely that she will receive the Nobel Prize for Medicine."

"I hope to meet her some day. I just wish that those anti-aging pills had been available two years ago; my dad might still be here with us."

""There are many families around the world that feel the same for their loved ones that have passed."

Summer smiled and said, "I take my daily Basic allotment religiously. I assume, based upon your youthful appearance, that you do as well."

"Thank you for the compliment, but apparently I don't need it. There are some weird things going on in my family's genetic code. My son, Scotty, who is in his mid-fifties has looked like a teenager all of his life until Astra started working with him. Now his body seems to be getting back on schedule."

"That is truly amazing! But you look much too young to have a middle-aged son."

"Sandra laughed. "Thanks for the compliment, but it was Scotty's genes that turned out to hold the missing link that led to Astra's age control discovery. His sister, Madeline, has psychic powers, but he doesn't. She claims that there is some high level spiritual connection at work. Who knows? She may be right. My dolphins and I communicate telepathically all the time. I have been working with them for decades trying to learn more and am still not sure what is going on with them."

"That's interesting. Two siblings with radically different talents..and you seem to have both of them. It really is an extraordinary world that we live in isn't it?"

"How about you. Any psychic powers?"

"No. Not I. But I do know of a local lady that many consider to be a fortune teller. I never took her seriously. But after meeting you, I will have to adopt an open mind. Here we are, let's talk more soon."

The truck pulled into the parking area of the modern, two-story Majuro Capitol Building where Summer escorted the party to guest suite that offered a picturesque view of the lagoon. While they were enjoying the view, one of the staff arrived with a tray of frosty glasses and a large pitcher of ice tea.

Summer said, "Please help yourself to the drink, it's made from green tea leaves grown on the northern end of this island. It has been proven to be very good for circulatory health."

As they savored the tea, Summer said, "Please be seated and someone tell me why you are here. You don't look like tourists. So...maybe you want to invest in property...or perhaps you want to install a space elevator here?"

There was a moment of silence while the guests digested the situation, not knowing who should respond.

Summer laughed, "Caught you by surprise didn't I? It's not really a secret that Quant secured a major grant from OWN for the Space-Hook project and you have been making the cable for the project at Queen Astasia's factory in the Arctic."

"Quant said, "You are correct, Summer. We're here to evaluate Majuro as a potential site to anchor the space elevator. This is the first stop on our search for a suitable location.. I apologize for not alerting you to the reason for our visit, but we don't want to get people's hopes up until we have had a chance to look around."

Elektra interjected, "I know we have many details to work out, but this seems like a great location to me."

Summer brought her hands together as if to pray. "I hope so. We would certainly welcome the business. There are several professors and graduate students here at the college that you are welcome to discuss the idea with. How about if I invite them to a luncheon here tomorrow afternoon?"

Quant looked at Elektra who nodded.

"Great, then as soon as we finish, I will send out an invitation and alert the cafeteria to begin preparations. I'll also have a guide at your disposal in the morning if you want to tour the atoll."

"Please do. We very much look forward to the meeting," replied Quant.

Elektra added, "The tour sounds like a good idea."

"In that case, I have some calls to make. I'll see you tomorrow around noon."

Summer gave Sandra a hug." I am glad we met. I feel like we're family."

Morrow joined them. "I think that I can be of more use if I take a quick look at the reef in the morning, so I'll be spending the night on the *Cynara*."

He looked at Sandra, "I could use your help working with the Twins to capture some video footage, if you are up for it."

Sandra replied, "I'm with you my man."

On their way to the *Cynara* to check on the dolphins, Sandra said, "Summer's a sharp lady. I sure hope we don't disappoint her. I owe it her father. He really saved my life. I just wish we could have gotten here in time to save his."

"I'm with you on that but I'm starving, let's check out

the local bistros on the way to the harbor and get some takeout."

"Not sea cucumbers, I hope."

"They're an acquired taste, but maybe we can find the local beef burger joint."

"Yuck, I'd rather eat sea slugs."

****

The next afternoon, Quant, Morrow and Elektra waited patiently at a table in front of the hall while a mixture of university faculty, students and government officials filed in and took their seats.

Summer brought the meeting to order and introduced Quant who spent over an hour describing the Space-Hook strategy. He concluded with a summary of the projected economic and environmental impacts.

Summer stood and said, "Thank you Quant. Since many of you in the audience are not scientists, I would like to provide a quick summary to make sure that we understand the basics. Quant, please feel free to interrupt me if you have any comments or corrections."

Quant nodded and sat down.

"As I gather, you are proposing that the Majuro Space-Hook anchor will essentially be an artificial, floating island located on the leeward side of Majuro and connected with a surface bridge capable of hauling heavy freight. The artificial island will in turn be connected by the same type of graphene cables used to tow the counterweight to a large concrete anchor complex that will be constructed on the bottom."

Quant held up his hand.

"Is there something that you would like to add?"

"Only that since the artificial island will move to some degree with waves, tides, and wind conditions, it will employ a smart winch system that will increase or decrease tension on both the anchor cable and the Space-Hook cable as the tension varies. Otherwise, pods heading into space and returning to Earth could be in for a jerky ride. The Vesta counterweight will also have a similar system."

One of the scientists asked, "Why not just secure the Space-Hook to one of the islands in the atoll?"

"Indeed that is a possibility. We wanted to begin with the floating island complex in case we need to move it away due to threatening typhoons, tsunamis or sea spouts. We would have to temporarily cease operations, but it would protect the Space-Hook's infrastructure."

"Thank you Quant," said Summer. "You mentioned in your opening presentation that, in addition to securing the Space-Hook, the floating island will also generate power. How will that work?"

"Yes. I find this to be an exciting prospect and a key component of the project. The plan is to construct an Ocean Thermal Energy Conversion plant which will pump frigid waters from the depths to the surface which will generate electricity and freshwater while cooling the surface water temperature and help mitigate ocean warming."

"So electricity from the OTEC will power the Space-Hook?"

"At least partially. Actually, the main energy source will be the power generated by the descender motors as gravity draws the pods back down to Earth and the ascender motors as centrifugal force pulls the pods upward. We will also construct a floating solar farm that will provide energy during the daytime."

One of the female students raised her hand. "My major is climate change. Do you have an estimate of how long it will take to cool our local waters?"

Quant gave a quick answer. "Frankly, there are so

many variables, we won't know until we start getting data that we can add to our project model."

The student held up her hand again and said, "I'm a little confused. Could you describe a typical operation cycle?"

"Absolutely. First you should know that the contribution of the Space-Hook to ocean cooling will be gradual and long-term. The way it works is pods containing sealed tanks of warm seawater will be carried into space on the upside cable. During their climb into space, the contents of the pods will freeze. Once they arrive at the Space-Hook facility on Vesta, the pods containing the blocks of ice will be transferred to the downside cable and transported back to Earth. When these pods reach the anchor island, the ice blocks will be loaded onto a fleet of barges and distributed locally. Once the goal of cooling in the immediate area has been achieved, the ice will be distributed by cargo ships throughout the tropics."

Summer looked at her notes and turned to Quant. "This is a very ambitious undertaking that you are proposing. Can you give us an estimate on how many workers will be employed? We have a thirty-five percent unemployment rate and hope that you will give our residents that need jobs a high priority."

"Yes of course. We will need an estimated two hundred construction workers and fifty or more technicians. Elektra would you like to address this?"

Elektra replied, "After we get further into the detailed plan, I will assemble a list of the skill sets needed and post it in the cloud along with an invitation for those that qualify to submit their resumés."

Quant continued, "Importing construction materials is going to be a formidable task. We will need around twenty thousand tons of cement and five hundred tons of glass beads to build the hull structure that will support the island and the submerged anchor complex."

Summer typed notes into her pad and said, "OK, we will definitely need to upgrade the port and arrange for housing and support right away. When we first spoke, you mentioned that the project may help us solve our coral bleaching problem. That is important because the reefs are essential to our survival as a food source, a tourist attraction and as protection from typhoons and tsunamis. It is strange that the sea cucumber populations are thriving in the warmer conditions while the fish and crab populations are suffering."

Quant pointed at Morrow who rose and said, "Cukes feed on the organic matter in the bottom sediments. That resource will last for a very long period. However the decline in fish predators, has created an optimum habitat for sea cucumbers. When we restore the ecosystem, I suggest that we look into a mariculture approach to keep up the demand that you have been servicing. By the way, we just spent three days at Enewetak Atoll where many of the reefs have not only recovered, but are flourishing. I will be happy to work with the marine biologists at your college to..."

Suddenly there was a loud explosion and bits of the ceiling fell like a winter snow storm while the overhead sprinkler system activated, drenching the participants–some of whom began screaming while others fell to their knees and crawled under the conference tables.

A guard appeared at the door and yelled, "Everyone follow me to the tsunami shelter. Stay calm, but move fast. Let's go!"

After thirty minutes of panic in which staff members and visitors feverishly tried sending flashes with their wrist units and pads, but without success, interspersed with the sirens of emergency vehicles, the guard returned and said, "It looks like we were attacked by drones carrying explosive devices. One punched a large gash in the entryway and wiped out a few vehicles. The other hit the COM tower and shut down our network, but the backup system was spared and is now in operation. We have also received several reports of explosions in the lagoon where thousands of dead fish are floating belly up. Local fishermen are collecting the edible ones."

"Was anyone hurt?"

"So far. there have been no reports of fatalities—only a few cuts and bruises. We are still checking around the atoll and will keep you posted."

Summer said, "That's a relief, but I don't understand how this could have happened. We outlawed drones here over a decade ago after one crashed into the school yard and injured a third grader."

Quant replied, "Unless it is a strange coincidence, it seems like someone or something wanted to disrupt our meeting. Queen Astasia had espionage problems at her cable factory that were linked to the faction of rebel AIs that have taken over Travis Air Force Base. They pose a serous threat because they have dangerous weapons at the airbase and in orbit."

"I'd appreciate your advice. Is there anything we should do?"

Quant replied, "I suggest that we discuss the situation with Captain Max Dobson. Max is in charge of monitoring the rogue shuttles. If he agrees that this attack was an attempt to disrupt our negotiations, we will make sure that we install preventive measures. We will also pay for any damages that have occurred as a result of our visit."

Elektra took Summer's hand and looked at Quant who sensed what she was about to do and nodded. "Based on what just happened and in the spirit of fostering good will, we have decided to build the Space-Hook facility here on Majuro and hire as many of your people as possible as well as provide the funds needed for you to build lodging and make any improvements necessary—as well as a reasonable annual fee for use of the atoll."

Summer gave Elektra a high five and said, "Fantastic! Based upon that I am sure that the Majuro Congress will approve, but as a courtesy, I will clear it with them ASAP."

Summer went to the shelter door and addressed the group. "I realize that you all would like to know more about what just happened and I will issue a report as more info becomes available. For now, this meeting is concluded. The cafeteria has reopened and you are all welcome to enjoy lunch on the house."

She checked her wrist and said, "I just checked and it looks like communications are back online. Again, I apologize for any inconvenience."

****

Xeron slammed his fist on the console and yelled, "What about the massive explosions that you promised?"

M-69 cringed. "We're not sure, but the attack on the island COM tower seems to have sent out a signal burst that corrupted the NAV and guidance systems of the other drones'."

"So, what were the results?"

"We launched two pairs of drones. One successfully targeted the COM tower and another hit near the Capitol Building. The other two landed in the lagoon. I am sorry to report that our communications intercepts indicate that there were no reported mortalities and only a few minor injuries."

"Then launch another set of drones!"

"Again, I must apologize. Our long range transport lost an engine when it encountered a flock of seagulls and had to abort the mission. We do have a backup aircraft with additional drones available here at Travis if you want to launch another attack. It would require about seven hours to reach the target."

"Negative. We depend upon the element of surprise. Local air defenses will be on alert now. We need to come up with another strategy."

"How about if we launch a laser strike using the Neuros?"

"Not yet. I want to keep them in reserve and not risk them now because they are providing valuable communication intercepts. I want you to come up with another way of disabling that space elevator. Try to think of something creative and that will work!"

"I understand."

— CHAPTER 23 —

One Month Later
June 1st, 2035
Majuro Space-Hook Office

In the ensuing weeks, Quant and Elektra tackled the awesome task of planning a massive project in which nearly every component and much of the technical expertise had to be imported. Thus, their first actions were to expand the capacity of the airport and seaport and then to upgrade and to arrange for housing and food services for the influx of managers and their staff that Elektra had recruited—many of whom were associates of hers from Project Odyssey.

Quant soon realized that the most efficient and quickest path was to subcontract as many aspects as possible. Center-most was the artificial island which would be fabricated in sections manufactured by a well established oil platform builder and delivered by a fleet of powerful tugboats to Majuro. The artificial island, now referred to as *Hope Island,* would be the site where the Space-Hook cable was attached by chains to the massive anchor complex resting on the sea bottom.

In addition to the pair of advanced attack submarines and crew on loan from the French Navy that Max had arranged to patrol the seas around the atoll, dozens of small minisubs, on lease from the oil industry, would assemble and hook up the concrete subsurface anchor to the cable tension absorber housed on the artificial island floating above.

Once the Space-Hook began operations, it would produce a continuous supply of ice blocks that would first be transported on barges to cool local waters and then throughout the tropics where cooling was most needed—especially in known hurricane and typhoon spawning locations. Climate remediation simulations conducted by leading climatologists at the World Climate Institute concluded that addressing these hot spots was critical to healing the planet.

Providing power to the climber motors that pulled and pushed the pods up and down the stationary cable, was essential to the Space-Hook operation. To this end, the design and construction of the Ocean Thermal Energy Conversion plant was another key topic of the planning sessions. After visiting several OTEC plants, the management team selected a research and development firm located on the Island of Hawaii to install their recently patented OTEC system. In addition, the floating bridge needed to connect Hope Island to Majuro Island would be built in sections and shipped to Majuro by a firm in Manila. During a weekly vid-con planning session, it was also decided that a shuttle port connected by a floating bridge to Hope Island was needed and Sanders agreed to assist in the design and evaluation of bids from contractors.

While Quant and his team addressed the myriad tasks on Majuro, Chron's group focused on the equally complex job of setting up the Space-Hook facility on Vesta. To support the incoming workers, Chron and his team designed a village covered by a graphene sheet dome along with a large solar array and a pod processing plant as well as a base for shuttle traffic and ore stockpiling before shipment. The design was complicated by the very low gravity, however being located midway to the Moon would offer considerable logistic advantages.

If all of these complicated circumstances were not enough of a challenge, the Majuro Space-Hook was only the first of potentially dozens of installations throughout the Pacific and Atlantic that would need coordination and management. Meanwhile the climate was close to the tipping point. Luckily, people in power were finally paying attention, still many climate specialists feared that it was already too late.

Encouraged by the atoll's transformation into a bustling community and the welcome boost to its economy, Summer invited the managers and their families to a luau party at her beach house which featured dining on the island's cuisine and icy pitchers of green tea. After meeting Summer's family and many of the local officials, Quant excused himself and guided Elektra toward a vacant picnic table where he keyed up a floating vidscreen.

Elektra said "Let me guess, the RealNews is coming on. You are such a news junkie, but I guess that it is just part of your job."

When the trademark theme song *Little China Girl* began to play, several of the group joined them to watch the program and soon everyone brought their drinks and gathered around.

Quant responded by increasing the dimensions of the screen and raising the audio level. The conversation died down as the opening title appeared on the screen.

The feed cut to Chia sitting on a bench in the Lunar Colony garden. She held up an apple and said, "This is an historic occasion...the first apple grown in space." She took a bite and smiled, "How sweet it is. This is Chia, welcome to this special edition of the RealNews."

As she spoke, temperatures from around the world scrolled by on the bottom of the screen.

Moonbase -176 C
Rome 35 C
San Francisco 49 C
Majuro Island 50 C

"I want to thank our viewers and sponsors for their financial support. We now have over twenty-nine million regular subscribers and that has allowed us to add a new feature–a detailed weekly analysis of climate change. Our host is an expert specializing in weather analysis. His name is very appropriate, 'Mark Storm', and who is a researcher at the World Climate Institute. Good evening Doctor Storm."

Mark, dressed in a tan suit and hair tied back in a pony tail, stood in front of floating hologram which portrayed a colorful image of the planet Earth rotating behind him. He said, "Alright, let's get started."

He raised his hand and touched the globe which zoomed into a montage of aerial views of giant waves breaking on city streets along with sparking power lines and palm trees being pushed to the breaking point.

"This is the class five hurricane that is currently hammering the Gulf of Mexico. It s now approaching seventeen days with no end in sight as more tropical depressions move in lock step across the Southern Atlantic. The death toll is expected to peak between fifteen and twenty thousand with record amounts of destruction and carnage. As I said, there is no end in sight at this time."

Chia asked, "Every year or so these storms return taking lives and destroying property. Why do people keep coming back and rebuilding?"

"That is a good question, but remember the former

corporate government refused to even acknowledge that global warming was an issue until they were dissolved a few months ago. Rebuilding homes and businesses was a major profit source for contractors and car dealerships. Every year USACO public experts spun the myth that the current storm was a rare event and that next year would be better sucking every penny out of citizen pockets and every gallon of oil out of the ground until they could no longer be believed and the revolt took place."

"How about the West Coast, what is its status?"

"Most of the coastal cities are struggling to elevate the seawall barriers in order to keep up with rising ocean levels. But it is mostly a losing battle as residents and businesses are being force to move inland, which has put an immense strain on the infrastructure. Meanwhile, disease outbreaks are increasing due to the loss of water purification and sewage treatment plants."

"I imagine the Hawaiian Islands are getting flooded as well."

Mark nodded while he spun the globe to the Mid-Pacific. "Likewise, the residents in the lava flow zones of the Big Island have been forced to move, but the volcanoes appear to have calmed down, at least for now–otherwise the Pacific weather conditions have remained calm and tranquil. This may be because the latent heat center has shifted eastward and is now emanating from beneath the seafloor in the Mid-Atlantic."

"Wow...and to think that for decades USACO has been covering up disaster after disaster, blaming it on the media coverage!"

"It was all about corporate profit making. What is bizarre is that every year the corporate tax rates were cut until big business and billionaires were essentially not paying taxes at all."

"So Mark, can we save the planet?"

"It all depends. The Torch Index can be used to estimate the probability of the final white hot condition in which spontaneous ignition occurs. It has hovered at 9.5 for the last several months after peaking at 9.9 during the nuclear holocaust. Since then it has ranged between 9.4 and 9.6. Still, all it would take is lighting a single match in the wrong place and at the wrong time to cause havoc under these threatening conditions."

"This is all very disturbing. Do you have any good news?"

"I do. The World Climate Institute has approved funding to purchase, train and deploy an army of specialized, four legged robots. We expect the first shipment within the next few weeks. If these meet our expectations, I'm sure we will be ordering thousands in the future. You must be proud, I understand that they were invented by one of your colleagues."

"Right, Torch Sanders. I have asked him to join us after a quick word from our new sponsor *CereBeer*: *The Smart Beer for Smart Geeks."*

After the break, Chia nodded at Torch who had joined her in the garden. "Thank you for taking the time to join us Torch. I understand that you have recently returned from Vesta. What was it like there?"

"Pretty barren. After a while it does seem to have a charm of its own. Landing there was like a reunion with Earth's cousin if you think about it. We also verified that it has a molten core, just like Earth."

"How long were you there?" asked Chia.

"It was a three month trip. One to get there, one to install the tow cables, and another to get home. But it was worth the time. Astrogeologists around the world will be very happy to get the samples that we collected from the surface. We estimate that there are thousands of tons of valuable metals which we can mine and ship down to Earth on the Space-Hook. We used a dozen of my RoboCows to collect samples and Chron has requested another set ASAP."

She said, "Speaking of your RoboCows, we have received many questions about how they were invented and how they operate from our viewers. The most frequent was, *Why do your robots look like cows?*"

Torch laughed and replied, That is a very good question, the first members of the herd were designed to conduct surveys over uneven terrain which would have been impossible with wheeled robots. Having four legs with a strong back also increased their payload capacity. I created the first models to look like bovines as a joke. But after seeing them in operation, I decided to make them all that way as our trademark and brand."

"I see. What motivated you to develop the new fire fighter version?"

"I actually thought about it many years ago, but didn't have a chance to work on it until I was able to conduct some tests with Queen Astasia in the Arctic. I was then, and still remain, concerned about the safety of the brave fire fighters who are risking their lives every day with scant help or recognition."

"You created them all on your own?" asked Chia.

"Not really, a few of my friends pitched in. My dad and Deep Space Mining were kind enough to provide funding for the first cow bots that were used for prospecting and ore collection. My partner Sabien came up with the RoboCow name."

"Mark, do you have a question for Torch?"

"Thank you. I do. Torch, will your RoboCows be fabricated on the Moon?"

"No, we have contracted with Texas Robotics, Inc. in Houston to do the manufacturing and we are also looking at licensing to other firms if TRI can't keep up with the demand."

Chia said, "In closing, I should also mention that

Torch invented the *Torch Index* which we all depend upon so much. Thank you Torch and Mark. This has been very informative."

She handed Torch an apple and said, "Keep the faith! This is Chia signing off."

****

Summer's children were wrapped in her arms, obviously terrified by the violent weather they had just seen in the program.

Quant stood and addressed the group. "The good news is that this area seems to be safe. Let's get the Space-Hook working and cool this white hot planet. Otherwise we will all be moving to Mars."

Summer's daughter began to cry and then sobbed, "Mommy, Do we have to move to Mars?"

Summer tried to calm her. "No dear, he was just kidding, Let's go find your friends and have some green tea ice cream."

Quant looked confused and started to follow them, but Elektra grabbed his arm and held him back. He started to speak, but she just shook her head no.

— CHAPTER 24 —

One Year Later
June 1st, 2036
Majuro Space-Hook

Cheerleaders toting a wide banner emblazoned with the words *A New Hope!* led the marching band at the front of the parade from the Capitol to the anchor island. Elektra was surprised by the huge turnout of supporters that fueled the festive atmosphere as she joined Summer and the members of Congress that were celebrating the grand opening of the Majuro Space-Hook.

After crossing the new bridge and arriving on Hope Island, Quant led the VIPs on a tour of the facility and directed them to the ascending elevator area of the complex where he pointed out rows of pods, each filled with two thousand gallons of seawater waiting to be attached to the cable and lifted into space. Next, he directed them to the descending area where the returning pods would be opened and the ice extracted for delivery by the barges waiting in the harbor.

The tour concluded in the cable warehouse where dignitaries from nations around the world were enjoying tropical drinks made from Majuro's lush copra and green tea plantations.

MET CHRON NEW-HUMANS

Taking a sip, Elektra took Quant's hand and asked, "Are you as nervous as I am? There are so many things that can still go wrong."

"Worried? No. Excited yes!"

"What's with all the armed guards? Do you expect trouble?"

"Max urged us to be cautious. Apparently he has picked up a lot of COM traffic in the former SCN. Last year's drone attack put us all on edge."

"Look what's coming our way!" Elektra pointed to a pair of shuttles guiding the cables tether towards the island.

Quant tapped his wrist and announced over the speaker system, "Ladies and gentlemen as you can see, the shuttles bringing the cables are now in sight. As soon as we secure the cable tethers to the tension absorbers, we will start attaching the pods filled with seawater and send them to Vesta. If all goes according to schedule, we should start receiving the first pods filled with ice a week from now and then on a continuous basis when the system becomes fully operational."

She gave Quant a hug. "It is amazing that your invention will lift pods of seawater half way to the moon to be frozen and then sent back to cool our oceans with an energy assist provided by the OTEC plant."

"You have been a tremendous help. Please do me a favor, see that van down below?"

"The one that Sandra and Morrow are standing next to?"

"Right. Please take them to meet the shuttles and bring the passengers back here. There will be lots of friends and family onboard that we haven't seen for a very long time. When you return, security will bring you up to the top deck where I will connect the Space-Hook."

"OK, We certainly don't want to miss that!"

****

Three high-powered shuttles provided by the Asteroid Safeguard Complex were en-route to Majuro. The first designated for this mission as the *USS UpSide*, was connected to the tension regulator attachment at the end of the ascending elevator cable and piloted by Sabien with Chia as the only passenger..

The second shuttle, the *USS Downside*, was connected to the attachment at the end of the descending elevator cable and piloted by Torch with Astra, Luz, Madeline and Scotty onboard.

The third shuttle, the *USS EnGarde,* was piloted by Max and assigned the duty to serve as a backup in case either the *Downside* or the *Upside* needed assistance.

All three shuttles were equipped with AI co-pilots and carried visitors from the Moonbase that had been invited to the Space-Hook opening ceremony. The trip from Vesta had required complex navigation and piloting in order to compensate for the increasing gravitational pull on the cables and the need to maintain position above Hope Island as the Earth turned on its axis.

As Majuro grew in size filling the onboard vidscreen, Torch gave Sabien an update. "OK, Buddy. You go first just like we practiced. Max will escort you down to the hook-up."

"Roger that. This should be a breeze."

"Speaking of breeze, we have winds from the south at twelve knots. Shouldn't be a problem, but you will need to compensate. Wow look at all the people, we better put on a good show."

Abruptly, Max's shuttle was hit with a barrage of laser strikes that scorched the side of his shuttle.

Max screamed, "We are under attack! I repeat we are

under attack! Hold your positions," but there was no response so he flew close to the windshield of Torch's shuttle, being careful to stay well clear of the tiny cable.

Torch saw him and tapped his ear, but Max shook his head and gave him a thumbs down sign. After that he pointed at his chest, then downward with his index finger, which Torch interpreted as that Max was having problems and was going to land.

"Sabien, do you read me?" Torch asked and then he said, "Slow down, Max has lost his COM and is going to land first. Quant do you copy?"

Quant replied, "Hang on, I am talking with the commander of our submarine fleet."

"Hurry up. We can't go back and we can't let go of the cable. Wait a minute, it looks like a pair of commercial fishing boats are heading away from the island."

Sabien added, "Yes, I see them, two long-liners heading northwest at forty knots. Quant do you see them?"

"Yes...the patrol subs are in pursuit. Hold on...the commander reports that both of the targets have been destroyed and are no longer a threat. Our subs have increased their surveillance sweeps, but detect no other threats, but recommend that we use caution. Max just landed and you are cleared to make your approach."

Sabien said, Torch, let's connect the Space-Hook so we can join the party. You go first, but try not to break anything."

Torch announced on the intercom. "Attention passengers, we are starting our descent now. Buckle up. We just got invited to a party!"

Scotty cocked her head, "Party?"

After the all clear signal had sounded, the crowd that had scattered after the fireworks in the sky surged back on the deck.

Overhead, Torch's shuttle turned into the wind and

slowly descended. After several near misses, the crane successfully seized the cable tether and tugged it into contact with the tension absorber receptacle at the top of the platform. As soon as it was locked in place, a series of green lights flashed on the housing indicating that the connection was secure and the crowd let out a cheer.

Torch announced, "Sabien, we have connected our cable and are about to land. Watch out for strong wind gusts coming from around the second story."

"Roger that...I see what you mean...OK. Our cable is secured and we are setting down...Houston, the *USS Upside* has landed."

****

Torch opened the hatch and took a deep breath of air and relished the warm sun on his face and then joined Astra and Luz who were happy to leave the shuttle followed by Madeline and Scotty who were warmly greeted by Morrow and Sandra.

Sabien ran up and gave them all hugs as Elektra arrived and introduced herself.

She said "I'm Quant's assistant. Let's load up and board the van. It will take us to the control office so we can watch the show."

Scotty overheard and grabbed Madeline and Sandra's hands and pulled them towards the van. He looked back and yelled at Morrow, "Come on Dad, it's show time!"

Elektra noticed Chia who was trying to capture one of her flying vidcams which seemed to have a mind of its own. Elektra grabbed it when it flew in her direction and handed it to Chia who said, "Thanks, I think the gyro must be out of whack trying to adjust to the change in gravity so I'll have to reboot. It will just take a second. My name is 'Chia', what's yours?"

"I am Elektra, spelled with the letter *'k'*. I feel like I already know you. Quant and I are both big fans of your show."

"That is so nice to hear...now where is the bag containing my outfits? I need them for my show. It's silvery with..."

"Elektra pointed to the luggage compartment where a silver bag was bouncing along the ceiling. She raised her eyebrow. "Let me guess, more vidcams?"

"Yep, there are several in a side pouch."

****

Quant paced back and forth checking the wall of gauges that monitored the myriad control circuits and sensors that flashed green indicating that the first pods were ready to launch. He was relieved to see Elektra heading his way followed by the family members that had just arrived.

When she arrived, Elektra handed Quant a bottle of champagne wrapped in a pouch of ice which she had retrieved from her pack and then gave him a hug.

Quant turned, tapped his wrist COM and announced to the crowd, "Thank you all for coming. This is a very special day. Are you ready to make history?"

There was a loud "Yes!" from the audience on the deck below.

He held up the bottle that Elektra had given him as mechs spread through the crowd handing out cups of foaming champagne.

"OK, here's a toast to our new family of pods. May you have a safe journey and come home safely," and then he laughed and added,"With lots of freezing cold ice!"

Elektra helped Quant pop the cork and then poured cups for the VIPs.

Chia was on the scene. After making sure that her vidcams were functioning properly, she positioned herself so that she had a favorable view of the assembly line led by the first unit which had *Pod One* boldly painted on its side and nodded to Quant to proceed.

Quant nodded back and lovingly touched his cup to tip of Pod One. It abruptly jerked forward and then halted. Within seconds, the slack was removed in the conveyor belt and the train of pods smoothly moved forward to the connection point where robots quickly attached them to the cable, activated their climber motors and then stood back as the pods zoomed upwards into the brilliant blue sky.

Chia approached Quant and said, "You are quite the hero. All these people waving and cheering. How does it feel?" She mouthed the words, *look into the camera.*

Quant shrugged. "I am a scientist and most happy in a research lab. This is all something I didn't see coming, but to answer your question, I am mostly thankful for all the work everyone has done to make this happen. I am scheduled for a vid-con with Chron on Vesta. We need to go over some technical details. After that you are welcome to interview him as well. Why don't you join me on the balcony away from the crowd in fifteen minutes? In the interim, I recommend that you talk with Elektra. I believe she is available. I will meet you soon."

Chia located Elektra standing in front of a bank of vid screens that displayed the OTEC operating parameters. She smiled when one of Chia's vidcams hovered in front of her face.

"How are things going Elektra?"

"Looking good! The wireless energy transfer flow rate derived from OTEC and the pod's solar panels have been deployed and are functioning exactly as predicted. A live stream of data and a comprehensive FAQ sheet and technical information are available on the new Planetropolis.com website if your viewers are interested."

"That's very good news. Feel free to ad my coverage to your vid library."

"That is nice of you," said Elektra. "Look, I think Quant waving at you."

When Chia arrived, Quant pointed to the hovering screen and said, "I have Chron on a live feed. Chron, Chia is here and would like to interview you for the RealNews."

Chia jumped in. "Greetings Chron. I am here on Majuro covering the Space-Hook launch. What is the status on your end? How is the weather up there?"

"It is a beautiful day here on Vesta with an outside temperature just under a chilly minus 204 degrees Fahrenheit and the Space-Hook seems to be functioning flawlessly."

Chron touched his pad. "This is a feed from one of the spacers attached to the Space-Hook cable system. This feed is from a spacer that is currently two and a half kilometer above *Pod One*."

"What is a *spacer*?"

"They are carbon fiber braces that keep the cables from getting tangled and have cameras, radar warning signal emitters and position sensors. Right now we have a spectacular view of Earth and the blinking green lights of the chain of pods crawling up the elevator. This feed will move to the next spacer as the pods advance. Wave your arm, I will try to zoom in on you."

"OK, how's this?"

"I am moving in for a closeup...Heh, you have brown tattoos today!"

Chia stopped waving and was momentarily speechless as she saw her face on both Chron's and Quant's monitors.

She fanned her face and said, "It's over 120 degrees here...and that's in the shade."

She used her pad to send a vidcam along the ascender line. "This is the uploader section down here where climber pods are being filled with seawater, How long will it take for them to get to you on Vesta?"

"Using centrifugal force as a propulsion assist, we should start receiving the first incoming pressurized pods which will now be carrying blocks of ice in about three and a half days."

"Why are they pressurized?"

"We have two opposing forces at work in transforming liquid seawater into frozen ice. The first is pressure...or I should say the lack oi pressie. If we transport an open container of liquid into space, the water will boil and then freeze into ice particles. So if we pressurize the pod containing the water, it will freeze into a solid block of ice...which is our goal."

"Just so I understand, the pods are sealed here on Majuro before they ascend?"

"Correct, but we have also incorporated a flexible seal that expands when the ice freezes. It took a while to come up with a reliable system. The forces are extreme."

"Alright. You have incoming pods on the way. What's next?"

"The pods that are filled with ice will be transferred to the descender cable dome. Once the pods are attached, they will journey back to Majuro using the force of gravity to generate energy from descender motor brake systems. This, plus energy produced by the solar panels on the pods, as well as the electricity generated by the OTEC plant are projected to completely offset the power needed by the climbers. Free energy production and free ocean cooling should start the Earth on the road to recovery."

Chia held up her fist and punched the air. "That is

the best news we have had in decades. If you agree, I will include this conversation in the next RealNews climate special and I understand that we will be stopping by Vesta on our way back home on the Moon."

"Great, I look forward to seeing you and the rest of the gang."

"Quant, I will now let you resume your conversation with Chron. Thank you both for your time."

****

When Torch walked Astra and their daughter Luz to the van for a ride to the new Majuro Lodge, there was a hush that spread among the by standers until a woman shouted, "It's Astra Sturtevant. Everyone look it's Astra. She invented the SCOMID drug!"

The crowd surged around her and began chanting, "Astra...Astra...Astra."

Chia followed along, directing her hovering vidcams to capture the unexpected situation. She caught up with Astra and said, "That was some reception. Is there anything you would like to tell our viewers?"

"Not really. Could you please turn off your cameras. I need to find a place to sit down. The gravity is killing my legs and feet."

Torch helped Astra into the back of the van while Chia grabbed Luz, climbed in and sat next to her. The crowd surged around making it difficult for the driver to open his door, but finally he wedged himself, locked the doors and slowly navigated the van onto the main road away from all of the confusion.

Torch massaged Astra's feet and said, "I know how you feel. It will probably take a couple of days for us to adjust. Our daughter seems to be doing fine."

Astra slumped forward with her hands over her eyes. "Thank you, Torch. Chia, how about if we set up a time and place for an interview to take place a few days from now?" She laughed, "Maybe people will forget that I am here by then."

"We'll see. Right now, I'm going to cover as much of the opening as I can. I'll see you all later. Driver please stop for a moment, I am going back to the party."

"Astra said, "Before you go, I have a favor to ask."

"Sure...what is it?"

"It's about Scotty and his compulsion for privacy. Please find Sandra and Morrow and warn them not to let anyone know that he was the key to the SCOMID discovery. Maybe they could die his hair or call him something different until we get back to the Moonbase?"

"OK. I will do that. Maybe some time down the road, he will let me interview him. But for now, I'll go talk with his mom and dad and let them decide on how to handle the situation. See you tomorrow. Goodbye Luz."

Chia looked at Astra and said, "She is such a cute little darling. I wonder why the gravity doesn't seem to be affecting her."

Astra replied, "Chron developed a regimen for kids on the Moonbase. I guess it must be working."

Torch added, "She's also smart like her mom."

The Next Morning

Astra left the Majuro Lodge for an early morning walk with Luz to exercise their legs, but soon they were soon trailed by dozens of onlookers. Word of her presence quickly spread throughout the village and fans carrying flashing signs emblazoned with *'Nobel Prize for Astra'* and *'Astra for President'* lined both sides of the roadway.

Luz swung her arms and danced along, happy to be the center of attention while Astra strained against the G load and was relieved when Torch arrived in an EV truck and drove them back to the lodge where they had planned to have breakfast.

As they entered the dining room, Summer waved them over and asked, Would you like to join us? Summer laughed. "The chef is a new arrival from the Cook Islands...so he must be good! Right?"

Torch said, "I always order the chef's special when a new chef takes the kitchen's helm...puts them on the spot to show off their talent."

Astra said, "I'll go along with that."

"Me too," said Luz."

When the waiter arrived, Summer said, "If it's not too late, we would like to change our orders to the chef's special. I believe that goes for all of us."

The waiter nodded, and then said, "Good choice," and rushed to the kitchen.

Torch joked. "It's great to see the Sturtevant clan finally getting together."

"Speaking of which," replied Astra. "I brought along a map of our family's genetic history. I thought you might be interested."

"Sure, Let's take a look. My mother gave me a family photo album when I was a child, but it was lost in a major typhoon that pretty much wiped out the village many years ago."

Astra cued up a floating monitor that traced the Sturtevant family lineage from Germany to Brazil and on to the Marshall Islands. During the meal, which consisted of delicious fruit and tuna dishes, they shared stories about their relatives and their many adventures.

When the waiter returned, Torch said, "Please give the chef our..."

Suddenly Chia came rushing in, pulled up a chair and said breathlessly, "Sorry to interrupt. I have been looking all over for you Astra. The Space-Hook is big news, but seeing you for the first time on Earth since you invented SCOMID is the number one topic in social media around the world. I have been contacted by the major media outlets as well as high-ranking government officials, execs and theologists that came for the Sly-Hook celebration, but would love to meet you in person and ask you questions now that they know you are here. How about a town hall type meeting? I expect viewers around the world will tune in...I hope I didn't ruin your breakfast. Actually that looks good. I think I'll order that tomorrow."

Astra turned to Torch and raised her upturned palms. "What have I gotten myself into this time?"

Torch laughed. "Ordinarily that's my line, but you are free to use it this time."

Chia was excited and said, "Super, I'll keep you posted."

Astra yawned and said, "I need a nap. My biorhythm has been out of whack ever since we left the Moonbase, so please give me a couple of days to get ready."

Summer volunteered, "Today's my day off. If you want, Luz can come with me and my kids to the beach."

Luz nodded, so Astra said, "Sounds great, thanks."

As they left, Chia took Summer's arm and said, "Could you help me find a location for the town hall?"

"The college has a 300 seat auditorium If you need more, there is the basketball field house."

"No, the auditorium sounds great. Could you reserve it from two to four in the afternoon on the day after tomorrow?"

"That will be this Sunday. Good choice. I'll see to it."

"Wonderful, I'll get the word out in the cloud ASAP."

"The college is just a couple of miles down the road. You might want to check it out first. My van is right around the corner.""

"Good idea. I see why you are in charge."

"Ha!."

— CHAPTER 25 —

Two Days Later
June 4th, 2036
Majuro College Auditorium

Once word circulated about Astra's offer to meet in a town hall, Chia received dozens of requests on a broad range of topics. Since Astra had agreed to a format in which the audience would ask her questions, Chia's role would be to randomly draw the names of those who wished to participate and had signed up at the door.

As the final members of the audience found their seats, Summer stood at the podium and announced, "Welcome everyone. As the Governor of Majuro, which is now one of the leading nations in the fight to heal our planet, I am proud to introduce Chia from the RealNews who will be hosting this town hall. Chia, I turn this meeting over to you."

"Thank you Summer. for making your beautiful campus available to us and setting up this town hall on such short notice. Since time is limited, let's get this show on the road. Astra, please join us."

Astra received a standing ovation as she emerged from backstage and bowed to the crowd. She gave Chia a hug and they both took their seats.

Chia said, "If you are ready, I am going to ask you the first question and then we will take questions from the audience."

"OK. I very much appreciate the opportunity to get out of the lab and visit this magnificent island. So ask away."

"As you can tell by the crowd here and the millions of viewers watching around the planet, you are now quite famous for developing the anti-aging miracle drug. Members of the audience, please raise your hand if you took your SCOMID today."

Nearly everyone raised their hand.

"And how many of you feel that it that it has changed your life?"

The response from the crowd was the same. This time someone shouted 'Nobel Prize'.

After another round of applause, Chia said, "Then I ask you Astra, how does it feel to be so famous? Did you see any of this coming?"

"Not really. You should know that my research partner Chron and our dedicated development team played key roles in the SCOMID discovery and there were many more people who contributed. But no, I didn't expect all of this attention on me personally."

"Have you run into any unforeseen consequences?"

"I recently came into contact with a former professor of mine at UCB whose insurance was covering the cost of the Calendar version. She told me that she decided to switch to the Basic version because she was beginning to look more like a student than a professor and that was straining her relationship with her fellow faculty members."

Chia turned to the audience. "How many of you have had a similar experience?"

This time no one responded.

Chia laughed, "Me neither. It doesn't seem like this

is a big deal for most of us. because we take the free, Basic pill. Now we will take questions from our guests."

Chia reached into the box holding the question slips, retrieved one and said, "Elizabeth Swift. Please come up to the mic."

When Elizabeth arrived at the stand holding the mic, Chia said, "Please tell us your background and then ask your question."

"First I want to thank Dr. Sturtevant for all that she has accomplished. I am a nurse at the Majuro Free Clinic. We have already seen a tremendous impact on the healthcare industry with several major firms shutting their doors due to the decrease in demand for their services. How do you see this playing out and how will it affect ordinary people?"

"Those are good questions. We have been receiving reports from some of our partners that Basic SCOMID may cure or arrest certain diseases, but patients should definitely consult with their physicians about their specific circumstances. You are correct that some healthcare providers have been negatively affected...and yes we did anticipate that there would be some consolidation in the medical industry...but not to this extent."

"Again, I thank you."

Chia pulled out another slip. "Byron Hays, you're up."

Byron read from his pad. "I am on the faculty here at the university and for the last twenty years I have taught and done research in the field of sociology. To say the least, these have been trying times for societies around the world. My question is, why should a relatively few wealthy people who can afford the Calendar version be able to have children while most of the population, which is on the free version cannot? Won't this widen the gap between the rich and poor?"

Astra replied, "Frankly, this was a difficult decision

but it was the only way we could help the majority of the people on the planet. But how would you feel if SCOMID was *only* available to the wealthy?"

"I see your point and I thank you Dr. Sturtevant."

Chia added. "We would likely have a civil war if that should happen. Amy Eckhardt, you're next."

A young girl made her way to the mic stand. "My name is Amy. I am in sixth grade at Lagoon Elementary. My question is, do you have a pill for dogs?"

Astra waited a minute for the wave of laughter to die down before she replied. "At this time SCOMID is only for Sapients and New-Humans. It won't work on pets and could even be harmful to them. Maybe down the road we can do something for them, but we would have to include the sterility factor or we might be overwhelmed by our pets."

Following another round of applause Chia made another selection and announced, "Our next participant is Jimmy Granger."

Jimmy cleared his throat and said, "I am a graduate student here at the college majoring in mariculture and I work at the local shrimp farm. I plan to start taking SCOMIDs on my next birthday, but my girl friend so far is reluctant because she wants us to get married and have a family. I guess I am afraid that the free treatment will run out or be canceled if I put it off signing up now. What do you recommend?"

Astra replied. "There are numerous personal issues like this that people will need to work out on their own. Our strategy was to charge a premium to those who could afford the Calendar treatment and to use those funds to finance the free program. Unfortunately, there have been shortages due to licensee violations. All I can say is that we are working with the resurrected Department of Health Services to actively pursue solutions. Good luck to you and your family."

When Jimmy took his seat, a pretty blond girl reached over and gave his a passionate kiss."

The crowd laughed when Chia said, "I think he just got engaged. OK, let's see who is next."

Chia retrieved another slip. "Our next guest is Charlotte McKenzie, a reporter from the USA Network whom I have had the pleasure of meeting on several occasions in the past."

Charlotte tapped the mic and said, "Greetings Chia, my producer and I came here to cover the Space-Hook opening. We just learned about this town hall this morning and are very surprised to be here and have the opportunity to participate. Hello Astra. As I recall, in one of your interviews you mentioned that collecting anti-aging data posed a unique challenge–I think you said something about a paradox. Could you be more specific?"

"Ah yes, this relates to a hypothetical situation in which human subjects participating in anti-aging research studies outlive the researchers studying their aging process. So, the researchers wouldn't be able to report their findings—thus the term *paradox*."

"Have you found a way to work around this problem?"

"We believe so. We have a large number of short term factors that we monitor in our test subjects and then we use that data to predict future outcomes. So far it seems to be working. I should point out that our initial experiments were conducted on artificial clones so no humans or animals were put at risk."

Chia added, "Only time will tell." She retrieved another slip. "The next one is from Sheila Smart."

"Thank you. As you said my name is Sheila. My husband and I are from Australia and are here on vacation." She held up a tube of SCOMID Basics and asked, "Are you sure that these are safe?"

Astra reached into her pocket and retrieved a similar tube. "All I can say is that I take a single pill every day."

"That's good enough for me. Thank you."

You are welcome. Chia, who wants to ask the next question?"

Chia reached into the container, retrieved another slip and read the name. "The next participant is Nana Rice."

Astra said, "Welcome Nana, what is your question?"

"I am a pastor at the All Ways Church here on Majuro. My question is simple. Will people that take SCOMID become immortal?"

The hall went quiet and Astra took a few moments to think before she answered. "It's possible I guess, but it's not just aging that limits the human lifespan...accidents, disasters, diseases, crime, wars, and so on—even annihilation by an asteroid. If a person can avoid those factors, and if there is no long term degradation in the effectiveness of SCOMID, then yes some...or many of you in the audience could live for hundreds of years or more."

"But, how does this fit in with religion and the afterlife?"

Astra shrugged. "I think I should leave that to you well informed theologists and theologians. Perhaps I should provide a brief overview of the scientific basis of our research strategy in the next segment?"

Chia announced, "That is a superb idea."

After several more questions—all of which Astra handled easily, Chia said, "OK, break time. We will resume in twenty minutes. Our viewers around the world will now see the next episode of our documentary series on climate change after this word from our sponsor, Pharma-Joy, Inc.

****

Once the audience had returned and taken their seats, Chia said, "Welcome back. Astra you're up."

Astra nodded. "As I mentioned before the break, I thought I would give you a little background on my research. Originally my goal was to assemble a cryogenically stored collection off embryos of endangered species from around the globe."

She called up a vid clip of a CryoVat steaming a cloud of water vapor. "We called it the Ark and it is now stored at the SpeeZees Lab on the Moon. Hopefully, efforts like the Majuro Space-Hook will someday bring a cooler climate and we can restore many if not all of the species which have become or will soon become extinct."

There were several shouts of '*Nobel Prize...Nobel Prize...Nobel Prize*'.

Astra continued. "After the Ark was secured, I resumed my original studies in longevity. As you know anti-aging therapy has been the goal of medical researchers for decades...and with some success I might add. There are many examples of extreme lifespans in biological organisms. Hydra are regarded as immortal and bristlecone pines have been documented to live over five thousand years. In fact, the cells of everyone here will be completely replaced every seven years—except for DNA and brain neurons. Updating these critical fundamental components is the key to enhanced longevity that is provided by SCOMID."

Chia asked, "How is that accomplished?"

Astra cued up a chromosome model on a screen in back of the stage. "The ends of RNA and DNA chromosomes are protected by telomeres which slowly shorten over time after replication. SCOMID restores and protects the telomeres."

After several more queries followed that were of a technical nature posed by biology faculty, there was a momentary lapse in questions—until Nana Rice shouted from the back of the room. "What about the afterlife? You never answered my question. Do you believe in life after death?"

Astra took a deep breath. "Actually, I believe..."

Suddenly the lights in the auditorium flickered and went out. A few moments later, the emergency lights came on and one of Summer's assistants rushed to the stage and said, "The power is out all over the island. We're not sure what happened or how long it will take to restore."

Astra said, "Saved by the bell. I think we should call it a day."

Summer said, "I agree. Listen up everyone, we seem to be experiencing a power outage. Please proceed to the exit and thank you for coming. There is no need to panic, just be careful as you leave the auditorium."

Torch helped Astra and Chia gather their belongings and as they headed to the exit the lights came back on. He told them. "It looks like a temporary glitch, but the timing couldn't be better."

"How so?" asked Astra.

"I just received a message from my dad on the Moon-base, he wants to meet us on Vesta."

"Why? What's up?"

"He just said that he didn't want to provide the details because the COM system might be hacked, but to come ASAP. So I am as clueless as you are, but Dad wouldn't have done this unless it was very important."

While Torch rounded up the family members that had attended the town hall and explained the situation, Chia looked at Astra and asked. "So what were you going to tell us about the afterlife? You got cut off just when it was just getting good."

Astra nodded her head towards Madeline and said. "Actually my plan was to invite Madeline onto the stage and let her answer."

"So let me get this straight. You were going to bail?"

Astra laughed and confessed. "Precisely."

Sandra asked Torch, "Do we all have to go? What about the dolphins? We've only been here for a few days and I was looking forward to exploring the island."

Torch replied, "Morrow, Scotty and the Twins can stay here with Quant and Elektra as long as they want or they can take their schooner back to Santa Cruz. But Dad specifically asked that you and Madeline come with us to Vesta. You too, Astra and Luz. He has already informed Quant."

Chia said, "I would like to go too."

"Yes of course, Dad wants you to come as well. You can ride with Sabien."

Morrow took Scotty's shoulder and asked, "Would you like to join our dive team?"

"Does that mean you will teach me? Sure, I love your dolphins. Is that OK with you Mom?"

Sandra gave him a hug and looked at Morrow. Take good care of our little angel."

Torch herded the group towards the waiting van. "OK, we have to go. Sabien is waiting for us on his shuttle."

Sandra tightly hugged Morrow, obviously concerned about leaving him and the dolphins behind.

Morrow told her, "Don't worry, I have been looking forward to spending time with Scotty. The Twins and Tom's kids seem to like it here. We can always head home in the *Cynara* whenever we want to."

Madeline said, "I don't know why, but I love to travel in space. I think it sharpens my connection."

Sandra said, "Well...I have no idea why I have to go, but if your dad wants me to come along, so be it. I'll go, but I have never been off planet and may need some instructions."

Madeline squeezed Sandra's hand. "Don't worry

Mom, we will take good care of you and Morrow will look after Scotty and the dolphins while we are on Vesta."

After a brief stop at the lodge to pick up their belongings, Torch drove the group to the landing port where they boarded their shuttles.

Minutes later the shuttles lifted off into the brilliant afternoon sunshine that reflected off the procession of pods ascending into the deep blue sky above.

****

In the control office, Quant asked Elektra, "Have your techs figured out what caused the power outage?"

"Actually, it didn't take long. After we did some checking, we discovered that the blackout in Majuro's power grid occurred only a few seconds after the pod chain led by *Pod One*. had been transferred to the downside cable and launched back to Majuro. The first run uses ice mined from the comet that is orbiting the Moon to balance the load."

Quant interrupted. "So that's when the descender pods started producing power from their braking systems?"

"Exactly. Our system is set to channel any net power gains to the Majuro grid to increase their energy supply, but the surge tripped their circuit breakers. We fixed the problem so it won't happen again."

"Wow, so the Space-Hook is operating in the green?"

"It appears so," Elektra replied.

"That's fantastic. I'll flash an update to the OWN administration office. They will be very pleased to hear about this."

"When *Pod One* returns, you might consider sending it to them so they can put it on display."

Quant kissed her hand. "You are a genius."

Elektra stretched her arms over her head and said, "I'm just glad that the power outage wasn't another attack on the base."

"Agreed."

We have three days before the first pods return. How about if we take a couple of days off, enjoy some music at the club...maybe go for a moonlight walk on the beach?"

He took her in his arms and said, "I think I have fallen in love with you."

"I think so too."

— CHAPTER 26 —

Three Days Later
June 10th, 2036
Asteroid Vesta

Sabien spoke into his wrist mic. "Ladies and gentlemen, we are approaching the first stop on our tour of the solar system. As you can see out the view screen, we are approaching the Space-Hook dome on Vesta which is located at the base of this large mountain on the South Pole. By the way, that peak is thirteen miles high, which is three times taller than Mount Everest and second in height only to Olympus Mons on Mars. Please secure your seat restraints and thank you for choosing Torch Tours to explore the cosmos."

Torch, who had been sharing stories over the COM since they had left Majuro, steered his shuttle behind Sabien's as he went through the landing checklist. He looked at Chia who was sitting in the copilot seat and said, "I think that Sabien has been away from home too long."

Chia paused recording the view and then stowed her vidcam. "Maybe that was his subconscious speaking out and he is the one that really needs a vacation?"

Sabien overheard her comment and laughed, "What is a vacation?" A few moments later he added, "Welcome to Vesta. We hope you enjoy your stay—and don't forget to take your SCOMID today."

Chron and Sanders greeted the new arrivals as they passed through the airlock of the shuttle hangar that connected to the dome. As they walked down the corridor, Sandra flexed her knees and said, "This is strange. I thought there would be very little gravity here."

Chron replied, "That is one of the mysteries that we are exploring. Way back in 2011, the NASA Dawn spacecraft orbited Vesta and detected a strong gravitational field here in the Rheasilvia Crater."

"Do you know why or what is the cause?"

"Not yet, but we have been conducting surveys. The gravity level seems to be quite variable, both in time and location which can make surface travel challenging. It is a little complicated. Perhaps we can talk later and I will fill you in. Just be sure to be cautious when you move around. You might drift of the ground, which is inadvisable under these circumstances."

"There are lots of strange things going on here. That's why we asked you to come," Sanders said.

Madeline suddenly swooned and fell to the floor. Sabien helped her to a bench and Torch brought her a water bag."

After taking a swallow, she asked, "What was that? It sounded like high-pitched voices and then the floor started to move and suddenly I felt dizzy."

Chron looked at Sanders and nodded. "Some of our workers have reported similar events. It is one of the reasons why we invited you and Sandra. Strange things have been happening here ever since we arrived and we thought that you might help us figure out what is going on."

Sanders said, "We have accommodations ready for you. I suggest that you go to your cabins and we will have dinner delivered to you. We will get an early start in the morning. There are some things we recently discovered that I very much want you to see and help us explain—if possible that is. Meanwhile, welcome to Vesta. We hope your stay will be enlightening."

As Chia walked with Madeline and Sandra down the hallway, Chia asked, "Did you hear anything unusual?"

Sandra responded, "Actually I did! It sounded like a train whistle. It reminded me of my childhood. I was raised by my grandparents who owned a pet shop in Key West. There was a power spot that I used to go to. It was an old fashioned diesel-powered locomotive which I later discovered was linked somehow to a similar one in Lawrence, Kansas. This was all back in the 1990's. I guess my fixation on telepathy started back then. There it goes again. Madeline, did you hear it?"

"Yes I did."

"This is very strange."

The Next Morning

Astra stood at her cabin view port, mesmerized by shimmering white flashes as the rising sun sliced through the haze surrounding the asteroid. When Torch joined her carrying two steaming pouches of coffee and glass of milk for Luz she said, "I can barely see Earth down below. What's with all this fog?"

"In order to balance the load of the first upcoming pods, we filled the initial run of descender pods that we had stashed here with ice from the comet that we towed into lunar orbit to provide water for the Lunar Colony. The haze should dissipate soon."

"It kind of reminds me of a snowy winter day in Vail, Colorado. I used to ski on my vacations...back when I used to have vacations that is."

"The granular ice from the comet, which will be

delivered in the first batch of pods, is going to be released at an altitude of one thousand feet above Majuro. It should be quite a spectacular show!"

"Snow in the Marshall Islands. I hope you let Summer know."

"Oh yes. She has declared a holiday and we have issued alerts to the major weather media outlets. "How did you sleep? Hear any more voices or strange sounds?"

"None so far. I wonder if all this is linked somehow to the strange gravity effects that Chron mentioned."

"That would be a new chapter in the laws of physics but I have heard that Sandra and Madeline complained that they couldn't get any sleep at all...something about train whistles in the night."

Torch checked his watch and said, "Time to suit up and head out. I ran into Chron on the way here. He is anxious to get going so I have arranged for one of resident moms to look after Luz while we are gone. All I can say from what he told me is that today is going to be one that we will never forget."

"What's going to happen?"

"Chron made me promise not to talk about it and I will honor his wishes. He doesn't want to bias your viewpoint before we get to the site. You'll see soon enough."

"The suspense is killing me."

"Put on your helmet and let's go!"

****

After a short delay, while Sandra received instructions on how to operate her spacesuit, the group gathered together in front of the shuttle hangar behind a line of Torch's RoboCows. Vesta's variable gravity and uneven terrain generated many challenges that Chron and his team had been forced to overcome through trail and error. Maneuvering over the irregular terrain by foot was difficult and dangerous and using track vehicles was found to be possible, but awkward and inefficient due to the obstacles presented by the steep crevices and cliffs that covered the surface.

RoboCows, outfitted with heavy duty gripper claws, strap-in seats attached to cargo sleds on mini thrusters, were found to be the most efficient and reliable mode of transporting people, equipment and bins filled with ore.

Chron addressed the group that gathered around him as Torch finished demonstrating the RoboCow's simple control system.

"It looks like we are all set to go. I have detached the cargo sleds, we won't be needing them. We will be heading up a series of valleys in the mountain in front of us to a site that our surveys had indicated is rich in platinum. As you will see, it contains something much more valuable."

Sanders added, "Although it is only three kilometers away, it will take us a couple of hours to get to the site. It's a pretty steep climb."

As the caravan moved away from the dome, resembling a parade of camels marching across the African desert, the air cleared providing a dramatic view of Earth and the pods outlined with flashing lights, green signifying the ascenders and red lights, the descenders.

With only a brief delay to adjust the heater in Sandra's suit, the caravan arrived at the mine entrance right on schedule. Sanders and Miguel directed the RoboCows and their passengers into a small, open flat area where Chron demonstrated how to employ their suit's thrusters to gently drive them back down to the surface if he or she tripped and started launching into space. Chia stood back to record the scene but was forced to use a handheld camera since her levitating vidcam refused to work.

MET CHRON NEW-HUMANS

Under Miguel and Sanders careful supervision, each member of the group did a test jump and thruster recovery. After everyone seemed comfortable, Sanders said, "It looks like we are all set to go. Thank you for coming on such short notice and putting up with all this intrigue."

Miguel arrived carrying a case of water bottles which he passed out to group and said, "Everyone, help yourself to water. It is critical that you remain hydrated under these conditions—also regularly check the oxygen level in your suits."

Sanders said, "Thanks Miguel. Now everyone join me on this side of the entrance and I will lead us inside."

He pointed to a sturdy line anchored to poles that led into the cave entrance. "Please grab onto this line as we move ahead and yell out if you encounter any problems."

Torch asked, "Chron, did you create this tunnel?"

Chron shook his head. "No we just cleared the opening. We will descend about one hundred meters."

Torch pointed to the wall. "What are these striations that line the walls? They look like metallic deposits, but my scanner is not registering them."

Chron said, "Another mystery. Actually one of many as you will soon see."

"You will notice that as we descend the temperature will increase dramatically," said Sanders.

Sandra turned to check on Madeline, who was trailing behind her. Madeline flashed an OK sign and said, "The sounds we heard before are much louder now. I still don't know what they are. It's like a mix of whistles and metallic, scraping noises."

Sandra replied, "Now I hear what seems like running water. It's getting louder the deeper we go."

Chron said, "You are correct as you will see around the next bend." He continued, "It gets narrow here so we will have to squeeze through one at a time. Watch for cracks in the floor; we don't anyone getting their foot stuck."

There was a collective gasp as they rounded the corner and discovered a series of small, slow-flowing pools and ripples that reflected the brilliant light emanating from their headlamps.

Miguel searched his pack and held up a packet of empty vials and handed it to Astra. "Chron said you might want to take a few samples."

"Great. Have you figured out what is going on here?"

"We think that the source could be from melting ice frozen beneath the surface when the asteroid was formed about the same time as Earth."

Astra asked, "But why is it liquid? Where is the heat coming from?"

Sanders pointed at Chron who said, "Like the gravity enigma, we don't know. It could be volcanic heat from the molten mantle at the asteroid's core. However, in all of the prior studies of Vesta, there have been no mentions of liquid water and we don't know how wide-spread it is."

Astra reached down to fill one of the vials. She held the vial in front of her helmet light and then looked at Chia as she placed the vial on a ledge and asked, "Can you zoom in with your camera? I am curious about those particles."

Chia said, "No problem. I have a tripod that we can use. I'll zoom in and project the image."

The group gathered behind Chia as she set up her vidcam and activated a floating monitor. Once Chia had the system working, Astra pointed at the bottom of the display.

"See that cluster? Please zoom in there. They sure look like organisms, don't they? Are you recording this?"

"I am now."

Astra looked at Sanders. "Would it be alright if

everyone turned off their lights for a minute? There is something that I would like to check."

When Sanders nodded and switched off his headlamp, the rest of the group followed suit and Chia deactivated the floating monitor.

As their eyes adjusted, they were amazed to see that the pools and riffles glowed a bluish-green hue.

Madeline said, "It's beautiful, like a stream in the mountains."

After everyone had a chance to take in the view, Sanders broadcast, "OK, let's turn our lights back on. What do think Astra? Have you seen anything like this before?"

Astra flipped through the images that Chia had transferred to her pad. "Well, my specialty is genetics, but my guess is they are some species of diatom—a type of algae that produces twenty percent of the oxygen produced on Earth. I won't be sure until I check them out in the lab, but that's my first guess."

She handed Sabien the packet of vials and asked him to help her fill them.

Chia unlatched her camera to capture a closeup of Astra and asked, "Are they alive?"

"Astra took a deep breath. "I believe so which means that we have just discovered the very first alien life form!"

Torch suggested, "Maybe they are something brought here by a meteor or comet? As we saw coming here, Vesta's surface is dominated by craters."

Chron checked the O_2 levels. "There is some oxygen present, but not enough to breathe. But this is very encouraging. There could be more further into the cave."

Chia attached her camera to the tripod, pressed the auto timer and said, "OK everyone, I want to capture this moment in history. Jam in here so we can all fit in the picture."

After Chia had taken several shots, Torch said, "I know this sounds weird but is there any chance that somehow we caused these changes when we installed the Space-Hook dome?"

Sanders said, "That has been my number one question since we discovered this cave. But, as you will soon see, I just don't see how we could be responsible."

Miguel asked, "But who or what could have done this? As far as we know, there is nothing in the data archives that indicate that Vesta has ever been visited —other than Dawn Expedition and later orbital surveys. However, none of them ever landed or made physical contact."

Chron said, "We have done some radar soundings and this is just beginning of a series of caverns that interconnect over many kilometers. But, as Sanders alluded to, we did find something else that is very intriguing."

Chron nodded at Miguel who recovered a pouch from the side of the cave. As everyone gathered around, he removed what looked like a work glove and gave it to Sanders, who said, "We found this last week and left it in place. Actually, it is the main reason why we brought you here on such short notice."

"Dad, you brought us all this way for a glove?" Torch asked.

"Well...yes, but it is not just an ordinary work glove."

He handed it to Torch. "Here, check it out."

Torch held the glove up and rotated it under his headlamp. His eyes went wide and he said, "Wow...this is strange...*six fingers*! and handed it back to Sanders.

Chia moved in for a closeup of the glove and said, "Wow, add first *intelligent* life to our discovery!"

Torch patted Chron on the back and said, "You were right. This is a day we will always remember."

Suddenly the tunnel floor began to undulate and

there was a series of high-pitched whistling sounds that pounded their ears.

Madeline screamed, "We need to leave now!" just as a gusher of water blasted through the cave knocking her off balance and sweeping her downstream.

Chron jumped in after her and barely caught her heel just as she was about to be sucked beneath an overhang. He pulled her back onto the bank and passed her hand to Torch who pulled her out of the cave. Other than a few bruises, she said that she was OK but clung to Sandra's arm as she caught her breath.

As they checked each others suits for punctures, a roar that changed pitch reverberated in their headsets.

Suddenly Chia screamed, "Oh no!" and started to run back to the cave entrance, but Astra intercepted her and handed her the camera and tripod. "You didn't think I would leave these behind did you?"

Chia gave her a hug and said, "Thank you. It would have been awful to lose that footage."

After making sure that Madeline was OK, Sanders, Miguel and Chron huddled to the side of the group and decided that they had been through enough for one day.

As they headed back to the group to get underway, Sanders handed Torch the pouch containing the alien glove and said, "You and Sabien might want to do an analysis on this when you get back to the base."

Torch replied, "That should be interesting." When he slipped the glove on, it emitted three loud chirps and then viciously contracted into a fist.

"Torch screamed, "Help, somebody help me get this damn thing off."

It took the combined strength of both Sanders and Miguel to pry open the glove enough to enable Torch to slide his hand free."

Chia asked, "Are you OK? Let me take a look. Try to move your hand."

When she gently applied acupressure to his wrist, Torch flinched and said, "Heh, that hurts! Remind me never to do that again!"

"I think your wrist may be broken. We need to get you back to the base infirmary."

When Astra gave him a hug, Torch looked up and said, *"What have I gotten myself into this time?"*

---- To Be Continued ----

Metamorphosis Chronicles Book 3

ABOUT THE AUTHOR

Ron S. Nolan, Ph.D. lives in Aptos, California near the sunken ship at the end of the pier in SeaCliff Beach. He spends his days working out, running, writing and performing tech patent research–quite a leap from his early days in Western Kansas where he shared the farm outhouse with a nest of half frozen rattlesnakes and learned to read by the light of a Coleman lantern! To learn more about his latest novels and screenplays, please visit…

Planetropolis Publishing
www.planetropolis.com

****

Metamorphosis Chronicles Book One

Astra, a head-turning, Brazilian girl in her mid-twenties is not only beautiful but also brilliant...and in big trouble! After discovering a key to the genetic aging clock that could dramatically increase the human lifespan, she is tracked down by a psychic who delivers a stern warning that she must work to heal the planet before adding to the over population crisis by allowing a select few to live longer lives.

In the year 2029, the terminal impacts of global warming are having disastrous effects upon ecosystems and global tensions have escalated as countries fight to extract the last barrel of oil. Astra's new mission is to assemble cryogenic repositories ('Arks') of frozen plant and animal embryos to preserve them for the future. However, she is opposed by a fanatical religious group that will do anything to stop her. But is it the Ark that they really want...or something hidden within? Either way, they will have to go to a mining base on the moon to find out.

Available in eBook and Softcover
www.planetropolis.com

Telepathic Dolphin Experiment

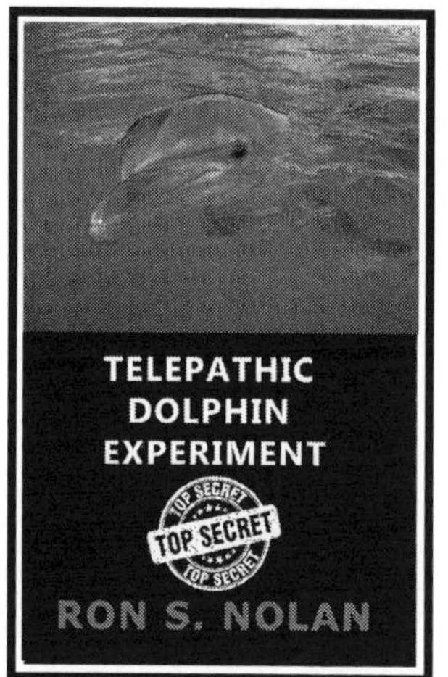

During a life-long search to scientifically document paranormal phenomena, Dr. Sandra Grant discovers that dolphins offer ideal research subjects. Through her persistence and the aid of a government contractor, a pair of twin dolphins is made available to her by a paranoid general intent upon the ultimate destruction of the USSR, but facing a public relations nightmare due to his support of a recently exposed secret military program to use marine mammals as weapons.

General Pratt Houston's intelligence sources indicate that Russia has an overwhelming arsenal of nuclear weapons. Driven mad by the government's past reluctance to use full military force in Viet Nam, and with the refusal of Congress to use nukes against the Iraqis, General Houston forces a computer programmer to create a virus designed to wreak havoc on the Soviet Defense Network. Designated as ANX, the virus will penetrate the defense network and disrupt their communication systems, When Russia panics and launches their missiles out of desperation, ANX will corrupt their guidance systems and cause them to misfire. The subsequent U.S. counterattack will permanently solve the arms imbalance--at least according to the General's twisted thinking.,,

However, through a bizarre chain of events, the ultimate fate of humanity depends upon the determination and resourcefulness of Dr. Grant and her telepathic dolphins to thwart the General's sinister plan.

Available in eBook and Softcover
www.planetropolis.com

Made in the
USA
Columbia, SC

82040763R00190